TREADED ON ME!

Robert C. Schubert

5-27-17

TREADED ON ME!

Rise of the United Constitutional Militia

ROBERT E. SCHUBERT

ISBN: 1533386021
ISBN 13: 9781533386021
Library of Congress Control Number: 2016909308
CreateSpace Independent Publishing Platform
North Charleston, South Carolina

THEY WERE BRAVE

With ears bleeding from the explosive power of the enemy artillery, the firing of weapons, and the detonation of grenades, Karnic knew that the only thing he could do was wait for the order to advance. With adrenaline rushing through his body like a bolt of electricity, Karnic checked his M4 rifle one more time as his mind began retracing the events of his life that had led him to the indescribable, challenging day he was now facing at the Battle of Saint Louis. He looked down at a black freckle on the palm of his hand and said to himself softly, "Just attack."

A whistle was blown and sounded as if Gabriel were blowing his trumpet. For many, it would be angels' trumpets calling them home. The line captain screamed, "Over the top!" Just like the soldiers of World War I, Karnic and the rest of the United Continental Militia climbed up and out of the creek bed they were in and charged the enemy.

Karnic thought it was strange to announce to the enemy that they were coming. But since the electromagnetic pulse, there were very few electronics that worked. With every finger grab and foothold he could find, Karnic followed his orders and fought just to get over the top. Once at the top, he took in a deep breath and rushed from the safety of the rocky Missouri land, which had provided him with some security from the enemy gunfire and artillery rounds that were exploding all around him. The one image that kept flashing in his mind was of how the long blond hair of the beautiful woman he had laid eyes upon as his company pulled away from the terminal in Kansas City for their short trip to the front.

Never before in the history of man had there been a turning point in a war as great as that which took place at the Battle of Saint Louis.

Chapter 1

KARNIC FAMILY HISTORY

F rom the time Sergeant Karnic was seven, he had known that he wanted to be in the military. That realization came while watching the movie *Red Dawn* with his father. His father had served in Vietnam and had shared a few stories of his time in the US Navy.

Karnic came from a long line of servicemen. His family had arrived in the United States from Germany shortly after World War I, and when World War II broke out with the invasion of Poland, half of the family returned to fight for Germany. After the attack on Pearl Harbor, the half who remained US citizens joined the US Armed Forces. Soon after that, they found themselves fighting against their former countrymen. Karl E. Karnic was one such relative of Sgt. Karnic—and the one he was to be named for.

Karl E. Karnic rose through the ranks of the Wehrmacht and eventually became a well-respected general. He was among some of the last German soldiers to die in battle on the Eastern Front. Because of Karl's love of country, he led a handful of brave men to defend a small village against the advancing Russian forces. With the current state of the war in his country, he knew that there would be no support or reinforcement coming to his aid. Understanding that those in the village probably thought as he did, Karl felt it was his duty to show them that there were people in the army still protecting them. With most men already taken by the war, all who remained were mostly women and children doing what they could to survive.

With the invading Red Army closing in on the village, General Karnic ordered his men to start making preparations for their arrival. With few supplies on hand or in the village, he felt that the fight would most likely be over within the first few minutes. The one thing he counted on was the healthy supply of 8mm rounds for the Mauser K98 bolt-action rifles that most soldiers had been issued. He would have given anything for more ammunition to operate the MG42, for which there were only eight hundred rounds. As the rifles had a firing rate of seven hundred rounds per minute, they would go fast. General Karnic had always believed that being a marksman was better than blowing through rounds in a machine gun and had trained his men accordingly. Today he prayed that his philosophy was a sound one.

Located midway up a high hill, the natural terrain provided protection on which they hoped to capitalize. The Russians moved in like ants going for candy, with no regard for any military tactics. They simply relied on sheer numbers to achieve their objective. That was evident after the MG42 opened up with its eight hundred rounds and laid waste to hundreds only to have them replaced instantly by double the amount—although the Russian troops did advance at about half the speed they had previously.

Karl only had twenty-seven men armed with the K98 8mm Mausers, but they were all well-trained, combat-hardened marksmen. The horde of Russians slowed their advance even more once the battle began—with every round fired by the Germans, one of theirs fell. It sets a different tone to a battle when you are confronting a machine gun rather than a group of highly trained marksmen. With a machine gun, many rounds that fly may never stick a target, but when men drop with every crack of their opponent's weapon, you have the feeling the next crack could be for you.

Karl's men gave them hell, but the Red Army kept getting closer. Karl's main problem was that the K98 Mauser rifle held only five rounds—five rounds that did not last long when fighting against overwhelming forces. Every time Karl watched as one of his men was hit, he felt part of himself die. Not long into the battle, which seemed to last all day, Karnic made the decision to save as many of his men as possible. The last people of the village had by now been given enough time to make it to the American front—he knew they would be safe. Now he made the decision to order the men who could still move to follow the same path of the villagers and surrender only to the Americans. The men under Karl's command had refused the order, but Karl had already anticipated their dedication.

"You men will do as I have ordered," Karl demanded his men "for it is my final one to give. I do not give it to save your life but to ensure the lives of our innocent countrymen of the village. You will do your duty and slow down the Russians if they make it past us. Our country has fallen, but we are still the protectorate of our people. So do your duty; honor those who have fallen before you and those yet to fall." With the words flowing from his lips, he understood that he was soon to join the ranks of the fallen.

General Karl E. Karnic sent every man he felt had the slightest chance of surviving the journey to the American front. That left only the dead and wounded. Even though six of his men were moments from death due to wounds, they were fighting hard. As those who were mobile were leaving, Karl asked a favor from his trusted sergeant who would be leading them: to give his son, who would be born any day now, a letter, accompanied with his service tag. As the sergeant was receiving the items he knew that the general would be staying with the men who were fighting still. The general could not ask them to sacrifice their lives if he were not willing to do the same. The sergeant shook the general's hand and replied "Good luck Sir" before leading the way to the American frontlines.

That was the last time anyone saw General Karl Eugene Karnic and his wounded men. The sergeant knew that they had fought hard and hurt the enemy before the end. Half an hour after the sergeants and the groups departure, they could still hear the crack of the Mausers, and with every crack, the sergeant knew it would be one fewer Russian following.

Chapter 2

YOUNG ANGELIQUE

The Carringer household was quite a peaceful place to grow up, and Angelique could not have asked for more loving parents. Her parents were truly children of the 1960's, peace, love, and community were a way of life. They were hippies. They tried many times to create the perfect communal society, but each time it started to thrive, members moved away, mostly to start their own families and work new lands. The farms in a way became the communal society they had been dreaming to create. Many families made their living by moving from one communal farm to another and helping with the planting, harvesting, and livestock.

Angelique would spend most days doing schoolwork and playing with other children on the farm, whenever they were around. Her family's farm was just outside of a little community on gravel called Four Mile Hill Road. There were very few other farms on the road. One of their neighboring families, the Bowmen's, lived directly across the street. The Bowmen's had a little boy named Chad around her age, to which she paid little attention.

When Angelique did play with Chad it was mostly due to long spans between children coming to her parent's farm from other families much like hers. During the times she would attempt to play with the neighbor boy it never lasted long before he would start to do things to impress her, like jumping off the barn. At that point, she would complement him on not getting hurt and politely leave.

Another boy lived just down the road at the bottom of the hill—he was a skinny, lanky, very tall boy for his age. Angelique knew very little about him—the only thing she knew for sure was that he enjoyed spending time in the woods.

Most of the time it was just Angelique and her parents, although often other members of the group would arrive, and it would be a communal society once again. There was always plenty that needed to be done—planting gardens, making pottery, and feeding the animals. The chores seemed to never end, except for when she had school.

She did not attend school like most children her age, although she very much wanted to. Angelique was homeschooled; since her parents had grown up in the 1960's they did not believe she needed to be part of the harsh world of public school. Her parents took great care with her education and always started the day with three to four hours of math, English, and science. After lunch, it was always literature—poetry mostly. Although her education was well rounded, Angelique felt as if she needed the experience of socializing with other children her own age. Although she enjoyed it when other families came to stay, very few had children close to her age.

Her greatest enjoyment came when Old Jerry and his wife came to help with the spring planting. Jerry was very different from the typical flower children in the community—he had been an army ranger in Vietnam. Since her parents' teachings on history seem to except everything having to do with conflicts and war, Jerry would fill in the blanks. While Angelique would be working hard at her chores alongside Old Jerry, he would tell her stories of adventures he'd had in Vietnam and of life in the military.

Old Jerry was not one to live off the land, weave baskets, and make pottery. He had married into the lifestyle. Jerry and his wife came around twice a year like clockwork, and Angelique was always excited to see them pulling up the driveway. When they would leave, she would begin counting down the days until his next visit with the same intensity and excitement of counting down the days until Christmas.

Neither of them knew how it started, but each time Jerry visited, he would teach Angelique a new fighting move. Jerry could tell from a young age that the girl had the spirit of a warrior. Upon his arrival each spring and fall, she could not wait to show him how well she could do the moves—she would practice them every day. Although Angelique practiced the fighting moves, she learned early on to keep it from her parents. She would never forget what had happened when they found out that Jerry was teaching her fighting moves and told her a story's about his time in the military. When she was nine and full of excitement. Jerry had returned home at the end of the planting season. Since Jerry had not been there, Angelique had decided to show her mother the fighting move—this was done by trying to sweep her mother's legs out from under her. Angelique had been unsuccessful at taking her mother down to the ground—she was just sixty pounds and not nearly big enough to take down a full-grown person.

The problem came when Angelique had been asked to explain what she was doing. After her mother had found out that it was a fighting technique that Jerry had taught Angelique, there had been chaos in the community. Mrs. Carringer had been very angry at Old Jerry, and that was almost the last time that Angelique saw him. Jerry and his wife did not arrive for the fall harvest, and Angelique asked her parents almost every day without fail, "Where is Old Jerry? Is he coming?" Each time there was a little more sadness in her voice.

Almost a year passed before Angelique saw Old Jerry and his wife again. It seemed that things that had finally blown over and were back to normal, except for one thing: Old Jerry no longer told his stories or showed her new moves. Not only did it break her heart that Jerry was not doing the things she so looked forward to, it also broke Old Jerry's. For the first three weeks, Angelique waited for her and Old Jerry to be alone and then begged him to tell her a story or show her a new move.

"Look, Old Jerry," she would say, and then perfectly demonstrate one of the last moves he had showed her.

Each time, Jerry would tell her, "You have to stop" or "Your mother and father do not want you learning those things" at the same time reminding her "There is nothing I can do." All the while, he would look around to make sure that no one saw her doing the moves. He, too, had the same sad face as Angelique.

A week later, Angelique broke Old Jerry. She had him telling stories and showing her new techniques. They both knew and understood that it would be life changing for both of them if anyone ever found out. Jerry remembered the scolding he had received from Angelique's father the year before and did not want a repeat of that.

After Old Jerry had finally relented, Angelique took him on a walk to the back of the field where the woods began. She was very excited to show him the training ground she had created. She had ropes, logs to run on for balance, trees she climbed regularly, and even a scarecrow stuffed with old clothes and hay. Jerry could tell by the bare ground, frayed rope, and missing bark from the trees that she had trained a great deal. Seeing the area reinforced Jerry's belief that Angelique was a warrior.

During the planting and harvesting seasons, Angelique learned everything Old Jerry wanted to show her. She was always sad to see the seasons come to an end, but she looked forward to practicing her new moves until Jerry's return.

Chapter 3

BIRTHDAY GIRL

On Angelique's twelfth birthday, Old Jerry had a gift for her that she could not have imagined. Like normal, Old Jerry and Martha pulled up the driveway under the watchful eyes of Angelique. No sooner had they stopped their truck and trailer than Angelique was at the driver's-side door. Old Jerry always played it cool with her, even though he, too, had become very excited to see how well her training had advanced. Very little gave him more excitement these days than working with Angelique. Jerry had always wanted children, but for some unknown reason, he and his wife could not conceive. The desire for the children they did not have eased when Angelique took an interest in Old Jerry's military past.

This year Jerry was more excited than most—Angelique was finally old enough in his eyes to move to the next level of her training. "I have a birthday surprise for you," he said and looked down.

Angelique was just a little puzzled by that, since her birthday had been months before and he had stopped getting her things years ago. She always told him that the training he gave her was the best gift she could ever ask for. With a grin, Angelique looked up at Jerry and did not say a word in return. She could tell by his tone that he did not want one. She gave both him and Martha hugs once they had exited the vehicle then ran around the house to let her parents know that they had arrived.

Three days passed. Jerry spent most of his time with Angelique's father. Thinking about what he might have got her as a gift, Angelique was about to lose her mind. She was also dying to show him how well she had mastered her last lesson. Jerry could see her watching him, waiting, waiting for him to give her a signal that it was time for a new lesson or, in this case, her gift. For the first three days, he stayed away from her as he had planned.

Jerry wanted nothing more than to get on with her lessons, but he had to be sure that she was capable of not giving away their secret—he knew that she was good at not speaking of it when things were going well; he just felt like she needed to be tested on self-control before moving to the next stage. Jerry understood that her parents had almost banished Martha and him over a few fighting moves and if they found out about what Old Jerry had planned for the next stage, then he figured that he would be murdered by hippies. As he was on his way to bed, Jerry stuck his head into Angelique's room and said ever so softly, "Tomorrow."

Angelique's eyes opened wide—excitement and wonder filled her for the next few hours. She had no clue what he had planned, and even when she awoke in the morning, her first thoughts were of what it could be. Old Jerry was already sitting at the table, having his morning breakfast and chatting with her father about some horses his buddy in the area had. From what she could hear of the conversation, Old Jerry was going to be gone for most of the day. Angelique was starting to feel a little drained from wondering what the gift would be—after all, they had arrived four days ago. She continued to control herself.

"I'll load the hay from the barn and run it over there—I'm sure his horses will love it. Should be a repeat buyer for you." That was the last thing Angelique heard Old Jerry say to her father as he stood and walked out the back door.

"Great, that'll take all day," Angelique exclaimed under her breath.

"What was that, Angel?" her father asked.

"I'm hungry. Are we having pancakes?" she asked and put a fake smile on her face.

When Angelique was close to being finished with her breakfast, Old Jerry stepped through the door and walked over to the counter where the coffee pot sat. He could feel her eyes following him as he walked through the door and crossed the room.

"You about done there Ange? We have to get moving soon," Jerry said as he filled his cup.

"D...done," she replied while chewing.

"Great. See you in the truck in five." Drinking his coffee, Jerry turned and gave her a wink as he headed for the door.

The excitement was more than Angelique could take—she had been waiting patiently for four days. Well, at least it *looked* like she was patient on the outside. As it turned out, five minutes for her to get in the truck were four and a half more than she needed. She didn't think Jerry would ever get in. Old Jerry walked over to the truck and gave the passenger side front tire one kick and then another. Angelique sat in the passenger seat and watched. He then slowly walked to the back tire on the same side and then gave it a light kick—he seemed to be checking the air in his tires.

That was it. She could not wait any longer. Angelique pressed her thumb quickly on the buckle release for the seat belt and it quickly retracted. But before it had fully finished, she was already on her way out the door. She ran to the driver's side, where she kicked the front tire; moved to the rear of the truck, where she kicked the rear driver's-side tire; moved to the trailer on the same side, where she kicked the tire; ran to the other side of the trailer, and again kicked passenger side tire; and then moved to the back of the truck, stretched her short legs under it, and kicked the spare tire.

"All good!" she said calmly, looking directly at Old Jerry, who was looking back at her with the biggest grin.

"OK," he replied as she turned and headed back to the passenger side.

Her short, blond hair bounced up and down, a bounce that made her hair look like a cheerleader's pom-poms. Jerry walked at a normal pace to the front of the truck and looked in at her buckling up—he still wore the grin on his face. He was done playing games with her. It was time to let her in on the surprise.

Jerry got in the truck, and they started down the road. He figured that after she asked, he would let Angelique know what the surprise was. He ran into a problem with that idea: she had decided to let him have the first word. They drove for almost half an hour, and then it happened.

"Damn Ange, you are one stubborn girl!" Jerry was the first to break. His buddy's place was less than a thirty-minute drive, but they were pulling a trailer, which was slowing them down.

"What is it?" she half yelled, unable to contain herself anymore. "Am I going to get to ride my first horse?" she asked with a smile.

"Yes," he replied. "That's not your birthday gift."

Angelique was puzzled. She wondered: How could taking her to ride her first horse not be the surprise?

"First you will learn to ride a horse," Jerry said, and then paused as they turned into the driveway of his friend's horse ranch. "Then we are going to spend the rest of the day with firearm training."

He began to get worried. Angelique's face just went blank, and all emotion left her expression. Jerry was so concerned that he brought the truck slowly to a stop. She looked almost catatonic. He turned to her.

"Angelique?" Jerry asked, as if he were looking for her.

She unbuckled her seat belt and leaped upon him in one swift movement. Jerry had no clue what was happening until he suddenly realized that she was hanging from his neck, hugging him. Angelique was speechless.

That planting season they made many trips out to Jerry's buddy's ranch for horse-riding lessons—that was the cover. Angelique did learn how to ride a horse but not nearly to the extent that she learned about firearms. Old Jerry and his buddy taught her everything, starting with firearm safety, pistols, tactical movements, and long-range marksmanship with big-bore rifles. Over the next few years, Angelique learned about reloading her rounds, ballistics, the purpose of different bullets, and much more. She also discovered that her favorite sidearm was a Colt 1911 .45ACP.

Chapter 4

ANGELIQUE GOES TO SCHOOL

Even though Angelique very much enjoyed her life, especially when Old Jerry came around, she felt that she was missing out by not attending public school. She watched every morning when the school bus would pick up the neighbor boy and wished that she, too, could get on the bus. Every day in Angelique's house started with begging her parents to attend public school, like the rest of the kids in the neighborhood. To her, it looked like the neighborhood kids were always having fun on the bus, and she wanted to have fun with friends. After about a year of this same daily routine, her parents gave in and allowed Angelique to give it a try. She was so very excited her first day that she was out at the end of the driveway and waiting for the bus a half hour before the bus arrived.

Oh, no! Angelique thought as she saw the neighbor boy coming out of his house. She had hoped to get on the bus before he came out. From what she had noticed, he was always running out of his front door when the bus had already stopped and begun to honk. *Today of all days he decides to come out before the bus arrives*, she thought to herself.

"What are you doing?" Chad, the neighbor boy, asked with a confused look. "You going to school?" he followed up, without giving her a chance to answer his first question. "I thought you did school at home. Why would you want to go to a real school?"

Angelique had no idea which of his many questions to answer first—they just kept coming from him, and he never gave her a chance to answer before asking another.

"Yes," she said with a beautiful smile.

She figured Chad had asked so many questions that he wouldn't know which one she was answering. Chad was a little, redheaded, freckled boy who annoyed Angelique most of the time, yet she never showed it.

"I hear the bus," she said with excitement, and she knew that her first day of school would soon begin.

Chapter 5

⸺⸙⸺

KARL AND ANGELIQUE

The world was stuck in a constant state of panic over nuclear war between the Soviet Union and the United States. All around the world, nations jockeyed for position on the world stage. Even though they were all waiting for the worst to happen due to the Soviets and the United States threatening to use nuclear weapons, the countries all raced to develop their own.

Young Karl, at age eleven, had no real understanding of what was happening. All he knew was that some guy on the TV was commanding somebody to "tear down that wall." For young Karl, there was only one thing on his mind: the girl who danced in the woods. He had moved into the area little more than a year ago, and he would see her as the school bus passed her house each day. He often wondered why she didn't ride the bus or go to his school, since she lived just atop the hill near his family's home. Often he would run through the woods and would see her in the same spot, doing what looked like a very strange dance. Sometimes she would do the same movements over and over and over. He didn't understand why girls did the things they did.

Karl would watch as Angelique jumped around and swung her arms wildly; he was too shy to speak to her even though he wanted to. Each time he saw her, he would dream of going over to the fence and calling out, if only to find out her name. It wouldn't take long before he would let fear take over and go back to the things young boys did in the woods, like climbing trees and swinging on vines.

Often he searched for arrowheads and other Indian artifacts. He was fascinated by history. Karl was always reading books about ancient Rome, Egypt, the old West—whatever he could get his hands on. When they first moved to the area, he found books on the town itself (Rock Town), mostly due to the strangeness of it. It seemed strange that anyone would name a town Rock Town. That was until he learned why.

It seemed that two families looking to make better lives for themselves had come over together from Germany. The two families had been large and had chosen two large sections of land to farm and build a small community on. The only problem was that when they arrived at their new sections of land, the ground covered in rocks. The two men who headed each family blamed the other for the poor land. Nobody knew exactly which man threw the first rock, but before anyone had realized it, they had thrown rocks at one another for most of the day. With everyone in the family throwing, areas were cleared as rocks flew through the air at the opposing family. Soon after these areas are where the city hall and the old school were built. From that day on, the town had been named Rock Town.

Today was the day every young boy despised: the first day of a new school year. No more running through the woods all day, climbing trees, fishing in the pond, or playing in the creeks. No, it was all cut down to only the weekends, which seemed so far apart that they would never come.

Karl's mother woke him up very early and made sure he had breakfast before school. She would drag him out of his bed by one foot, and right before he smacked the floor, he would surrender to her will. "I'm up. I'm up," he would moan. Then he would start getting himself ready.

Karl went through what would become his morning routine, but this morning was special: he could smell his mother cooking pancakes. He hurried and ran to the kitchen before she was done. He always felt like if he didn't ask her, she would not make them the way he liked them—crispy around the edges— but his mother would smile every time, as she knew that was how he liked them. After Karl applied just enough syrup to cover the top to the edge of his pancakes (spreading the syrup with his fork so that very little ever touched his plate), his mother would laugh.

No matter how early Karl was awakened, it seemed that he was still running to catch the bus. He either spent too long getting out of bed, getting dressed, or eating breakfast—it was always something. Every once in a while, he would take a glance out the window to the top of the hill—on many mornings, a little yellow from the bus would show through the trees.

To Karl, getting on the school bus felt like anything but what he wanted to do—in fact, it was the last thing. Sometimes he would start out as soon as he heard the bus, but by then, it would still be too late. On most mornings, he would find himself running for the end of the driveway. However, after getting on the bus this morning, he would be the one waiting at the end of the driveway to get on from then on—the bus would no longer be waiting for him. Today she was on the bus: the girl who did the funny dances in the woods.

Chapter 6

———— ✺ ————

KARL AND ANGELIQUE MEET

As he was walking to the back of the bus, Karl stopped in his tracks. He could not believe that it was Angelique and that she was sitting alone. He normally would walk to the back of the bus to sit; in the mornings, Karl could sit wherever he wanted on the bus since he and Angelique were among the first people on. Due to the shock of seeing the girl and freezing in the aisle, that changed as his heart began to beat fast and a queasy feeling came over him. The bus started moving, and Karl almost fell to the floor—instead, he did a little roll and landed in the seat across from her.

"Hi, I am Angelique," she said in the sweetest voice he had ever heard.

Karl's heart started pounding hard in his chest, and he began to feel a little queasy. Then he realized, *Angelique, Angelique. I know her name. Angelique.*

"Karl," he finally got out, after what seemed like minutes had passed. Then he turned quickly to the window and watched the trees as they streaked by.

Not knowing what was wrong with the boy, Angelique turned her attention to the bus ride and thought about how happy she was to be on her way to school.

Karl just could not believe it: at school, she seemed to be following him. She was assigned to virtually every class he was in. Although it made him happy, he was also very scared. In every class she attended with him that day, he could not think of anything but her, and all day he kept telling himself to talk to her. Each time Karl wanted to talk to Angelique, he could not get the courage up to do so, and now it was the last class of the day.

Karl sat in his seat near the back of the class and hoped that she would walk through the door. He lost hope when the bell rang and she had not entered the classroom. Then there she was—just on the other side of the door's glass. Karl felt his pulse start to race, not only because she was entering the room for this class but also because there were only two seats left in the class. There was one open desk in front, and the other was behind him. This was his chance—he just had to find the right opening.

Angelique was with Charlotte the guidance counselor, who had been checking on her for most of the day. This being the last class of the day, the counselor wanted to check with Angelique before the class. The counselor knew that once the bell rang for school to let out, it was like opening a cage filled with hundreds of angry squirrels.

Even though Angelique had wanted to attend public school, she was excited for the day to be finished—she wanted to tell her parents all about it. After the counselor left, Angelique entered the class and spoke with the teacher about why she was late. She had been briefed on the tardiness policy and wanted to follow the rules to the best of her ability. Her teacher had already seen that Angelique was with the counselor and just directed her to have a seat.

When Angelique turned away from the teacher and looked for an empty seat, she was happy to see one by the neighbor boy. She walked over and took the seat in front of his, placing her books on the desktop before sitting down. Her pencil fell to the floor without her noticing—someone else noticed, though: Karl. Angelique felt a tap on her arm, and she knew it had to be the neighbor boy. With one quick movement, she spun with excitement to see what he needed, hoping it was to pass her a note. But instead she felt her hand make contact with something other than the back of her seat. Then she heard it.

"Ouch!" Karl screeched.

When Angelique was fully turned around, she saw it: her white pencil with little pink hearts, dangling from his open hand. She could tell it was in very deep, and as he pulled it out, the pencil had no lead.

Karl was stunned. *How did that happen?* he thought to himself. He had opened his hand as soon as he'd felt the pain, almost instinctively, like he had grabbed something hot. The only problem was, this something was sticking in his hand. When he looked at it, Karl could see a cone-shaped bump on the back of his hand, which was when he realized what had happened. He turned his hand palm up, and the pencil remained.

As the teacher was moving to Karl with a box of Kleenex, he pulled the pencil from his palm. Once the pencil was free, he could see what looked like a black hole in his hand. It took no time for the hole to vanish in a pool of red, and by that time, the teacher was already pulling tissues from the box to apply pressure. Within seconds, Karl was off to see the school nurse.

Nurse Janet cleaned Karl's hand, made sure everything was functional, and applied antibacterial ointment and a bandage. Karl's hand didn't bother him as much as the thought that he would not get to ride the bus home. The injury was not bad enough to be sent out for medical treatment, but it was enough to have his parents come and pick him up. Karl sat and watched out the window while the other children boarded the buses—a little while after they left, his father showed up. After talking to the nurse Janet about how Karl received the wound by attempting to pass a pencil to Angelique. Karl's father Eugen walked over to where young Karl sat.

"Ready to head home, Son?" Karl's father asked with his slight German accent.

"Yes, Father," Karl replied in a depressed voice, his head hung low.

This gave his father a cause for concern. "Let's go, Son—we can talk about it on the way home." Walking to the truck Eugen could see that his son had something on his mind and was pretty sure what it was. Young Karl walked silently his head down holding his injured hand. Eugen wait for Karl to speak first but after a few miles he decided to speak first. Glancing over to Karl he asked, "You want to talk now?"

"No," Karl said.

"OK, can you answer a question?"

Karl bobbed his head up and down once in reply.

"Is Angelique the daughter of the family next door?" The moment Karl's father said Angelique's name, he knew that he was right about the problem. Karl took in a deep breath at the sound of Angelique's name and looked up and out the windshield.

"Yes," Karl reluctantly replied.

"Is she the reason you now have a hole in your hand?" his father asked with amusement.

"Yes, but it wasn't her fault. It was mine. I was returning her pencil the wrong way. When she turned, it was bumped, and being very sharp, it went in my hand. I swear, Dad, it was an accident. She had noth—"

His father had to cut Karl off, or he would have gone on like that for the rest of the ride home.

"That explains everything."

With confusion in his eyes, Karl asked, "What explains everything?"

Eugene looked at Karl and said one word: *women*. After a few seconds (during which he looked lost in thought), Karl's father continued: "They are the one thing that—no matter how big, strong, and tough a man is—can cause him to climb to great heights or lose everything." After another second, Karl's father continued, "Making us look like fools is what happens most of the time."

"Son," Karl's father continued, remembering how it felt to be in love at Karl's age. "Your Opa" what you Karl called his grandfather "gave me a piece of advice that my father passed to him during the war. Attack!"

Karl jumped in his seat startled by his father's voice as he said the word loudly—his father's point had been made.

"Son, what he meant was, whenever there is something in your life that causes you anxiety or fear, just attack it. Had it not been for Opa's advice, you wouldn't be here now," Karl's father said, beaming with pride.

The next morning, Karl was waiting at the end of his driveway for the bus, bandaged hand and all. He didn't know what he was going to do when he got on the bus, and it had been driving him crazy all morning. One second he decided to sit in the same seat as Angelique and talk to her—the next, he decided to walk past her to the rear of the bus without giving her another thought. He had to decide what he was going to do and soon.

Karl could hear the bus and see it from the end of his driveway, and panic started to set in. He began pacing; his thoughts began racing—he didn't know what to do and wished he had more time, but the bus had just come to a complete stop in front of him. Karl froze and looked up at the bus driver, who was puzzled to see him standing there and not running down the driveway.

Karl suddenly remembered the advice his father had given him: "Just attack!" Karl looked at his hand as one foot went in front of the other, and before he knew it, there he was. He was standing by the seat that contained Angelique, who had a very worried expression on her face.

"How is your hand, Karl? I so did not mean to do that. I hope you believe me." Angelique said in the sweetest voice Karl had ever heard.

"Oh it is nothing and I should have been more careful."

Feeling confident that this was his opening Karl sat down beside her with butterfly's flying around in the pit of his stomach, unsure what to say next.

"What do you do for fun after school?" Angelique asked breaking the silence. Karl relaxed at the question and the two began talking without stopping all the way to school. Karl could not help from thinking while they talked *The greatest two things about yesterday—this hole in my hand and Opa's advice*. From that point forward Karl and Angelique were inseparable.

Karl had become what he perceived to be a man—a man with new beliefs and a new way of life. Leaving the shy little boy in the past, he was filled with confidence. Little did he know that even though he and Angelique had made a connection, their young love would soon be separated. The following summer Karl's parents had decided to move hundreds of miles away in order to be closer to his aging grandfather, Karl and Angelique lost all contact with each other.

Chapter 7

CREATING HISTORY

E veryone saw it coming, yet it seemed that nobody did anything to stop it: war! Only this time it was not just a war overseas—there was a war brewing in the United States as well. It was strange. It seemed that the majority of the country had no idea just how bad things had become and how corrupt and inept the government was—the very same government they had elected. It was to be expected, since most of the votes the politicians received were from those who received entitlements.

The amazing part was how the government and political parties seemed to have total control over the news. In the United States, there were, at any one time, six major news outlets. Of those six, all would have very similar news broadcast dealing with the same subjects—approved subjects, dictated to them from their respective political parties. Very few people seemed to recognize this was even happening. People in the United States cared more about *Keeping Up with the Kardashians* and the new government handouts they could receive than what the politicians were doing.

The government had turned into a get-rich-quick scheme. Each congressman or congresswoman worked the system to increase his or her wealth and the wealth of those around them. Many of the programs such as payments made to colleges and universities were mere fronts for moving taxpayer money to the congress people's respective organizations. Much of this was not that well disguised, yet the people did not do anything, because they were being paid off through entitlements.

Slowly, just as during the American Revolution, those who paid attention to what was going on started to speak up and be heard. The people once again spoke out against scandals and corrupt policies, only to find both tied up in courts until the people had lost interest, and this became the government's normal operating procedure.

Many of the veterans coming back from decade-long wars in Iraq and Afghanistan paid close attention to what the government was up to—this was mostly why they were placed atop of the National security watch list created by Homeland Security as the number-one threat to the United States. Just under the veterans on the National security watch list by Homeland Security were gun owners. In a time when the government kept telling the people about the fight against terrorism, how come the terrorists were not at the top of National security watch list?

Chapter 8

THE SPARK

Texas. Texas was the first to say *enough is enough*. Enough with all the corruption in the government at the federal level and the destruction of the Constitution. Texas was not the only state to feel this way—it was just the first to act and take the lead. Texans became nervous with the removal of the Posse Comitatus Act, which prevented the use of federal troops on US soil. Not only that, but Texans were nervous about the use of Texas and a few surrounding states as enemy territories for the war games conducted by the US military over the last two years.

The games put people in Bastrop Texas on edge, and even more so when they started seeing the C-130s dropping paratroopers and supplies and seeing soldiers repelling in from Black Hawk helicopters. The whole sight made it seem more like an invasion than training. The military had plenty of land on which to conduct mass drills at this level—areas that would not cause panic.

And if all those activities were not bad enough, there were the black-ops personnel, who walked the streets trying to blend in with the good people of Texas. But Special Operations guys were easier to spot than they thought—they commonly asked the same questions of people, their feelings about the current government or the weapons the citizens of Bastrop possessed, and in small towns this was a dead giveaway that the strangers were not locals. People in the rule areas of west Texas were much harder for the Special Operations personal to fool than those in cities such as New York or L.A. where citizens were much more liberal.

Because of the general ill feeling the citizens of Texas held, the governor requested that the head of the Texas National Guard keep an eye on all military activities by federal troops in the state. The year started out just like the last few, with the announcement that Texas and the same surrounding states would once again be treated as enemy territory. Over the last two training years, there had been more and more equipment brought into Texas and the surrounding areas, but little of it ever seemed to leave. The amount of personnel trained in the area also seemed to increase, along with the duration of the training.

This was the third year that Texas was going to be used as enemy territory. Like the previous years, the governor put out his request to the Texas National Guard, and they worked at keeping tabs on the whereabouts and logistics of the training. Everything played out along the same lines as the previous years, but that was before the incident causing Texas to begin seceding from the Union.

The Bureau of Land Management, also known as the BLM, had been doing what most people felt was land grabbing. There were tens of thousands of acres along the Texas-Oklahoma border, stretching throughout the Red River Valley. The ranchers had utilized the open range for their farms for hundreds of years. The BLM had recently been trying to confiscate the land for federal use by classifying it as federal property. This would remove the farmers, who relied on the thousands of acres for their livelihood. To those ranchers, it was unacceptable to be forced off land that their families had worked on for multiple generations.

For those who don't know, a popular saying in Texas is "Don't mess with Texas." Apparently no one told the BLM this. Early one day they came in strong, under the cover of night, with semis and ATVs, and rounded up cattle and horses that belonged to the ranchers of the Texas side of the Red River Valley.

The BLM had already suffered an embarrassment in New Mexico when they tried to remove a rancher from state land that had been worked by a family for generations. They had rounded up the farmer's livestock the ATVs and helicopters, killing many cattle in the process. After doing so, the ranchers had refused to leave and staged a protest that had drawn in hundreds of people from all around the country. Veterans and civilians had armed themselves, ready to defend the rancher rights. After a short standoff, the cattle had been returned, and the BLM had worked to scrub the situation from the news. The BLM were very determined not to make the same mistake again—their solution was to come in faster, with more personnel and more equipment.

The size of the land that the BLM was trying to appropriate from the Texas ranchers was approximately seventy thousand acres, and it would be the first grab of many. They split up into five teams, all five being an equal distance apart, at specific areas that had the highest quantity of ranches raising cattle. They moved into their positions at 0330 hours. It was not until 0430 hours that everything was set up and ready for the operation to be executed. Everything had been staged; the operation was set to begin, and the big push to round up all the livestock was on.

Chapter 9

LIFE BEGINS FOR ANGELIQUE

Old Jerry not only trained Angelique in hand-to-hand combat and weapons—he also instilled in her a strong sense of patriotism. She really listened to what he had to say and took everything to heart. In her world of flower children and everyone being special, Jerry was the only person Angelique really cared for (other than her parents). She also knew that if anyone found out about the things Jerry was teaching her, well, it would be the last time she would see Jerry. Violence had no row in the communal society her parents lived in and they had chosen the path of nonaggression, even knowing how to protect oneself against it was to her parents a form of aggression.

It was the love she had for her parents and the education she received from Jerry that caused a rift between her and her family. For a week after graduating high school, Angelique worked on the farm with her family, planting crops and tending to the livestock. That was as long as she could take the idea of this being her life. As she put the last of the spring seeds in the ground, Angelique looked up at her mother and father. Wondering how they were going to take what she had decided was to be her path in life, she could not wait any longer.

"I'm joining the army," Angelique said with such speed that it was almost too fast to hear but not too fast for the ears of a parent when it came to a subject like the army.

Both of Angelique's parents turned in her direction and said at precisely the same time, "WHAT?"

Now that it was out there, Angelique's relationship with her parents changed forever. Her parents hadn't thought that she would stay on the farm, but running off and joining the army—they just hadn't seen that coming.

The following week a friend of Angelique's drove her to a recruiter's office. She knew what she wanted to do—she wanted the infantry. She was very aware of what was involved, but Jerry had trained her well. Now it was time to show the world what she could do. When they arrived at the army recruiter's office, Angelique did not have a second thought about what she wanted.

They pulled up, and before the car was in park, she was out of the passenger door. Full of excitement, she walked into the office, and it almost took her breath away. Looking around the office at the posters, cardboard cutouts of soldiers, and the men and women in uniform, Angelique froze in place—not with fear, but with the excitement of the experiences she was about to embark upon.

"Hello, I am Sergeant Soper." The man reached out his hand to her, but Angelique did not even acknowledge that he was there. He cleared his voice and addressed her again. This time he had her complete attention.

"Hello," Angelique replied in a voice she did not recognize. She then brought herself back to this time and place, looked directly at the sergeant, and said, "I want to enlist."

"Then you have come to the right place. Follow me." Sgt. Soper directed her to his desk. Once she was settled, he walked over to the brochure rack, removed several brochures, and walked back behind his desk.

"OK, now here are a few jobs I think you would like." He began laying them out in front of her on his desk.

"Medic, parachute rigger, cook—"

"Wait," she said, bringing his presentation to a quick halt.

"I know what I want to do. Infantry," she said with pride.

When he heard the words come from Angelique's mouth, Sgt. Soper froze. All he could think was, *How could someone this beautiful want to join the infantry?* Then he thought that she must be mistaking the infantry for something else, another job. He decided that he did not want to hurt her feelings about the mistake. He would just move on with the brochures he was showing. "Transportation—"

"No, I am sorry, Sergeant, but I want the infantry." As she cut him off this time, he could hear that her tone had become much more serious.

Sgt. Soper looked at Angelique and thought, *This blond-haired, blue-eyed girl wants the infantry?* It puzzled him.

"I want to fight," Angelique said as she leaned forward and slowly kept eye contact with the sergeant.

"Very well then," he said at the same time as he broke her stare. He then gathered up the brochures that were on the table and walked back to the rack they had come from. Angelique watched as he did so and watched as he put them back in their places on the rack and took out one and only one brochure.

The excitement was starting to build in her again as she watched him come over with the single brochure, one that had to be for the infantry.

This time the sergeant sat down in his seat before addressing her. He looked into her eyes and said, "I am sorry, but at this time women are not allowed in the infantry."

After hearing the words come from his mouth, Angelique was outraged. She could feel her hopes and dreams crashing. Her path in life had been so clear just a few moments ago—now it was fading.

Sgt. Soper then began speaking again. "Although—"

Angelique's attention focused closely on that word.

"There is a position I think you would like, if you are interested," he said in a questioning tone, as if she were going to leave since she could not have what she wanted.

Little did the sergeant know, Angelique was not the kind of person to just quit when things didn't go her way. She was very disappointed about not being allowed in the infantry because she was female, but that had not changed her plans about enlisting.

"Yes," she said, as if also saying *get on with it, man!*

"Military police."

He had her attention now.

Sgt. Soper placed the brochure on the desk in front of Angelique.

"What all do they do?" she asked, interested in the prospect.

"It is as close to the fight as you can get without being infantry." He paused to read her reaction. After seeing that this was going to be the right fit for her, the sergeant began pulling out the paperwork for her to fill out.

Angelique spent two hours filling out her enlistment papers—by the time she was done, she was excited than when she had gone inside the recruitment office. Her excitement last week had been nothing compared to today. Today she was at Military Entrance Processing, where she would undergo her Armed Services Vocational Aptitude Battery test and physical exam. The bus picked her up at the recruiting office, and the entire ride there she looked out the window and had thoughts about what to expect tomorrow. Tonight she would take the ASVAB, and tomorrow the physical.

The test that night was easy for Angelique, with each question she answered she knew there could be no chance if failing. But by the end of the next day, Angelique wished that they had allowed her to bring a book to read. There was so much waiting around. This was not how she had expected the day to go. She had expected to be moving from one thing to the next all day, not doing one thing and waiting thirty minutes for the next part of the exam. Then Angelique remembered Jerry often saying that in the military there was always a lot of "hurry up and wait"—she was beginning to understand what he had been talking about.

After the physical, they had another stack of papers for her to sign. Before today, she'd had no clue what her social security number was, but after today, she would no longer forget it. She wrote it almost as much as she signed her name. After choosing her job as military police, Angelique moved to the next and final step of the day, one she had not been aware would happen on that day: the swearing in. The oath of enlistment that every service member took. When Angelique was told that the oath would happen at the end of her day, a cold chill ran all through her body, as if a hundred ghosts had passed through her.

After an hour of waiting, it was time. They led her to a room at the other end of the building, and there were many others waiting as well. They all looked around at one another until an officer walked into the room and to the front.

"I will be conducting your swearing in today," he said as he looked around the room.

"If there are any among you who wish to change your minds, now is the time to do so." He then waited for just a few seconds for his audience to con-ssider what they were about to participate in. Once again he spoke. "Let's begin. When I say *insert name*, you will insert your name. We clear?"

Everyone replied "yes" Angelique though had doubts that a few in the room could follow the simple instructions. Her blood pressure and emotions began to run high with excitement, and then they started. With her right hand raised, Angelique repeated after the officer: "I Angelique Rose Carringer, do solemn-ly swear that I will support and defend the Constitution of the United States against all enemies, foreign and domestic; that I will bear true faith and alle-giance to the same; and that I will obey the orders of the president of the United States and the orders of the officers appointed over me, according to regulations and the Uniform Code of Military Justice. So help me God."

By the end, Angelique had never felt so much excitement. Her life was truly changing. Angelique understood that it wouldn't be easy, but for her, that was part of the attraction.

Chapter 10

SQUIRES FAMILY FARM

I t was a beautiful Texas morning; Bill Squires and his son Richey were gearing up the horses for rounding up the cattle. Bill checked the saddle of his horse once more pulling the leather straps tight as he ran through a check list of supplies in his mind.

"You have the fencing staples?" Bill asked his son who he was sure had other things on his mind.

"Right here." Richey was very excited that day—as of midnight, he was now sixteen. He had planned for the last six months to be posted outside the DMV door at 8:50 a.m. on Monday. Even though he had been driving around the ranch for years, Richey could not wait to take the ranch truck to town. Bill had everything checked within minutes; the two of them were ready and waiting patiently for the rest of the work group. Bill's brother Tom; Tom's son, Robert and his daughter, Sierra, were also pitching in that morning. Like most ranch families, they helped one another with the work as much as possible.

The Squires family they preferred to round up the cattle for branding and for castrating the bulls in the early morning. They had their packs loaded up, for they knew it would be a long day—the gear consisted of the day's meals, two canteens of water, and the tools needed for the day. Each family member carried a firearm—you never knew when a cow would have to be put down or a predator would be after the cattle. Bill always carried his grandfather's Winchester .30-30 while Richey preferred carrying a semiautomatic .44 Magnum Ruger rifle—both were carried in sheaths attached to their saddles. Tom was a six-gun man—somehow, he always had one on his side and was still able to wrestle the bulls to the ground without it getting in the way.

The most skilled with a rifle was Robert, who had served as a sniper with the 101st Airborne. After thirteen years of military service, with six of those years spent overseas, he was ready to do nothing but work on the ranch, although he still loved his weapons. When it came to Robert's rifle, he carried something that was a great deal different than the rest of his family's firearms and not even close to traditional. His rifle of choice was the Noreen BN36 in .30-06 cartridge. The rifle was constructed in the AR-15 rifle style—it was semiautomatic, with a twenty-round capacity.

Robert had fallen in love with this rifle the first time he had laid his finger on the trigger at the range. His weapon of choice in the military had been the M24 sniper rifle, which shot a .308 cartridge. The two rifles had nothing in common, except for the thirty-caliber bullet. Since he was young, Robert had loved the .30-06 round, and with the BN36, after moving through the twenty-four-inch barrel, it had a much greater effective range than the .308 cartridge. It was tricked out with a Mark 4 Leupold LR/T scope. Robert never used it for hunting—after his time overseas, the only thing he loved to do was take out Pepsi cans and fire cold bore at 1,100 yards. He had a target set up at the ranch and, making all the calculations needed beforehand, took a shot once a day.

Robert took his love affair with firearms seriously. For the Noreen rifle, he used a machine gun–rated silencer from SilencerCo with a Specwar suppressor, and he made subsonic rounds for his .30-06, which he dubbed "silent nights." They greatly reduced his range, but he could still put the bullet on target at four hundred yards without disturbing the silent of night. The main issue he had was that the rifle did not fit in any of the standard sheath designs for saddles.

So Robert did the only thing he could and had a local leather smith design a sheath that accommodated the shape of the rifle. It did take a little while for his horse to get used to the awkwardness, but he had been able to adjust. Big Boy was a purebred palomino, standing sixteen hands with seven hundred pounds of muscle. His coat was a golden tan with a long, blond mane. Robert was there when the monstrous horse was born and had cared for him during his first month on Earth, which created a bond with the horse. Even though he had left for his last tour in Afghanistan after that month, when he returned, Robert and the horse were still connected, almost at a spiritual level.

Robert's sister, Sierra, was a senior in high school and was in love with creating short documentaries. Her pack was much like the rest. She had her gloves, rope, and other gear for the day's work. Sierra was never known to sit back and let others do the work. She may have been the homecoming queen, but she had no problem getting her hands dirty, or any other part for that matter.

She tied back her long, dark-brown hair and ran it through the ball cap she always wore when going out to work the range. Her cap had once said *Willie's Feed Store. We supply the feed so you can supply the meat.* After years of use and wear, about all that could be made out was *Willie's Feed Sto* and a few other letters. Nobody knew why the cap meant so much to her, but it was always on her head when there was work to be done.

There were two things that were different about Sierra's pack, the most notable difference being that she only carried a .22-caliber pistol with her—an old Blackhawk revolver her father used to quick draw with. She never wanted to move up to anything bigger, not that she couldn't handle the larger calibers— she just chose not to. The other difference would be the camera she had attached to her old cap. It was small but still very noticeable.

"Sierra," Bill called out when they had finally arrived. It was still dark, but as Sierra got closer to her uncle and he went to give her a hug, he noticed the camera on the cap's bill. He was always giving her a hard time about one thing or another—in fact, he gave everyone a hard time. Uncle Bill's hard times were always in good humor and made people around him enjoy his company. "Sierra," he said, "don't you know cameras are mounted on the left side of the bill, not the right? After all, it is just proper etiquette."

"Well, Uncle Bill," she replied in a sassy tone as she pushed out of his hug. "You never could tell left from right."

After the banter subsided, Bill showed his interest. "What documentary are you working on now?" he asked, with true interest in her work.

The family always enjoyed Sierra's work, except when the documentary was focused on them. She seemed to have taken after Bill with the witty banter and a funny style of sarcasm.

"This one is not really defined yet," she said, somehow with confidence and uncertainty at the same time.

Bill raised an eyebrow and gave her a puzzled look. "How can you not know what the documentary is about?"

Sierra created the smile that always made men melt—she was great at that and knew it. "I wanted to take a new approach and shoot the footage and then decide what it will be about."

Bill always had a good sense for bullshit and called her on it. "So you got a new camera and wanted to try it out."

With a look that said *busted*, Sierra laughed and replied, "I have to go help Robert unload the horses. Don't make this doc about you." She let out a laugh and pointed at him while walking over to the trailer.

The five of them started the day by riding the ridge, making it easier to spot. For most of the ride, they rode in silence; as the hint of dawn began to break, there was a little more chatting. For the last few minutes, they had been hearing something but none of them could place it—none of them felt like it was anything to bring up at the time. They were listening for the cattle in the darkness. All five of them enjoyed the twilight hour—they believed that five in the morning had to be the most peaceful part of the day. They enjoyed nothing more than being out in the fresh air with no worries other than working the cattle. This, on the other hand, would not be one of those mornings.

They had just started to reach the area where they suspected the cattle would be, where they typically always were, when the group heard it—the sound they had heard earlier had become loud enough to make out: it was mo-torcycles or ATVs. They often had issues with people getting lost riding trails in the area, and on more than one occasion, they had helped to point those people in the right direction.

Speaking in a soft voice, Robert inquired, "What do you think, Dad? Little early for riders, isn't it?"

Tom just squinted his eyes, as if he was focusing to hear clearer and see bet-ter—he took in all that his senses could tell him before replying, "Wouldn't be the normal lost city riders. That is for sure."

Bill's face also had a puzzled look. "Let's move in that direction, slowly." He pointed his gloved finger to the east, along the ridge. It was hard to make out in the very dim light, but those who couldn't see the direction he pointed at just followed him.

As they were just reaching the top of the ridge, it was immediately clear what was happening.

"Rustlers!" Bill whispered with urgency. After cresting the top of the ridge and seeing the lights from three ATVs, the others came to the same conclu-sion. They saw the rustlers moving back and forth in a circle pattern behind the cattle, pushing them to the east. It was easy to tell from the cry of the cattle that they were not having a great day.

The group's first instinct was to rush down and put a stop to what was a hanging offence. They knew there was no point in checking for cell phone cov-erage: they were too far out.

Bill turned slowly to address the others. "I want nothing more than to ride down there, but it's much too dangerous." He spoke in a low tone that was barely audible. With all the noise from the ATVs and cattle, he did not fear that the men down below would hear them.

"I do have a plan," Bill continued. He then looked at Robert and asked, "Did you bring your suppressor?"

Robert was surprised at the question and wondered if Bill was talking about killing the men silently. The last thing Robert wanted was to shoot men for stealing cattle. Even if that was what his uncle was thinking, it did not matter.

Robert just slightly dipped his head and said, "No, I did not see a need for the extra weight."

Bill looked down the valley and back at Robert "OK. With the noise down there, I don't think they would even hear a shot. So this is what I want you to do…"

Robert felt a sigh of relief until he heard his uncle say, "This is what I want you to do…" He had done his duty without pause overseas—Robert knew that every shot he took there was justified. Shooting a man for cattle rustling was not right, and Robert was going to say so when he heard the next part of Bill's plan.

As he was laying out his plan, Bill looked over at Robert and noticed the way Robert's face was distorted, almost like he was extremely constipated. Then Bill realized what Robert must have been thinking.

Speaking a little louder, Bill addressed Robert, who was looking down in thought. "Robert! Look at me, son."

Robert looked up to tell his uncle how he felt. "I will n—"

"I want you to shoot the ATVs. Can you make that shot, son?"

Just as Bill's words rolled out of his mouth, Robert was silently relieved and said "Hell, yeah." He then started mumbling under his breath: "Too easy, too easy."

Bill continued to explain what he wanted to happen. "When Robert disables the ATV's, in the poor light, it should look like the motor threw a rod." He paused to make sure everyone understood that they were only shooting the motor and not any of the men down below, no matter if they were cattle rustlers or not. "The idea is that since they are down one, they will want to get out of here and call it a day."

While Bill was explaining the rest of the plan, Robert was unstrapping his rifle and looking for a place to tie Big Boy to.

Everyone seemed to be good with the plan, especially Sierra. From the moment they had all come to the conclusion that the people were rustlers, her blood had started pumping. This was going to be her best documentary ever. Sierra had already developed the name for the rustlers: Red River Rustlers. The triple *R*'s. *Nah*, she thought. Sierra thought the whole breaking-things-down-to-letters thing had been done to death—it had lost meaning. By the time Uncle Bill had finished his plan, she had already checked everything a dozen times. This was footage she did not want to miss.

The five of them kept just below the backside of the ridge from the rustlers, preventing their outlines from being seen from below. The first thing the rustlers would see, if anything would be the twenty-gallon hat that Bill wore. In the right light, it looked like a condor perched upon his head. The rustlers were not moving at a quick pace, and for the most part, they did seem to have the knowledge needed to move cattle. Then again, the people who got into cattle rustling were not normally the brightest.

After Bill was through talking, Robert rode east, a little ahead of the ATVs. He found a nice clump of twisted cedar trees, which would provide great cover and help hide the flash. There was enough light to make the shot easy enough, but there was just enough darkness for the flash to give him away. Robert tied Big Boy about twenty yards down the ridge, and with his rifle in hand, he grabbed his pack, which contained a small sandbag, water, a range finder, and one extra magazine. He knew he would not need the extra magazine—it was just force of habit.

Robert eased himself between the cedars and settled into position. Every movement he made was slow and direct at this point—his military training was kicking in even though this was not a combat situation. He raised his range finder up and spotted two objects 635 yards down below: a large rock at 635 yards and a shrub ranging 602 yards. Now he knew just what setting he would place his scope. He had everything he needed to know to include slope of the ridge, wind, and temp. Now it was just time to wait for the right opportunity.

The rustlers moved forward, driving the cattle. Robert knew that there would be only a small window between the cattle passing his range marks and the ATVs moving by them.

It seemed like the cattle were never going to move past Robert's range marks—these men really did not know what they were doing. Suddenly

Robert saw it: the shrub—it was his first opportunity for a shot. The cattle were past it, and here came one of the men riding up to a cow that was munching on it. Robert moved his finger to the inside of the trigger guard and then started moving it to the trigger. All the while, he focused on his breathing and peered through the scope at the front of the engine of the ATV. His breathing was almost to the natural pause, right before taking in more air, which was the optimal time to fire, and his finger was almost to the trigger. Robert did not want his finger to reach the trigger before the pause in breathing, due to the trigger's sensitivity. Everything was timed to perfection—almost there.

"What the...!" he exclaimed. The cow started walking away with the shrub. *Was it in even close to the same spot?* Robert thought to himself. Then he immediately started scanning for the rock. "Hopefully one of the other damned cows is not that hungry," he said.

Robert then zeroed in where he thought the rock would show, and not a second too soon. *There it is*, he thought as a little smirk curled the corner of his mouth. One of the ATV's was about to ride past his mark. He was ready—it didn't take much adjusting from the last mark to this one. His breathing was on track, his trigger finger almost there. Just one last calculation needed: the speed of the ATV. Robert could only guess the speed, but at this distance, he knew it would not be that difficult for him.

He fired. The rifled recoiled, and he was back on target. Success. The ATV was no longer mobile, and a fine mist of smoke was coming from the engine.

Robert felt great satisfaction with the shot. Indeed it was a great feeling, destroying the dreams of a cattle rustler. All three of the ATVs were together now, and it appeared that the plan was a success; the three of them had not heard the shot or seen the muzzle flash.

Robert knew that this was going to make a great story for Uncle Bill to tell down at the feed store. Robert turned to make sure Uncle Bill had seen that his plan had worked. He sure had. Even at this distance, you could see the grin on Bill's face.

Suddenly it appeared that Bill's hat was caught by a gust of wind, only after it had been pushed up by a fountain of blood spouting from between his shoulders.

His body know just standing there headless holding the Winchester .30-30. Robert was in disbelief and really did not know what to make of the sight until he heard the crack of a rifle. It had only been a second, but it seemed like minutes had gone by.

All of a sudden, everything started moving faster and faster. Robert pulled himself together quickly and looked down at the men—they were holding radios and had begun scanning the ridge. From what seemed out of nowhere, Robert could see that they had M4 rifles with ACOG scopes. He also found it strange that the cattle rustlers were wearing all black and tactical gear. He kept watching the men and could tell that the shot had not come from them.

The remaining ATV's started up the ridge in the direction of Robert's family, with rifles pointed in their direction. The rustler whose ATV Robert had disabled was now on the back of the closest ATV started firing, and Robert could hear the explosive power of his cousin's .44 Magnum from down the ridge and his father's revolvers. He decided not to let the men get any closer and took sight of the lead ATV driver—at that moment he received a face full of dirt.

SHOOTER, Robert thought, and then spun to the west. He knew this had to be the shooter who had killed Bill. Robert scanned the valley—he knew the shot had come from the valley below. There. He spotted the shooter down the valley, on top of the semitrailer they had spotted earlier.

Now that the sun had crested, Robert could see three semis and a large makeshift corral. *No time for that*, he thought as another round zipped just past his head. Robert reached over and grabbed his range finder: 935 yards to his uncles killer. He did not bother changing the setting on the scope and moved between the first and second mil dot down in his scope. Exhaling, Robert slowly squeezed the trigger. It was hard to tell if the bullet struck. The shooter seemed to just fall asleep on his rifle.

Robert could still hear the gun battle going on just over from him on the ridge. Jumping to his feet, he stealthily began moving in that direction at a faster pace than he normally would have in similar situations.

After Robert cleared about fifty yards, the gunfire grew silent. Fear and panic set in, as thoughts of his sister, father, and cousin flashed to the forefront of Robert's thoughts. The next one hundred yards seemed like one giant step he cleared with ease. Then Robert could see the results of the battle. Two of the rustlers were standing over his family's motionless bodies.

Robert's stride never slowed for an instant. His Noreen was up and already firing before he had even given it a thought. One round, two round, three rounds...the 179-grain rounds just kept leaving the barrel as Robert continued to get closer and closer. The two rustlers were dancing as if controlled by a drunken marionette. That was until the last round left and the bolt locked open. Then it appeared that their strings had been cut, and they fell to the ground.

Robert came right up to the bodies on the ground, dropped to one knee, reloaded with the extra mag from his pouch, and began scanning the area for another target. He dare not look down at the bodies for fear of losing his alertness. Robert just let his instincts and training take over—he scanned in all directions, smelling and listening for movement. He snapped around to the direction from which he had charged. His only thought was: *movement*. With his rifle at the ready, he began looking for a kill shot.

Out of nowhere, it seemed, his sister rose from the fine Texas dirt.

Robert dropped his rifle and ran to her—he snatched her up from the ground like a hawk getting a field mouse for dinner. He squeezed her tight and then threw her to about arm's length.

"Are you hit? Hurt? Anywhere? Are you?"

She just shook her head no. He could tell that she was going into shock.

It was at that point that Robert began to really take in the horrific sight of his family. He did his best not to look very closely. Robert had one thing on his mind, and that was Uncle Bill's saddle pack. Robert could see all the horses around were dead, so it did not take long to find what he wanted. Uncle Bill always kept a bottle of Old Crow in his bag—he used it to cut the dust from his throat on the windy days out on the range. The bottle was at least seven years old by now—you couldn't even read the label anymore. This was going to be a lifesaver—Robert gave a shot to Sierra. She didn't even flinch—because of that, he had her do another, and this got the reaction he wanted to see. It was almost a soothing feeling, seeing her start to pull around.

Robert knew that he had to find out what the hell had just happened. Before turning around, he took a hit from the bottle himself. Robert took in a deep breath and turned. "OH, GOD!" he said.

Robert could clearly see that his cousin and father were dead, yet he checked for a pulse nevertheless. Uncle Bill never knew what had happened to him—his death was so fast. Robert moved on to the men, all in black tactical gear. *These are not typical cattle rustlers*, he thought. He turned the first one over and reached for the man's wallet.

"That won't be any help," Robert said to himself when he noticed that a round from the .30-06 had passed through the man, expanding and shredded his wallet when it exited. Robert moved on to one of the others. The next man was lying on his stomach already—Robert reached down and found his wallet and got a very sick feeling when he opened it.

Inside were credentials for the Bureau of Land Management. These men were not cattle rustlers—they worked for the government. Robert looked at the men again, searching for anything they might have missed that would have identified them as being from the BLM. There was nothing. Not even name tags.

Robert looked at his sister and knew they had to get out of there. First he had to find the third ATV rider. He moved down the hill and found him fairly quickly. He was under the ATV with more than one bullet wound—clearly the man was dead.

Robert grabbed his rifle and sister and ran for Big Boy, who was still tied up where he had left him. It was a four-mile ride back to Uncle Bill's farmhouse, but Big Boy would have no problem carrying the two of them.

Robert and Sierra spoke very little on the way back and mostly just drank water and ran through the morning's events until they reached the archway over the driveway to Uncle Bill's farmhouse—they knew that they were about to confront their aunt Margaret. Neither one knew how to tell her what had just happened, and neither one wanted to be the one to tell her. Margaret and

Bill had been high school sweethearts and had married the day after graduation. That was forty-five years ago.

As they got closer to the house, Aunt Margaret yelled from the barn. "What are you two doing back so early? One of you sick?"

Both of them jumped at the sound of her voice and turned to her. Margaret knew that the news was not going to be good, and her normally smiling face turned to one of concern. She began almost running to the children.

Sierra had started crying at the sight of her aunt, and Robert helped her off the horse. Margaret grabbed her and just kept asking, "What happened? What happened?"

Sierra tried to gain her composure and said with a quavering voice, "They are all dead."

Chapter 11

—⁂—

DARRIAN MICHAELS

D arrian Michaels was a young man from Saint Louis. He lived just off Kings Highway with his elderly grandmother, whom he affectionately called Moms. She was, after all, the only mother he had known. His father had served one tour in Afghanistan and two in Iraq. But Darrian was too young to realize just what his father had been doing all those years. The one thing he did know was that he loved his father and his father was fighting for his country.

Moms would read the letters Darrian's father would write to Darrian and would talk about his father daily. She would tell him stories of the trouble his father had got in as a young man and the ways that Darrian was just like him. Just down the street from their home was a National Guard Armory, where the 138th Bravo Company infantry unit was located. To help Darrian feel closer to his father, she would take him to Forest Park once a month and let him get to know the soldiers, who did physical fitness tests there once a month. Darrian watched them with amazement and dreamed of the day that he, too, could serve like his father.

By his father's last tour, Darrian was fourteen and would run the three miles from his grandmother's front door to the park once a month where the unite exercised in preparation for their biyearly physical fitness test. By then, he had already made friends with many of the soldiers and was even made to feel like part of Bravo Company. Whenever the company passed out the score cards to conducted the biyearly physical fitness test, he to received one and took the test alongside them. The only thing that concerned Darrian was a six-foot-four-inch platoon staff sergeant, Sgt. Karnic. Every time their eyes met, Darrian felt half his age. No other man made him fill that way—the closest had been coming eye to eye with a timber rattler after tripping over a log on a camping trip with his father.

"Darrian!"

Darrian heard the call coming from far off as he was approaching. He knew who it was in an instant. Spc. Marks. Spc. Marks had become Darrian's appointed battle buddy. He helped Darrian feel more like part of the company.

"Movin', Specialist!" Darrian yelled back and took off at a full run. He loved using the military terminology whenever he could. But since he was not really in uniform, he felt a little unnerved about it, especially when Sgt. Karnic was about.

"Glad you could join us today, Michaels," said Spc. Marks. He always used Darrian's last name once he was with the group in order to help make Darrian a part of the team.

"OK. Now that we are all finally awake, out of bed, and shaved and have decided to join the rest of the team, Michaels, I believe we have a physical fitness test waiting for us." Spc. Marks enjoyed calling out the last man to the formation. It made them fight to get there first, or at least not last for fear of their name being called.

"Can anyone tell me what the first event will be?" Spc. Marks asked.

All of their hands started going up before the specialist even finished because, once again, you did not want to be last. For once, it was a question that none of them had to think about.

And as one, they all said loudly, "The push-ups!"

"Excellent!" replied Marks.

"Now on the command of *fall out*, you will get in your designated lines in single file and await further instructions. Any questions? Group attention! Fall out!"

Darrian knew that his participation was limited, since this was a scored test, so he moved to his spot off to the side. He would wait there until the first person from his adopted team finished and would conduct the event with him off to the side.

Chapter 12

BACK AT THE RANCH

Sierra looked up at her aunt, who had not said anything since those three terrifying words had been spoken. Slowly raising her head and clearing her vision from her own tears that had started once again, Sierra looked directly at her aunt. Sierra had had a long ride back to the ranch house to cope with what had taken place. Aunt Margaret, on the other hand, had just been told and was visibly ill from the news. Margaret was a woman of Native American descent, yet she was very pale white at the moment.

Robert jumped down from Big Boy and made his way around to his aunt. Robert and Sierra guided Aunt Margaret to the house. Once in, they thought it best to lay her down in her bedroom, which was just off the living room. Margaret had still not uttered a word, nor had she shown a reaction to the news other than turning white.

With great concern for her aunt, Sierra thought only for a second about giving her the whiskey that had helped her through the shock. Margaret was diabetic and had many other health problems, many of which were not being helped by the current news. Sierra decided that the best thing she could do would be to get her aunt talking.

After a few minutes of sitting on the edge of her bed, Margaret was able to ask, "H...how?" It was as if the words were too big to exit her mouth. "Was it a stampede?" she continued.

Sierra wanted nothing more than to cry at being confronted with the question—however, she knew she had to be strong. The days of crying were over for her.

While Sierra was taking care of Aunt Margaret, Robert was pacing through the living room and trying to figure out the next move. "What to do and whom to contact?" he just kept repeating to himself, as if suddenly an unknown person would jump out of the corner and give him the answer. Due to the scope of the situation, he knew that local law enforcement would not do. He also knew that no federal law enforcement would give them any justice. Luckily he had a third option, and it was the best one that any Texan could hope for: the Texas Rangers.

Robert knew that waiting would only make this strange and horrific problem worse—using the Internet on his phone, he began quickly searching for the number. Once he located it, he dialed immediately, without knowing just what he was going to say. What do you say when you are calling law enforcement due to killing several federal agents? Robert did not know, but he knew it was a call that he'd never thought he would ever be making.

Before he knew it, Robert heard a voice say, "Texas Rangers, how may I direct your call?"

He still did not know. After trying to gather his thoughts for a second, Robert heard the voice again. "Texas Rangers, how may I direct your call?"

Suddenly he thought, *Simple and to the point.* He said, "There are three government employees—correction, four government employees—shot and three family members. Please direct my call to whomever it is I need to speak with. Thank you."

The operator had apparently heard it all because she just transferred the call without any further comments. After two rings, a ranger came on. Robert once again thought to himself, *Keep it short and to the point.* He did not want to spend a lot of time going over the situation on the phone.

When the officer answered, it was with a hint of confusion in his voice.

"Hello, I am Ranger Sepulveda. How may I help you today?"

Robert took a deep breath and exhaled then started. "I am Robert Squires. My family and I went out this morning to tend the cattle on our ranch. We came across what appeared to be cattle rustlers rounding up our cattle. I disabled one of their ATVs with my rifle. A fight ensued, and now my uncle, sixteen-year-old cousin, and father are all dead."

Ranger Sepulveda could not believe what he was hearing. The story seemed unreal, and it was hard for him to believe, due to the calmness in the voice telling it. He thought to himself that this had to be somebody screwing around. Who could have this happen to him and not be hysterical when calling? The ranger continued to listen.

"They also killed our horses. After the firefight, I saw that it appears the men were BLM agents. This is going to require a great number of rangers to sort out. Come quickly. I do not like leaving my family lying dead out there."

After Robert had finished, the ranger had only one thought. *This had to be a joke, a prank, something.* The caller was just too calm and collected for such a brutal event to have taken place. The whole thing was unbelievable—most likely it was somebody on a bad trip. It would not be the first time. In no big hurry, the ranger opened up the calendar for the day on his computer.

It was a shared calendar for everyone to keep informed of the whereabouts of fellow rangers in case of emergencies. It was a new system that his young new supervisor had implemented. Like most changes in the station, everyone had fought it, but then it had turned out to be very useful—yet nobody ever commented on that aspect.

The ranger took all the information from Robert and said, "I am on my way to your location," the address showing on the call system. "Stay calm." The ranger rolled his eyes when those words started coming from his mouth. This was by no means an out-of-control caller.

On the shared calendar for the day he simply put down *Cattle rustlers?* and then right beside it *Addicts?* There were also three boxes, under which he posted the call he was responding to—they were marked "low," "medium," and "high." They represented the threat level of the call. Ranger Sepulveda marked Robert's call as "low." He pretty much figured he would run into a few addicts who were high or tripping playing video games, thinking the shit had really happened. It had happened before.

Once Robert hung up the phone, he still did not quite know how to explain exactly what had happened to the ranger. He himself did not know exactly what had happened, how everything had spiraled so far out of control so fast. He went to check on Aunt Margaret, but Sierra had it all under control. Sierra seemed to have moved past the shock of the morning's events and had newfound calmness—Margaret, on the other hand, was still shaking slightly, but at least a little of her color had started to return.

Sierra stood up from her aunt's bed and made her way past Robert. She walked to the kitchen area, just past the living room, in search of something to relax her. As Sierra was walking by, Robert, who was still in deep thought about how to tell the story, saw it: they both had forgotten that all this time, Sierra had been wearing her new camera on the bill of her hat—it was so small that they had forgotten it was even there. He developed a lump in his throat and asked himself, "Had it been recording?"

Before alerting his sister to his possible discovery, Robert realized that he did not want his aunt to know that there was possible video. He was certain that watching that would be the death of her. She looked drained and was lying on her bed. Slowly walking over to her bed, he leaned and gave her a kiss on her forehead.

"I have to do something, but I am right outside your door if you need me," he said.

As Robert slowly shut her door upon exiting her room, Margaret stared out into nothingness. He walked across the kitchen to where Sierra was reaching for a bottle of whiskey. He stood by her, and with a voice just above a whisper, he started to ask, "Is your camera…"

That was all it took; Sierra gasped and stood up straight. At that moment, he knew that she had been recording. Everything was now on her phone, the whole encounter, the entire morning. Since the camera worked from Bluetooth, she had forgotten it was even there, mostly due to the shock of the events. Robert grabbed her arm and put his finger up to his lips, then pointed slowly to Aunt Margaret's room and wiggled his finger back and forth. Knowing exactly what he was gesturing about, Sierra nodded.

Robert again softly spoke to her: "Check the video. Make sure you got it."

Then it occurred to him that Sierra might not want to watch it, either. Before a moment had passed, he followed up with another question. "Do you want me to check so you do not have to relive it again?"

Sierra looked Robert straight in the eyes—it was a look he had never seen before, at least not from her. The only time he had seen that look was overseas in combat. It was the thousand-yard stare, the one that said to others, "I have seen shit. I will not take shit. Nothing is too tough for me. Mess with me, and I will fuck your world up."

Robert was watching his little sister change before him, and he only hoped that it was not for the worse.

Sierra pulled her phone from her pack—it was still recording. She hit the stop button. It had been recording for a very long time. She was a little nervous and hoped her phone would not have trouble processing the video. After about ten minutes, it was finished. Now it was time for the moment of truth: Sierra tapped play. There it was—footage from the moment she had turned the camera on in the truck after arriving at Uncle Bill's. Then, there she was, face-to-face with Uncle Bill—it seemed like an eternity ago. Sierra hit pause.

At that moment, the majority of people would have broken down and sobbed like a baby, but Sierra had been hardened by the day's events. She was so full of anger that she couldn't let another teardrop roll from her eyes. She fast-forwarded to approximately one hour after that, then twenty minutes, and then thirty. She did not want to watch the whole thing—she just wanted to verify that the footage was there. Sierra looked over at Robert and gave him a slight nod.

Robert's thoughts about how he would explain what had happened to the rangers when they arrived subsided—he now had video proof of what had gone down. The next thought Robert had been of it being the only copy. He did not want Sierra's copy of the video to be the only copy. He stepped in and checked on their aunt, who was still having a difficult time coping with the news.

Once he had addressed his aunt's needs, Robert filled the time waiting for the rangers with downloading the video from Sierra's phone, making copies, and storing them on different websites and e-mail servers. He also made DVD's of the video. He wanted to be sure that no matter what, he could obtain another copy. Robert knew that his and Sierra's lives had now been changed forever.

Ranger Carlos Sepulveda arrived at the ranch house approximately an hour and twenty minutes after the time Robert had spoken with him. Robert had estimated that it would take Sepulveda half an hour to forty-five minutes to get to the ranch. Even though it had taken longer than anticipated, Robert was grateful to see the ranger vehicle was the first to arrive. He felt that if the BLM had arrived first they would all be killed. He was also certain that the BLM agents were already in rout.

Chapter 13

WOMACK

Colonel Womack was a potbellied colonel to whom little responsibility was given. Stationed at the Jefferson Barracks Military Post in Saint Louis, he had dreams of making general one day but knew that was virtually impossible. He had not even taken the army physical fitness test in the last five years—on paper, it appeared that he had taken the test, but everyone knew that his tests were just the magic of the pencil in a young lieutenant's hand. At this stage of his career, the chance of advancement could only come from something dramatic.

At night, he simply sat in front of his television with a microwave dinner and watched war movies. The movies he enjoyed the most featured generals such as George Patton as they conquered the enemy. He often imagined himself as the one in charge, with the respect of his men—respect he had not felt for some time.

Colonel Womack walked up and down the halls of the barracks, day in and day out. Drinking a large cup of coffee, he filled his time until mandatory retirement with talk of the past to any person who would listen—however, people at the barracks knew to avoid the MacAttack (a nickname not given for the many Big Macs he could eat but for his size). Not all were lucky enough to avoid his meaningless conversations, conversation in which personal would nearly vomit from the smell of the colonel's coffee and cigarette breath as he spoke.

For Colonel Womack, this day started out much the same, but by the end, he would feel like a new man. He stopped at his local station, the TLC One Stop, where he refilled his thirty-two-ounce coffee mug and bought two packs of Camel filtered cigarettes. He thought that today was just going to be just another day closer to retirement. He worked his way into his SUV, pulled out, and headed for the barracks, the place he knew would be the last station of his career.

Driving in the left lane of the two easts bound lanes, the colonel worked a Camel from its pack and fumbled it around in his fingers before placing it between his lips. As he reached for the lighter lying in the cubby next to the SUV's stick shift, the colonel noticed that his phone was ringing and thought that he must have forgotten to turn the ringer back on at some point. Not used to receiving calls, he was excited to answer it.

"Wooom...Colonel Womack," he said in a weak voice. He didn't recognize himself.

"If you want to make it *general*, pull over," the voice on the other end replied. Then the voice was gone.

Chapter 14

─────⌘─────

TEXAS RANGER

Robert did not know how to feel. He was excited that the rangers had arrived, but he was also very worried and concerned for his and the others' safety. All of that changed when only one ranger pulled up; there were no others following. Now he knew how he felt—very confused.

"A single ranger?" Robert mumbled. "Who does he think he is, Chuck Norris?"

Sierra heard the vehicle pull up the driveway—her attention was on Robert, who was standing by the door and looking out the front window through the thin white curtains.

"What was that?" Sierra asked—she could tell that Robert said something but could not hear what he had said.

Robert reached back with his arm outstretched and moved his hand with the palm facedown. He then moved it up and down, signaling her to lower her voice—all without taking his eyes off the ranger in the driveway.

"There is only one ranger out there," he repeated, knowing it was better to keep his sister informed.

"One ranger?" she asked. "Who does he think he is, Chuck Norris?" Sierra let out an exaggerated breath and rolled her eyes.

Robert stood with a smirk on his face as he stared at the ranger. The ranger almost looked as if he were searching for a lost dog rather than walking into a pretty damned messed up situation. Robert was so confused—he thought he had been really clear and to the point when talking to the ranger on the phone. He wanted nothing more than to swing the door open and ask where the hell the other rangers were, but Robert resisted, knowing how it would look and knowing that he would lose all credibility if he provoked the wandering ranger.

Once the ranger reached the door, Robert opened it after the first knock. He had been standing on the other side with his hand on the knob since the ranger had pulled up. Robert opened the door, and the ranger introduced himself.

"Good day, I am Officer Sepulveda with the Texas Rangers." As he introduced himself, he was looking at Robert's eyes for signs that he might be on something. He was sure this was the person he had spoken with on the phone—he recognized Robert's voice.

Without identifying drug use, the ranger continued: "I am responding to a phone call from one Robert Squires. Would that be you?"

As Sepulveda studied the scene, he began to feel he might have misjudged the call.

Robert fought to control his emotions at the sight of only a single ranger showing after the type of information Robert had relayed over the phone. He pushed those feelings down and just worked with the here and now.

"Yes, thank you for coming," Robert said in the most sincere voice he could muster. As he motioned toward his sister, he continued, "And this is my sister, Sierra. She also was there and—"

He was abruptly cut off.

"Whoa, whoa, whoa!" Sepulveda said quickly while throwing his hand up in the sign of halt. "You were for real when I spoke with you on the phone?" Without even realizing it, Sepulveda's hand had moved to his sidearm. Robert noticing the movement started to feel like this had been the wrong call.

Robert now understood why there was only one ranger: the story seemed ridiculous. Sierra also saw the ranger's hand move—the last thing she wanted was for this to get out of control, like things had done that morning. She had already set the video up to grab the ranger's attention.

Sierra slowly reached down and hit the play button, starting the video. Sepulveda's attention snapped to Sierra. "Don't move!" he said with a commanding voice as he pointed his finger at her and began to draw his side-arm. At that moment, he saw on the computer screen a man's head vanish and heard screaming from a very frightened girl. That girl was the one standing in front of him now. It was obvious by her body language.

Sierra had been looking directly at Uncle Bill when he had been shot by the sniper who was positioned on the semitrailer.

Robert's muscles had tensed up, and he was ready to charge the ranger, who was drawing a pistol on his sister before the video had started stopping the ranger in his tracks. Now Sepulveda was just standing there, pistol half drawn, watching the video on the computer monitor. He seemed to be in disbelief that what he had been told was in fact true.

After the video came to the part where Robert and Sierra were riding off on a horse, the ranger moved again, but now his pistol was back fully in the holster. He looked at Sierra and could not believe that the girl in the video was the one standing in front of him now. The brown-haired, green-eyed woman in front of him was no longer the girl she had been just this morning—this was one thing Sepulveda knew for sure.

When she noticed the ranger staring at her, Sierra hit pause. Inside, she was screaming for the video to be over, but on the outside, she was all business.

Sepulveda stared at Sierra and then Robert—he wondered how the two of them were able to stay so levelheaded at this moment. Robert, he had guessed at this point, was military. The ranger also assumed that Robert had been in a combat zone. That was why Sepulveda had so badly misjudged the call and Robert's demeanor on the phone.

Sierra, on the other hand, was an enigma—she appeared to be only sixteen or seventeen, too young for the service. Yet she had seen brutality this day that would have turned most into babblings fools. The ranger wondered how anyone her age could keep her kind of composure.

After a few seconds of contemplation, Sepulveda looked over at Robert, and with his outstretched arm and finger pointing at Robert, he asked slowly, "Did you not say you were the one who fired first?"

Robert looked directly at Sepulveda and replied, "Yes, I took out one of their ATVs. As we were coming over the ridge, we could hear the ATVs running. The men presented themselves as cattle rustlers. After discussing what to do about them, we decided the best course of action would be to disable one of their ATVs. We hoped they would pack it up and go home without further conflict."

Apparently that was an epic fail, Robert thought.

Sepulveda's training was telling him to put handcuffs on the two for now, but his gut and heart were what he chose to follow. Something about the two just made him believe they were on the side of right. Before he could make his final judgment on that, the ranger felt that he needed to see the shot that started it all from the beginning. He turned his attention from Robert over to Sierra and noticed that she was already rewinding the video for him to watch from the start. She had anticipated he would want to see it—after all, why would he just take their word for it when they had video?

Sepulveda had almost watched the video up to the same spot as before, but this time he had Sierra stop it on a frame that showed the two agents Robert had killed at the end. Sepulveda could clearly see that they had no identifying marks. At that moment, Robert stepped over, pointed to the screen, and said, "As you can see, there are no insignias, nothing, no identification on their clothing. Nothing indicated that they were anything other than high-tech cattle rustlers."

Sepulveda was opening his mouth to acknowledge his agreement when, at the same time, all three had their attention drawn to vehicles approaching. Robert suddenly thought that he had been wrong before and that there were indeed other rangers arriving.

That was until Sepulveda asked, "Are you expecting anyone?" as he moved toward the front door. Sepulveda opened the door. As he did so, there was a searing pain in his shoulder, which was followed by a very loud noise. Reflexes slammed the door shut again, and they all fell to the floor like swimmers after the firing of a starter pistol.

Robert grabbed his Noreen rifle and moved to the front window of the living room, a window that no longer existed. Sepulveda had pulled his pistol and was lying on the floor and contemplating his next move while bandaging his shoulder.

Sierra had been startled for an instant—she had not expected that they would be shot at here. As she dropped to the floor, she was trying to think of where her weapon was. Then she remembered that it was still on her horse in the field. She looked over at Uncle Bill's display case across the room and began a low crawl.

Sierra moved with great speed and was soon at the case, where Bill kept his prized possessions: twin Colt .357 Magnums—they were in a glass case on display. With them were six rounds each. The rounds were of nickel casing and were quick-expansion Barnes 157-grain hollow-points. Uncle Bill had reloaded them himself and often said that they would stop anything from breathing.

After breaking the case, Sierra quickly began working to loud bullets into the revolvers. She had twelve shots total, and she intended on making each and every one count. Though soon as she slid the first round in, the kitchen door was kicked open with a loud, thunderous crack. Sierra quickly spun the cylinder with the single bullet so that it would be in the right position to fire—at least she hoped so.

Sierra fired, and the round struck the upper thigh of the man who was charging through the door—right where she had planned on placing it and the destruction was unimaginable. As soon as her bullet struck the man, he cried out in agony like no man she had heard before, or any animal for that matter.

With only one chance, she did not want the bullet to strike body armor, but she knew that most people did not wear it on their thighs. Due to the explosive power of a .357 Magnum and the Barnes quick-expansion copper rounds, the man who had started to do them harm would not have an opportunity to make that mistake twice. Sierra finished loading the pistols and was ready for action. By that time, the man had stopped moving, and a river of blood was running across the kitchen floor.

As soon as Sierra fired, Robert and Sepulveda snapped their heads in her direction, then at the screaming man on the floor, and next at each other. Both had the same expression on their faces, as if to say, "Is this really fucking happening?"

Robert thought to himself that he was glad Sierra had his back. He still could not get over how fast she had adapted. He then wondered if she might still be in some state of shock.

Sepulveda, on the other hand, thought, *What the hell is happening? These are clearly federal agents.* But they had fired upon him, and they were not doing warning shots.

Sierra was now focused on the back door, and suddenly even with the bullets flying through the front of the house looking for flesh, her thoughts turned to her aunt, who was in her bedroom just off the living room. With all the noise from the shooting and the dying screams, Sierra became concerned that her aunt was terrified. She slowly crawled across the floor to the bedroom where she had left her aunt.

While lying flat on the floor with her pistol out front, Sierra began opening the door. A bullet had already destroyed the frame, and the door was unlatched. After a gentle nudge with the gun's barrel, the door swung open, and on the other side, an all-black figure had opened fire about waist high on the door. Sierra immediately returned fire. He noticed her down low and began adjusting his fire in her direction. Her first shot missed, but her second was true—the shot came up at an angle that struck right between the nostrils, removing the top of his head and the Kevlar helmet the man was wearing.

Sierra's attention quickly went to what she knew was her aunt lying twisted in her own blood on the floor. Sierra's eyes shut with the pain of seeing her aunt lying on the floor, and she knew yet again that on this day she had lost another precious member of her family. Sierra moved over and covered her aunt with a blanket from the bed, and then Sierra lay next to Margaret on the floor, the pistols firmly in her hands.

The men outside firing at the house had now killed Sierra's aunt, uncle, cousin, father, and horse. Now they were trying to kill her and her brother. It had taken some time from the beginning of the day's events, but a transformation had started taking place inside her, one that at this moment was completed. Now she only wanted justice at any cost. All the years of Robert teaching her hand-to-hand combat, wrestling with her, and instructing her in firearms and survival techniques crystallized in her mind. Nothing short of death could stop her.

Sepulveda and Robert could not hear the fight in the bedroom due to the gunfire out front. Sepulveda kept trying to attract the attention of the agents outside by waving his hat just out the door. He gave up after the second try—all he achieved was a hat full of holes. The ranger then concluded that the only way out was by taking them out first. The problem was that he had no shot to take or even to try to take. Every time he prepared to open the door to fire, he received a blast of gunfire. Sepulveda was stuck and retreated to behind a thicker part of the wall.

Robert, on other hand, had a plan—he moved over to where he knew the wall was thinner. With the agents only fifty yards away from the house, Robert knew that his plan had a great chance of success. After three attempts, he was able to signal to Sepulveda. Once they locked eyes, Sepulveda knew that Robert had a plan.

Robert explained his plan just loud enough for the ranger to hear. It was simple. The ranger would fire randomly out the door to get a fix on the position of an agent and would relay it, and then Robert would open up with his Noreen rifle. Robert knew practically every object, nook, cranny, dip, or mole hole in the yard. Lying on the floor, Sepulveda described where the first man was located. There were four in front of the house.

First target. "The swing set!" Sepulveda said, as he retracted his head from the slight opening just in time to feel the heat of the passing bullet.

Robert closed his eyes and imagined that he was standing, looking out of what was left of the front window. He swiveled his Noreen .30-06 just a little to the left and squeezed off three rounds so quickly it sounded like full auto.

Sepulveda held his breath and took only a split second glance around the doorframe. "CONTACT!" he yelled excitedly.

Robert looked over at him. "Next!"

"Give me a damned second. I almost lost my head the last time I stuck it out." Sepulveda was looking around for something reflective to use. Luckily for him, there was plenty of glass on the floor, so he didn't have to go far.

"NEXT!" Robert ordered.

"Hey, I am not Chuck Norris, damn it," Sepulveda growled back as he used the glass to spot the next target. "Behind the gnome wearing the red pointed hat."

Robert adjusted his aim only by visualization and let out with three quick blasts.

"Low, but you got the gnome!" Sepulveda directed once more.

"Damn! Sorry, Albert," Robert murmured apologizing to the gnome as he adjusted his rifle and let out three more powerful blasts.

"Contact!"

Robert saw movement through the hole he had just put through the wall, so he quickly fired two more rounds.

"Contact!" Sepulveda acknowledged once again. He was astounded by Robert's ability with the rifle.

Movement outside had stopped, and the area around farm house fell quiet. Everything had happened so quickly that Sepulveda realized he had not called for backup—there had not been time. Well, there was time now. He reached up to his left shoulder for the radio, only to find nothing but the wire where it once had been. He had a bullet in his other shoulder—Sepulveda felt lucky that was all that he'd received. The call would have to be made from his truck. As Sepulveda stood, he felt his feet get kicked right out from under him, and he landed on his wounded arm.

Still in her dead aunt's room, Sierra stayed low to the floor and slowly peeked out of the door into the living room just in time to see Sepulveda land on the glass-covered floor. She knew that if Robert were not on his feet, she wouldn't move hers.

Sepulveda cringed at the pain shooting through his body and growled at Robert but said nothing—at this point, he had to trust Robert.

Robert was lying on his back with a big doll of his aunt's, which usually sat in a small rocking chair in the corner. He raised it up slowly and moved it back and forth, keeping it well below the window.

"It is not high enough," Sepulveda suggested, then watched the doll lose its stuffing.

"Snipers shoot from high, Chuck," Robert said with a grin on his face.

Sepulveda figured the sniper must not be able see him—so why move?

Robert, on the other hand, had the information he needed—he knew there were only two places the shooter could have taken that shot from. Both were about five hundred yards away. He knew it from years of testing out new equipment like his range finders. Robert crawled between Sepulveda and what was left of the couch and moved slowly to the kitchen. On his way, he signaled to Sierra to move back into the bedroom she had just exited.

He moved behind the counter and faced the front window. Most of the pots and pans that had been stored in there had been blown out by the firefight. Robert slowly moved debris out of his path and began looking for what he needed. After a quick scan, he saw it: a spot in the upper part of the lower kitchen cabinet, just under the counter, where two bullets had hit and formed an upright figure eight.

"Perfect," Robert said under his breath as he raised his rifle up and placed only the very end of the barrel at the bottom of the eight.

He began scanning the old wooden water tower first, believing it would be one of two spots with the right view into the living room. He zeroed in on the tower, and after a few seconds, thanks to the way two squirrels were playing tag on the tower, it was clear to Robert that the sniper was in the barn. Robert adjusted his fire just in time to see a flash. Sepulveda let out a yelp.

The agent was not anticipating a counter sniper threat—he was lying atop a black mat spread over two square bales of hay. It was apparent to Robert that this guy had never spent time in a combat zone.

Robert placed his crosshairs right on the bridge of the man's nose and began his trigger pull. Right before his finger met the trigger, he stopped and thought, *Intel*. Robert had to find out what the hell was going on. He adjusted aim to the shoulder—the shot would destroy the shoulder, but the man would live.

Again Robert began the slow trigger pull. The round was sent. One shot was all Robert needed—he jumped up from his spot and moved quickly to Sepulveda on the floor. Both of them gave the other a quick check for unwanted holes. Except for the original bullet Sepulveda had received, they both looked OK.

"On me!" Robert commanded.

Staying low, Sierra exited the bedroom, and Sepulveda stood up and looked at Robert.

"We are moving five hundred yards to the barn," Robert commanded. "I have front left. You have front right, Chuck. Sierra, you bring up the rear."

Before Sepulveda could protest, they were already moving, and Sepulveda found himself saying softly under his breath, "Fucking TV show."

They moved over the distance between the house and the barn in little time and encountered no resistance. Robert did not slow when he came to the entrance of the barn—instead, he just moved on in, not knowing if there were others or not. He did, however, feel that if there were, they would not expect Robert, Sepulveda, and Sierra to move in as a team and present overwhelming force.

Before Robert knew it, he was at the wooden ladder leading up to the loft, where the man Robert had just wounded was thrashing around in pain. Robert looked at the other two and pointed at Sierra.

"Keep us covered from down here," he ordered. Sierra nodded her compliance with his directive. With the two Colt .357 Magnums, one in each hand, she moved back to the entrance and took up post to one side, looking out.

Robert knew that the ranger was not going to stay, so he gave him a follow-me movement with his head and began climbing the ladder. Robert slowly raised his head up through the opening and scanned the wounded man for weapons. After being satisfied that there was nothing in the man's good hand, Robert moved on up and began walking across the loft. He could see that his bullet had done a great amount of damage. The damage started at the top of the shoulder and ran down the full length of the bicep. Lucky for the guy, though, it had not made contact with bone. He probably did not feel so lucky, with the greater part of his bicep split open down to the bone.

Robert went over, knelt alongside the man, and reached out to a pouch on the man's vest. The agent tried to move and fight back, but he was in too much pain. Robert slapped the agent's hand away, commanding, "Calm down"—he removed the man's first aid kit from its pouch. Sorting out the contents without saying a word, Robert found what he was looking for. The tourniquet.

The wounded man did not know what to make of the situation. First he had been following his orders to neutralize the personnel in the house—now they were dressing the wound he had received from them. He was almost as confused about this day as the others were.

Once Robert had taken care of the agent's wound with a tourniquet and a pressure bandage, he set the man upright against hay bales. He had not asked the man one question before treating his arm. Sepulveda just watched and thought it best to let Robert handle the man. He just wanted to dangle the man out the front of the barn loft until he explained what the hell was going on and why they were firing on a Texas Ranger.

Without saying a word, Robert walked around the man a few times while collecting his thoughts. He then paced side to side before turning and looking directly down at the man. "Why are you here?" he asked in a calm voice.

The agent looked up at him. "You and your family killed four agents this morning."

Robert heard somebody coming up the ladder. As he looked over, he could see Sierra's ratty old cap coming though the opening in the floor. Sierra had noticed Sepulveda had taken up post by the opening above her; she felt it was a good time to move up now that she knew why they had moved to the barn. She wanted answers, too.

Robert waited until she was nearby to begin again. The agent could not stop staring at the hourglass-figured, brown-haired, green-eyed girl with matching pistols in each hand. She walked across the loft like a giant—she may have only been five foot eleven but a giant nonetheless. Watching Sierra approach he thought how never before in his life he seen such beauty though she terrified him.

Robert returned his attention to the agent. "Why were they not wearing any identifying markings?" he asked, with a hint of disgust in his tone.

"What are you talking about? Agents always wear some type of identification when doing fieldwork." The agent's anger toward his captors was starting to show.

"Well, you gutless lump of shit, had they been wearing it, you wouldn't be lying there with a gimp arm, and I wouldn't have just killed two of your buddies!" Sierra said in a voice and tone that any other time might have been attractive. For the agent on the floor, he wished that he could slide through the cracks in the floor to get away.

"That was the intel we received at the briefing before moving out. The crime scene photos I saw of what you people did back it up. You will not get away with it, and I will not be saying another word." The agent fell silent and looked down at the floor.

Robert looked at his sister and then at Sepulveda. "Let's take him to the house," Robert said. Sepulveda nodded.

On the way, they stopped at Sepulveda's truck—this was his chance to call for support. As he looked in the truck and shouted, "Shit!" Sepulveda turned, grabbed the agent, and continued to the house. The radio in the vehicle had been permanently disabled.

Once in the house, they positioned the agent in front of the computer, which thankfully was still working. They hit play from the point where the group was coming up with a solution for the cattle rustlers and let it play to where the two of them rode off. Once at the end, the agent had no words. Unable to find words to express his thoughts, he just looked around the room.

After a few minutes of aimless thought, it all came together for him. He knew he had been manipulated by the agency. Now he had to do something. The agent looked at the three of them. "I need to call this in now—otherwise, I cannot help," he said. He pointed at the radio on the man Sierra had shot as he had been coming through the back door and made a give-me sign, opening and shutting his good hand.

The three of them stood motionlessly and stared at him like the guy was nuts. "Look," he said as he threw up his good hand in an I-surrender posture. "Do you plan on killing me?" he then sarcastically asked.

They looked at one another like the guy had lost it.

The agent then put his arm down. "Look, I am going to help you the best way I can, and that is from the inside. If I do not call it in now, somebody might get suspicious, and then I am no good to you."

The agent gave the three of them a moment to think about what he had just said.

Of the three Sierra didn't need a moment—she was already moving to get the radio for the agent. She was like a human lie detector. Nothing got by her.

When Sepulveda saw Sierra toss the radio to the agent, he moved to stop her. Feeling Robert place his hand on his shoulder, taking care not to inflame his wound, Sepulveda froze and turned to Robert. In the very short time they had known each other, not even an hour, they had already got each other's body language down. Sepulveda then relaxed as the agent prepared to make the call, but the ranger had his hand on his sidearm, just in case.

"By the way, you can call me Sam," the agent said, then began the call.

Once the agent had completed the call, they felt more confident that he was truly on their side and intended on helping them. "Now you have no more than twenty minutes to disappear," he said as a surge of pain ran through his arm. "Grab what you need and move. I will say I was unconscious when you escaped."

Sam looked over at Sepulveda. "I know you want to call in, but you must not. They have you marked the same as the other two—you are all now fugitives wanted for the murder of multiple federal agents."

"Give me a good number to call you in a few days for updates," Sepulveda said—he was not going to be without information from the inside. "We will contact you from a clean phone."

As the three of them gathered up weapons, ammunition, gear, and other supplies, Sam filled them in on his plan. "I will take the video and post it on the Internet for everyone to see. Right after I get a copy of the new video the BLM made."

Sam paused, making sure there were no questions. Then he continued, "It will take time, and I will keep you updated—in the meantime, stay safe and out of sight."

"Robert," Sam called out, then motioned for him to come in close. As Robert leaned in to hear what Sam had to say, he saw Sam's hand holding something and moving up quick. There was no time to react—Robert was in too close.

Sam's hand stopped just short of Robert's chest as he opened it.

"Cash." Robert's breathing returned to normal, and he relaxed as much as he could.

"It is all I have on me," Sam said. "Make sure you do not use anything traceable."

"Got it," Robert replied.

Sam looked into the eyes of the man standing in front of him. "Robert, have you ever heard of the Battle of Concord during the Revolutionary War?"

Stunned by such an odd question, Robert replied, "Sure, it's where the saying 'the shot heard around the world' comes from." He was still puzzled by the question.

Sam's eyes locked on Robert's. "Yes," Sam said. "And the moment your bullet exited your rifle this morning, I am afraid, it became the same as the one fired in 1775."

Chapter 15

138TH ANNUAL
TRAINING

Tension was mounting everywhere these days. Americans had become more and more divided on a great deal of issues, including race relations—something most of the country felt had been dealt with in the fifties and sixties, but something that had become a major topic. Everyone understood that you cannot stamp out racism altogether and that there will always be people who are racist.

The problem came with the election of a President Howard who made everything about race, no matter how small an issue it was. This was by no means the only disagreement people had—the list seemed to be endless these days. For most, it was the blatant violation of the US Constitution by those in power. It seemed not to matter who was in control, either: Republican or Democrat, they all disregarded the Constitution as if it were no more than a list of suggestions.

Republicans seem to be all for doing away with the First and Fourth Amendments. They were always passing surveillance bills, bills they said would help in the fight against terrorism. Everyone cheered for the surveillance, but when put into effect, it would only be American citizens who were under surveillance. America had been transformed into a communistic country where people were afraid to speak their minds over the phone—at least not without the fear that someone would soon be around to gather them up.

Democrats had started a campaign of government intervention—shutting down power plants, using the IRS to attack people, creating new regulations and laws without congressional approval, creating an ever-increasing dependence on government assistance. Then there was the big one: the Second Amendment to the Bill of Rights, the right to keep and bear arms. For some reason, the party had decided that people no longer needed guns and the Second Amendment was outdated.

There were two parties bidding for power in Washington, DC, but everyone began to see that there were no real differences between the two. Members of the parties would trash talk one another and preach how they would stop the other party from destroying the nation. Then they would turn around and approve one another's bills. Even if the bills passed, they were unconstitutional. The two parties were actually part of the same party—most people just could not see it.

The agenda out of Washington was currently to remove guns from the everyday citizen and establish all possible control over the land.

It was now June and the time of year when the 138th Bravo Company of the Missouri National Guard conducted annual training for two weeks. This year due to much civil unrest, the decision was made to cancel the training that normally took place at Fort Chaffee Maneuver Training Center in Arkansas and moved it to Camp Clark in Nevada, Missouri. Arkansas was one of the first states to side with Texas after a great number of federal agents were killed at what had become known as the Battle of Squires.

It was not the first time in history that government agents had been killed in a shoot-out, but this one made national news because of the alleged cover-up. Shortly after the shoot-out, in which only one agent survived, news of the shoot-out was broadcast on every station. The headline was "Agents Gunned down While Removing Cattle from Government Property." The country was in shock that something like this could happen.

The real problem came after the story had run for a few weeks, when footage of the event started emerging. The footage told a different version of the story. One showed a family protecting cattle from rustlers, not government agents. For two weeks, the news presented footage and photographs of the aftermath. The problem was that in the footage and photos presented the first two weeks, all the dead agents at the ranch had on insignias of their agencies. The footage being shown now told a different story—one where the agents did not have insignias of their agencies. It was very clear that things had been staged.

Arkansas was only the first to follow Texas—only hours after, Oklahoma followed. Missouri, on the other, seemed split, although the people were fed up with the direction the leadership in Washington was taking the country in. A Democrat was in the White House, and the state had a Democratic governor. Even with that being the case, the only thing keeping the state from siding with Texas were the Democratic cities of Saint Louis and Kansas City. They even began to swing to the side of Texas after the original footage surfaced.

Nevertheless the news broadcasts in most states had photos of the country's three most wanted up every fifteen minutes—the three were Robert Squires, who was former military; his sister, Sierra Squires, high school senior; and her older lover, Carlos Sepulveda, who was with the Texas Rangers. It was believed that Carlos had helped them escape in a Texas Ranger vehicle pulling a horse trailer, and the vehicle was heading south. Though Carlos Sepulveda and Sierra had never met before, the News agencies presented it as if they had, purely for ratings.

Washington had already done away with the Posse Comitatus Act, which prevented federal troops from performing military operations on US soil. This put everyone on edge, because up to that point, the only military authority that could legally operate within the borders of the United States was each state's national guardsmen. This had become problematic because the states of Texas, Arkansas, and Oklahoma had activated all of their guard units because of heightened tensions between their states and Washington.

The men of the 138th Bravo Company only had one thing on their minds today, and that was the beginning of their annual training. Sgt. Karnic always arrived early the mornings of training—he was normally two hours early to ensure that everything was ready for the day of training and that he was there before any of his men. After receiving notice from his squad leaders of full accountability of the men, he moved them all to the armory to check out their weapons—the men typically carried M4 rifles with ACOG sighting systems. After taking a quick weapons check he had his squad leaders load the men onto the transport that would take them to Camp Clark. It would be about a five-hour ride on the white Blue Bird buses the military was so fond of.

Sgt. Karnic sat in the front seat of the bus with the company commander. They were just twenty minutes from Camp Clark when they noticed the road-block ahead—they really didn't think much of it, until as they were approaching, they noticed Cougar 4x4 MRAPs sitting two deep on each side of the road. Two were blocking the road. Off to the side of the road were the white Blue Birds carrying the other half of Bravo Company and the first sergeant. Confusion set in, and Sgt. Karnic and the commander looked at each other. They looked most puzzled after they spotted the MRADs. They saw all the occupants of the lead bus, including the first sergeant. All were restrained with zip ties.

As they came to a complete stop at the place where a soldier in front of the bus guided it to park, Commander Sawyer and Sgt. Karnic jumped off the bus. With rage and confusion in his voice, Cdr. Sawyer bellowed out, "I demand to know what in the hell is going on here! Why are my men restrained? And who the fuck is in charge here?"

At that moment, a man came from around the other side of a Humvee and said, "That would be me, Commander. The name is General Arthur Womack." He had a big grin on his large cheeked face. "You, Commander, and your men are under arrest for treason against the US government."

Chapter 16

138TH ANNUAL TRAINING RETURN TRIP

U pon hearing the charges, Commander Sawyer seemed to lose all control of his facial muscles, and his jaw seemed to come unhinged. He pivoted his head slowly from the general to Sgt. Karnic to his side. To his surprise, the man did not show any emotion upon hearing the news. Now Commander Sawyer didn't know what was more surprising: being arrested as a traitor or Karnic's reaction. A man who had served in Iraq and Afghanistan, where he had received two Purple Hearts and a Silver Star for heroism, a man who loved his country like a religion—that very man was not showing the slightest sign of emotion at being called a traitor to his own country.

Sgt. Karnic's thoughts were crystal clear at that moment, as if a switch had been flipped and everything he had read in the papers, seen during his service, watched on alternative media, and heard as a rumor became clear and organized. Karnic had one thought: *This is not an act of the country I love but of the government I now despise.* From that moment, Karnic felt he would truly be fighting for *his* United States of America.

It was purely absurd that anybody would think that the men of the 138th were traitors to their country—80 percent of the company of 146 men had served in combat in both Middle East campaigns, and one had even served in

Vietnam. Yet here they were, being handcuffed and detained. Emotions were running high on both sides. On the one side, there were the men of the Bravo Company believing that they were going to training. A few even thought that this might be part of it. They didn't think that they were going to end up in handcuffs, struggling against brothers of the same armed forces.

Womack had at each side of him four handpicked MPs for this situation. The four of them knew what they were going to be doing and were following their orders, for they believed that they were on the right side and they believed that the information they had was correct. After all, three states had activated their guard units already. To them, these men were going against the oath they had taken to serve and defend the Constitution of United States from all enemies foreign and domestic. To them, the men of the 138th Bravo Company were the domestic enemy.

Sergeant Karnic stood tall and strong beside the commander, who was now face-to-face with General Womack. On each side were the four very well built and armed military policeman. The commander and Sgt. Karnic looked at one another—both knew by the look in Womack's eyes what he wanted. The man wanted somebody to give them a reason to escalate the situation and thus prove the righteousness of the arrest and make him a hero for squashing the traitorous act.

Commander Sawyer took a look around at his men and saw that many were beginning to struggle against the restraint of the unfounded detention. Both he and Karnic seemed to be having the same thought.

"Men of Bravo Company!" Sawyer said in a thunderous voice. He paused to ensure that they were all focused on Sgt. Karnic and himself.

Startled by the sound of his voice, the MPs on each side of Womack moved their hands to their sidearms. Everyone became calm and silent. Each man of Bravo Company could feel his heart pounding, his pulse racing, his adrenaline surging, and his fists clenching, and they all waited for the commander to give the order to resist.

Then suddenly the order came from the commander: "Do as you are instructed. Do not resist." At that moment he and Sgt. Karnic put their hands out to be cuffed. The commander knew his men would fight, but he also knew that was what Womack wanted. The one thing he was not going to do was play into this sick game.

The men of Bravo Company reluctantly followed the orders laid out by the commander. They may not have agreed with the orders, but they were sure he had a plan. Sgt. Karnic ordered his men to relax—this was not the time or place.

Sgt. Karnic had noticed while the MPs were collecting cell phones that Spc. Marks retained his Apple watch. Karnic's only hope was that the phone was still active and within proximity. Sgt. Karnic knew exactly who to call. He knew he could not call the armory, for they would have also been arrested. He knew it would not be wise to contact anybody who was military, for at this point, everyone he trusted was in handcuffs. There was one person who he knew could help Bravo Company and who would be faithful to the company. That was Darrian.

Once the men of the 138th were being loaded onto the buses, Sgt. Karnic moved away from the captain and started slowly and methodically moving positions to get next to Marks. He looked down slightly as he came alongside the specialist and noticed that Marks had covered up his watch and was making sure that it was not noticeable. That was a good sign to Sgt. Karnic. Once on the bus and seated about five rows back, Sgt. Karnic motioned to Marks.

By reaching over and pointing at his wrist and then giving the thumbs-up sign, Karnic silently asked the question, "Is it operational?" The specialist knew exactly what Karnic was asking and slowly looked at his watch without making much movement in its direction. As he moved his sleeve up slowly, Marks feared the phone would not be in range. Suddenly he saw it: three bars of cell signal strength—the greatest three bars he had ever seen.

Commander Sawyer was very curious about what Sgt. Karnic was up to, although he knew it had to be something to do with their current situation. The man was always formulating plans and strategies and was one of the best at doing so Commander Sawyer had ever seen. Sawyer positioned himself to where he could see Sgt. Karnic through the mirror just above the windshield. This gave him the advantage of keeping in contact without turning in his seat.

It did not take long for Sawyer and Karnic to make eye contact by use of the mirror. The lines of communication between the two were now complete. This made both men feel much better about their chances. At this point, they had figured there would be nothing good waiting at the other end of this trip. When Karnic had come up with a strategy that he felt comfortable with, he watched the mirror until he knew that Sawyer was watching. At that moment, he moved his lips with no sound. Commander Sawyer knew exactly what words Karnic was mouthing: *Distraction. Wait one.*

General Womack slowly turned and cocked his head to the side and addressed Commander Sawyer across the aisle. "Commander, I think we are going to take a slight detour."

Womack gave a smirk and bobbed his head, which made his second chin bounce like a turkeys. Then he turned to address the MP driving the bus, and he said in a very audible voice that most could hear, "Take us slowly through Forest Park. I would like for the people there to see these men now." Letting out a chuckle, Womack continued, "See them for the traitors they now are." He chuckled even more.

Sawyer slowly moved his sight from the general to the far right and slowly to the mirror in the hopes that Karnic had heard what was in store for them. With just a little of the mirror in his vision, he could tell by Karnic's slightest nod that he had.

It was time. Sgt. Karnic had all the information he needed to formulate his plan. At that point, he had Marks call Darrian, and then he prayed that the company's unofficial man would answer.

Marks knew that Darrian would answer his phone—Darrian always did and was always excited to hear from Marks. This most important call Marks had ever made to Darrian had to be answered. *Ring, ring, ring.* Then voice mail.

Karnic and Marks slowly wrinkled their brows and let out their breath silently, as if all hope was now lost. Karnic struggled to think of whom they could contact for help. The worst thing was that he knew a few people he trusted with his life, but this was not his phone—therefore, he had no numbers to call. Karnic thought fast, and right when the voice mail greeting ended and the beep happened, Karnic signaled that he was ready.

At the same time that Darrian's greeting ended, Karnic looked up to the mirror and gave the slightest nod to Commander Sawyer. Sawyer knew he need not reply, for his actions would soon confirm that the message had been received.

With his commanding voice, which did not command respect but summoned it, Sawyer spoke, "Hey, General Dipshit." The breaking of the silence by the man's voice shocked the guards, even those in the back of the bus. The general's head whipped around so fast that it took time for his chin to catch up. Sawyer took no break after addressing him. "Do you really believe these trumped-up bullshit charges are going to hold up?"

Sawyer did not wait for a response, a response he did not need or care for— after all, this was to create a distraction, not to get answers. "Is there any lower pile of..." He was determined to carry on as long as he could.

As soon as the words *General Dipshit* were heard, Karnic started leaving his message. "This is Staff Sergeant Karl Eugene Karnic of the 138th Bravo Company. We have a situation. Bravo Company under arrest, charge treason, on company-transport white buses. Destination Jefferson Barracks. Route to be taken through Forest Park. Mission, notify Family readiness group, Bring community and Family readiness group to Forest Park. Confront convoy. As many people as possible. Get the word out. Over." His message was short, clear, and precise.

Even though it seemed like an eternity since they had placed the failed call to Darrian, it in fact was only seconds before Marks's watch lit up and displayed "Darrian calling" across the screen. Both men felt the sense of urgency, and as Marks raised his bound wrist slowly toward Karnic, Karnic knew he would have to convince Darrian quickly. The distraction up front was not going to last much longer.

"Darrian, this is Sergeant Karnic." After that statement, he waited just a second because he knew that Darrian most likely would consider this a prank, especially since it was coming from Marks's phone. Then Karnic repeated even more gruffly, "I said, this is Sergeant Karnic."

Darrian had been doing his chores around the house when the phone started ringing. His hands were wet from doing dishes, and he could not answer his phone straightaway. By the time he got finished drying off his hands, the call had already gone to voice mail. He knew that Marks never called while out for training, and once he saw that it was a missed call from Marks, he wondered what the call could be about.

Without even considering if he should or should not, Darrian dialed Marks's number, and to his surprise, the voice on the other end was not Marks's. The sound of S. Sgt. Karnic's voice was startling—Darrian could not for the life of him figure out why Sgt. Karnic would be calling him, much less why he would be calling from Marks's phone.

Then Darrian heard it again: Sgt. Karnic repeating himself. That snapped Darrian out of the daze he was in. He had been around the company long enough to know that if Sgt. Karnic was speaking to him, he had better be listening, so that was exactly what he did. Once Karnic was satisfied that he possibly had Darrian's attention, he relayed the message. "Darrian, I left a voice mail. Listen to it and do what it says. I…"

Everything for Karnic went black.

Karnic started to regain his consciousness from the attack on the back of his head right about the time the bus started calming back down. "Apparently they do not allow phone calls," Karnic said in a sarcastic tone, as both a jab at their captors and a way to reassure the men that he was OK.

Karnic looked over at Marks's empty hands. He knew the watch was gone, but he still had to look. Marks just raised his hands slightly off his lap and put them back down, showing he was no longer in possession of communication. Neither knew if the plan had been set in motion. Only time would tell from here—an hour and thirty minutes of time: that was how long they estimated it would take before entering Forest Park, where the general no doubt already had news cameras set to show their capture, albeit on false charges. But that did not matter when only one side was telling the story.

Chapter 17

FOREST PARK

The general took detours so that he could have the buses pass right through the main drive of the park. He wanted the biggest show he could put on and was not going to settle for anything less. From the moment they turned off the interstate, he started fixing his uniform, removing lint, straightening his ribbons, and polishing his single General star.

They were still a few miles from Forest Park, but the roads were already becoming packed with cars and pedestrians. Reporters were at every corner, and all along the street, their vans deployed their satellite uplinks. Everyone wanted to get the story of the rogue military unit—it was going to make the news for weeks to come, and the star would be General Womack. At the front of the bus stood Womack, holding a pole, with one hand about shoulder high and the other on his very wide hip. He stood with one foot on the top step and the other one step down, as he attempted to present himself as a courageous figure, even though there were no courageous qualities about the man.

Karnic sat in his seat and surveyed the crowd passing by. He wondered if they were there to support Womack and the government's apparent move or if Darrian had directed them here. Karnic had no doubt that the boy would do what was asked of him—he just was not sure if Darrian had received the message before Karnic's rifle buttstock had hit the back of his head, which, an hour and a half later, was still throbbing.

Karnic looked to Sawyer by way of the mirror at the front of the bus—the two had kept constant eye contact since Karnic had awakened from his sudden nap. They knew that nothing needed to be said to the rest of the men about the plan, not only because it was being made up on the fly but also because they knew the men would follow their lead.

As Karnic was casually looking in no particular direction, he softly whispered, "Be prepared to move."

That was all it took. One by one, they repeated the message ever so softly without looking at anyone or making much of a lip movement. Most of the men had already loosened their zip-tie restraints enough to free one hand by removing their longest fingernail and working it under the catch that locked the ties into place. It was a trick Karnic had showed them over a year ago, and when he showed the men a trick like that, they remembered and practiced it.

The ride back to Saint Louis was quiet, with the exception of Karnic and the MP. The soldiers knew only two things: the country was dividing, and they had just been falsely arrested for treason. Sawyer did not know what could be done at this point, but he was beginning to get a better picture of what really had happened on the cattle ranch in Texas. He stared ahead, deep in thought, his brain rolling over one scenario after another, strategizing a way out that would not get the majority of his men killed. One thing he was sure of: this was not an approved route—if it were, there would be security along the road they were taking into the park.

"What the…" Sawyer trailed off lightly as he saw a man who looked like Darrian holding a sign just off the street that read *PT field*.

Sawyer instantly knew this had to be part of Karnic's plan. He wondered how he could let Karnic know that he understood—he sure as hell wasn't going to accomplish this by blinking it out in Morse code. *Nobody knows that shit anymore*, he thought, and then he thought to himself, *Karnic probably does.* But that didn't help.

Sawyer did the only thing he could. He blurted out, "Guess we aren't going to be on time to meet Darrian on the PT field to take his test." And then Sawyer started laughing very loudly, like he had told a joke.

"Quiet! Everybody!" Womack attempted a pathetic command voice.

Karnic gave a single half nod at Sawyer—he knew exactly what the joke was. Sawyer had to have seen Darrian and somehow had received a message from him about the PT field they used in Forest Park.

The crowd was becoming more dense as the buses moved even more slowly. General Womack was beginning to look a little panicked about so many people showing up. The fact that this was not what he had planned was evident by the sweat beading up on his forehead. The slower the buses moved, the more he sweated.

They were only a block from the area Bravo Company called their PT grounds; they could see the crowds ahead were endless. Karnic felt that something was going to happen at this point, he just had no clue what it was. Then, the crowed slammed into the side of the bus—it felt like the bus had been hit by a tsunami. Womack lost his footing and fell, with his full body weight on one knee that caught the edge of a step. This sent a wave of electric shock up through the core of Womack's body—one of pure pain.

With the buses now at a full stop, people began chanting, "Let our men go! Let our men go! Let our men go!" The roar was so thunderous that it vibrated the bus like it was a speaker pounding out a beat. A great majority of Bravo Company lived and worked in the area. The people of Saint Louis held their National Guardsmen in high esteem. Now the National Guardsmen were being paraded around like criminals, and the people were not going to stand for it—they may not have even known about this until it showed on the ten o'clock news had it not been for Darrian getting the word out.

"Stop it! Get back!" Womack yelled repeatedly. He grabbed the radio and called for the MPs to clear a path. Eight well-armed MPs disembarked and began charging forward from the back of the convoy. With their M4s charged and at the ready, they began moving the crowd back. Once they moved the crowd away from the door, Womack opened it and stepped to the bottom step. The roar of the crowd was so loud that it was hard for Womack to breathe. There were just so many people, and they were not there to support him. No, they were there to retrieve what he had taken.

As far as Womack could see were people chanting, "Let our men go!" He tried his best to speak but he could not tell if any words were actually coming out of his mouth. Womack's head kept twisting side to side—he looked at the MPs, who looked back at him for direction and then back at the crowd. Reaching down to his sidearm, the general thought of firing a round in the air to get the crowd's attention and quiet them down.

A second after Womack had the thought, his hand was already pulling a 9mm Beretta from its holster and was pointing it at the sky. His finger squeezed the trigger. The firing pin struck the primer and ignited the powder, and the bullet left the barrel with a very loud *boom*. Almost instantly, Womack realized that he had made a major mistake, for his was not the only bullet to leave the barrel.

The MPs, who were standing a few feet away from Womack when he fired just above their heads, had no clue where the sound had come from—they only knew that it was gunfire and very close. Panic, fear, and adrenaline surged through their bodies. Almost as soon as Womack fired, so did the MPs. Their bullets moved at an average speed of three thousand feet per second.

With tungsten steel cores, the bullets did not slow down after striking the first objects in their path. Once one MP had fired, they all did, again and again. The dead lay all around, almost stacked like sandbags, and encircled the MPs, who were covered with the blood of those they had just killed. Many of the dead appeared to still be standing unable to fall.

"Move! Move! Move!" was all Sgt. Karnic yelled when the firing started.

He had seen Womack raising his pistol in the air and thought, *This fool can't believe that the shit you see in the movies works.* Then the shot rang out. This was the moment!

Had there been those among the company who might have stayed behind and taken their chances with the courts? Well, at this point, there was no doubt that there would be none. Every man moved quickly. The MPs on the bus were subdued in seconds. Sawyer started for Womack, who was standing on the bottom step, almost resembling a mannequin staring at all the death he had caused with one shot.

Then Sawyer heard it: another round of fire—this time it was incoming. Womack collapsed and rolled out of the doorway, landing on eight dead MPs. Everyone on the bus dropped down—they believed that being taken in was no longer going to be their fate. Sgt. Karnic was the first to look out to see who was shooting. Then Cdr. Sawyer followed.

What they saw was a little unbelievable.

"Darrian!" Marks called out.

Darrian and four others were coming from around cars in the front of the convoy. Their guns were still trained on the MPs lying on the ground, as dead as those they had just murdered. They moved through the great number of wounded civilians to the rear of the convoy. As they were approaching each bus, they could see that Bravo Company had taken control of the buses and moved on to the five-ton truck in the rear. After seeing what had happen to the others, the driver and remaining MP exited with hands held as high as they possibly could be.

"Are there any others?" Darrian asked those around him, the little boy vanishing in an instant.

"No, No. I'm a medic. Let me help," the MP from the five-ton truck said as he pointed at the wounded civilians covering the ground for a hundred yards.

Darrian gestured for him to go, and then he felt someone's hand on his shoulder. Turning to see whose hand it belonged to, Darrian's eyes met with Sgt. Karnic's just as Karnic said, "Good job, soldier. We have it from here."

Darrian suddenly felt like a little boy again. Sgt. Karnic had that effect on many men.

People were returning, and doctors poured from the nearby hospitals to help those who were wounded. There were so many. It was an absolute massacre.

Commander Sawyer could hear the sirens coming and knew that with all the people and cars, they would have a hard time getting in the area. He turned to order the men to help the wounded, but he saw that there would be no need for that—they were already providing care. He and his men knew that the window for their escape was closing, but the civilians would always come above their own needs. Sawyer felt great pride when looking out at his company and only wished that he had been commanding them under very different circumstances.

Chapter 18

ESCAPE FROM SAINT LOUIS

A ll of the men from the 138th Bravo Company were also trained as medics—
their most important task was being able to take care of their wounded.
After all, they were always first on the scene. Due to their training, it did not
take long for things to get organized and for the most critically injured to be
seen by the multitude of doctors and nurses in the area.

"Commander!" Karnic bellowed out while pointing off in the distance. He
was drawing Sawyer's attention to the wall of people in the distance. It was very
strange—it looked like all of them had their arms locked together and like a
small group was running his way.

"Get out of here! Go!" the small group was yelling frantically.

Many of the wounded started calling for them to flee as well. "You men
must go now, or this will have been for nothing. GO! GO! GO NOW!"

Sawyer turned to Karnic—without saying a word, they both agreed that it
was time.

"Load 'em up, men. Both buses! MOVE! MOVE! MOVE!" Sawyer ordered
in his most commanding voice. "Sgt. Karnic, man the five-ton."

Sawyer felt great pride in his company and was proud to lead them now.
He just wished there had not been so many lives lost in the process. He and his

men would never forget the sacrifice the people of Saint Louis had paid on this ground for their freedom.

As Karnic moved quickly to the five-ton, he grabbed Darrian by the arm. "You are coming with me. Get in," Karnic said as he practically threw Darrian at the massive truck. He turned to those who had fought with Darrian, thus becoming outlaws, and addressed them with the most sorrowful tone of voice that could come from a soldier. "You men!" Well, three men and one woman. "You might as well join us—there is nothing for you here now." It was the kind of voice that said *thank you for your help—sorry it had to be against our own.*

The group jumped in the back, and Darrian followed. Their names were still unknown to Karnic, but they were closer than old friends.

From the time Womack fired his fateful shot until Bravo Company fired up the convoy, only thirty minutes had elapsed. It was the longest thirty minutes of their lives up until now. All three of the vehicles in the convoy were equipped with radios, and Sawyer had given new frequencies to all the RTOs (radio telephone operators) before they left the once-peaceful area they had once shared with the people of Saint Louis.

After radio checks were done, Sawyer gave the order to move out. "Sergeant Karnic, you have the lead. Get us out of here."

"Roger," Karnic replied and gave the huge vehicle full power. The thing was not fast, but little could stop it. This was good news since there were many cars he had to move in order to get the buses moving. Driving around the two buses, Karnic then plowed right through two cars parked along the curb and drove out on the field where they had, up until now, conducted physical training. Karnic dodged a few trees, and then they were heading down the running path that took them back to the street. The one thought Karnic had was how great it felt to be moving and not in restraints. That was something he was sure he would not allow to happen again.

The police were of little worry—they had so many people surrounding them that there was nothing they could do but watch the buses drive off. That is, if they even wanted to stop them. With all the noise the people were making, the police radios were pointless.

Karnic was not sure where to go—he just kept the convoy off the main roads and headed to the center of the state. He figured it would be harder for them to be tracked through the Ozarks, and most of these men knew the area well. After they were thirty minutes southwest of Saint Louis, he radioed for guidance.

"Cardinal, this is Ridge Runner. Over."

Sawyer heard the radio call and knew that had to be Karnic. Only Karnic would take it upon himself to give himself and the commander a new code name. Sawyer let out a little chuckle when he heard the call, and so did the rest of the men—all three vehicles had been riding in utter silence and glumness, and this was the mood changer the men needed.

Sawyer replied, "Ridge Runner, this is Cardinal. Over."

"Cardinal, can I get a heading? Over."

Sawyer stopped to think; he was so glad to be out of Saint Louis that he had not really thought of a destination. Then it came to him. "South. Arkansas. Ridge Runner, looks like we are now what they said we are, Traitors." Sawyer knew that every man could hear his voice and that each was listening closely, so he followed with, "Men, listen up! Today ends our faith in the government of this once-great nation."

Sawyer paused and let it sink in.

"Men, we all took an oath of service."

He paused.

"Today is the day. Today we uphold our oath, to the death, we shall—"

He paused.

"I shall defend the Constitution from ALL ENEMIES!"

He repeated even louder.

"ALL ENEMIES—foreign and DOMESTIC, so help me God."

The words rolled from Sawyers's lips over the radio like a Southern Baptist preacher on Good Friday.

"MEN! Today we have seen that it will be domestic enemies we must fight."

He paused.

"We have no other path."

He paused.

"And we have been labeled as traitors."

Sawyer wanted those words to strike home, and they did.

"Today we join the ranks of TRAITORS! Proudly we are TRAITORS! Traitors such as George Washington, Benjamin Franklin, Sam Adams! Traitors such as Patrick Henry, the traitor who said, 'Give me liberty or give me death!'"

A wave of electricity flowed over the men of Bravo Company as they all roared the roar of men with deep desire and purpose, a roar of fighting men!

"Those men were all traitors. Most importantly they were all PATRIOTS!"

They roared once more as Sawyer paused.

Sawyer came back on the radio, this time with a softer voice. "Men."

Sawyer waited and gave them a moment to listen before continuing.

"Men, I am sorry to say that I do not know what has become of the rest of the 138th Bravo Company. We can only hope that they are well."

He looked down at the floor in deep thought and then he began again.

"One thing I am sure of is that they will fight! And fight hard! However, as of now, we will no longer be part of the 138th."

The men looked at each other and continued to listen to the commander.

"Today we will be known by a new designation, one fitting to our new fight to keep the oath we all swore."

Sawyer's head hung low by the time the last word left his lips, almost as if he had begun to pray. Then almost as if he had been resurrected, he snapped to attention.

"From today forth, we will be known to the world as the United Constitutional Militia!"

The roar on the buses rivaled that of any rock concert. Then Sawyer gave his first order as the commander of the United Constitutional Militia.

"Ridge Runner, this is Cardinal. Over."

"Cardinal, this is Ridge Runner, over."

"Ridge Runner, take us to Arkansas!"

Chapter 19

ANGELIQUE'S CAREER

No sooner had Angelique finished basic and MP training than she began taking college courses online. She was setting higher and higher goals for herself, and a college degree would help her get there. She also began to study Russian as a second language. Even though the Cold War had been over for some time, she still recognized that the Russians could be a possible future issue.

After four years in the army, where she received two Purple Hearts and accommodations for bravery during her tour in Iraq, Angelique decided that it was time to move on. Rather than enlisting, she applied to the Department of Homeland Security. She felt that it was time for her to protect the people of the United States on US soil, rather than protect the interest of the United States on foreign soil.

Service to her country was very important for Angelique and left little time for a personal life, although from time to time, she would find herself wondering whatever had happened to the tall, lanky boy who lived down the road. She had been very close friends with him for years. From her first day riding the bus to the day he and his family moved away, they had done everything together. She had even taught him most of the fighting moves she knew, and he would show her tricks like starting fires with rocks or getting out of rope when tied up. Karl was his name, but all that had abruptly ended one day when his family had decided that they needed to be closer to his grandfather, who was up there in years. From that day forth, she had never seen Karl again.

Once hired by Homeland Security, Angelique moved through the ranks quickly. In just a matter of years, she was heading up her own field office in Dallas, Texas—the very state in which the battle at Squires Ranch occurred. The very state that had, at this point, begun separating itself from the United States. Everyone wanted the assignment, but the FBI had taken jurisdiction. That didn't stop many from looking into it, including Angelique. That was until the memos were circulated indicating that anybody investigating Squires Ranch would be subject to prosecution.

That did not stop Angelique from viewing the public information on the subject. She found it interesting and was quite curious as to how someone could fake a video so precisely and with so much detail while on the run. She was also fascinated with how the news agencies received what the head office was calling fake footage, especially since nobody had heard or seen the three suspects in weeks. Other than the two suspects, only one other person made it out alive from the ranch, and he was a Texas Ranger, Carlos Sepulveda.

The battle at Squires Ranch continued to amaze her, and Angelique's senses told her that something was not right on the ranch. Work around the office went on, even though Texas was boycotting everything from the federal government. Most people saw the recent events as just more political posturing and figured it would not be more than a few more weeks until things went back to normal. That was until the new video was tested and was then labeled as "original with no tampering."

That led to Texas calling out the state's National Guard and assuming control of all military bases within its borders. The stakes became even higher when, days later, Oklahoma and Arkansas did the same. Panic set in at Angelique's branch office, and the information they received was severely restricted. Angelique fought to keep her office together, but no matter her argument, she understood the need many had to leave the state. Within days, her office staff was cut to less than half. She did not doubt that by the end of the week, it would be reduced to half its size again.

The following two weeks proved difficult, not due to overwhelming work but due to the lack of it. It was as if her office had been forgotten. Few calls came in, and even fewer went out—cases had been pulled, or they just went nowhere since communication had been severely restricted. At least nobody was forced to remain in Texas. People were still free to come and go through the checkpoints set up along the state lines.

Angelique spent a great deal of her time just gathering what information she possibly could. The Internet was only down at the office. In fact, if a person didn't watch the news or follow current events, he or she would be hard pressed to notice anything had changed. Most of Angelique's work was done at her favorite lunch restaurant, where she was now seated in order to access the free Wi-Fi.

On most days, information was limited—very little information came from the main office. E-mails mainly consisted of Angelique requesting information and sending daily updates that she found pointless, since there were no open cases to report upon. Her office staff was little more than a skeleton crew—most had gone to offices in other states. Angelique had often thought of going to an office in another state herself, but she did not want to give up her posting.

The days were becoming longer and longer and there was less work to do. Much of the time, she just watched the local news while eating lunch. Today, though, was shaping up to be a little different. Something had happened in Saint Louis. The screen read: "Breaking News Alert: Missouri Army National Guard Unit Goes Rogue." This grabbed Angelique's attention even more since she was from Rock Town, Missouri.

She had followed current events closely—there were no indications that Missouri was going to side with Texas. It also didn't make sense to her that one unit of the Missouri Guard would go rogue. The broadcast went on to present the reports and evidence linking the unit, particularly 138th Bravo Company, with plans of joining the military of Arkansas. It also went on to report that the traitors were in custody and being transported, along with their gear and weapons, back to Saint Louis. Angelique was fascinated by the news and wondered what would possess an entire unit to leave their home state to join another state.

Then the next Breaking news alert really captured Angelique's attention, along with everyone else in the restaurant. "Saint Louis Massacre: Ninety-Three Reported Casualties; Forty-Two Confirmed Deaths." Angelique suddenly stopped breathing. When she began breathing again, all she could think was: *What the hell happened?*

On the screen, they were playing cell phone footage of the massacre. She was watching the television screen intently. As she was watching, she could not help but think about how the country faced threats from abroad, about how they were always in fear of another terror attack like the one that had happened on September 11, 2001.

Angelique's thoughts also went to larger threats—threats that North Korea had recently made possibly coming true and how that country could, once again, not only strike South Korea but also possibly the shorelines of the United States. Then again, there was the alliance being built between Russia and China, and both countries were becoming much more aggressive on the world stage. One of many things that did not make sense these days was how the current administration reacted. With more threats to the United States than at any time in history, Washington decided that what the country needed most was to reduce the size of the military.

While watching the news broadcast, Angelique came to one conclusion. With the current state of the Union and its internal problems, none of that mattered. People had feared attack from those outside of the country, and here the country was, attacking itself from within.

Angelique was a combat vet, yet the images on the screen still bothered her greatly. These were American citizens lying in pools of their own blood, caused by those who had taken a solemn oath to protect them. That was truly the part that bothered her the most. As she listened to the report on the Saint Louis massacre, Angelique could not help but get confused about what had happened. From what she could make out, those who had been arrested for treason had saved the people being massacred, massacred by those who had captured the rouge unit. The whole situation was madness.

Angelique stayed glued to the seat in the restaurant for hours—she really had nowhere else to be since there was few staff left in her office. Hours passed with the news reporting on victims of the massacre and asking people to call in if they "have information on the whereabouts of 138th Bravo Company, Missouri National Guard, last seen driving two white buses and one five-ton military vehicle." *That shouldn't be hard to locate*, Angelique thought as the reporter went on to say "The suspects are to be considered heavily armed and well supplied."

After watching more details on the possible supplies that the rogue company had recovered, Angelique could only speculate how the unit had recovered so much after being arrested. From what she could gather, all of their field and personal gear had remained on the buses. The five-ton possessed all of their weapons, ammunition, heavy equipment, and MREs. *Somebody really fucked the pooch on that one*, she thought with a smirk.

Angelique grew tired of sitting in the booth since the news soon began to get very repetitive. She paid her tab, which made the server who was waiting on her very grateful. As she walked home, she tried to make sense of what was happing to the country she so dearly loved. The problem was that there was no order or reason for the chaos. Her thoughts turned to those who had given so much in defense of the country, especially those who had given all. What would those men and women who had sacrificed their lives think of the current state of the Union?

Angelique was in such deep thought that she didn't even realize there were tears rolling down her face. Angelique was a tough woman, tougher than most men, but when it came to those in the armed forces present and past, she found it hard to control her emotions. Once she saw her reflection in the glass door of her apartment building, Angelique's thoughts moved straight to embarrassment. She did not usually cry, and the last people to see her cry were her parents at Old Jerry's funeral.

After arriving at her apartment, Angelique scanned it for anything out of place. It was a habit she had developed over the years. She just figured the habit had formed from everything she had seen and experienced up until now. After making sure that everything was in its place, Angelique turned on the news.

Things had changed in the twenty-minute walk from the restaurant to her apartment. Angelique could not believe what she was hearing and seeing on the television. Across bottom of the screen scrolled in bold print, "Martial law declared in Saint Louis and surrounding counties."

Then she listened closely to the speaker. "By order of the president of the United States, Saint Louis County and all connecting counties are hereby placed under martial law by the order of General Arthur T. Womack."

Chapter 20

WHAT NEXT?

I t had been an hour since Commander Sawyer's blood-pumping, adrenaline-charged speech, and now, instead of being the commander of 138th Bravo Company, he was now the commander of the United Constitutional Militia. That didn't solve any of their problems, but it did give them a new purpose and set of beliefs. The men of the newly formed UCM wanted nothing more than to go home. It was the main thing on all of their minds. The men also wondered why someone in the government had decided to mark them all as traitors. They knew that home would never be the same. The government had tried to sacrifice them to further a cause—a cause that was not clear to them and was of no consequence at this point. From here to the day they would be laid in the earth, the one thing that would matter would be keeping their oath and protecting the Constitution.

The militia's first concern was fuel. They had been on the road for hours. Taking the back roads added time, and the hills of the Ozarks burned a great deal of fuel. Sawyer had entered into a world that very few had experienced. He had a new fighting force and no idea how to resupply it. There were no forms to fill out or people to call—he and his men were it. As they were driving through what he believed to be Mark Twain National Forest, Sawyer observed what appeared to be isolated roads going into the forest and had an idea. He picked up the radio, held the mic firmly in his hand, and began his communications.

"Ridge Runner, this is Cardinal. Over." He shook his head a little when he said his call sign. *Leave it to Karnic*, he thought.

A few moments later, Sawyer received a reply: "Cardinal, this is Ridge Runner. Over."

"Ridge Runner, have you noticed the roads going off into the forest, the ones with gates blocking them? Over."

"Cardinal, I sure have, and I have just the key for them. Over." Karnic could already tell what the commander was thinking.

"Make it happen, Sergeant. Cardinal out."

Karnic passed a few of the gated roads before choosing one—he wanted to be sure that it would go far enough off the main road so that passing cars could not see them, and he looked for concealment overhead. The trees had nice bushy tops, so they would not be easily seen by air, even with the big white buses.

Karnic was in the five-ton truck, so he was in the lead. The five-ton was not the lead vehicle because it was the biggest but because it was the slowest. The rule in the infantry was that you are only as fast as your slowest man, which was true of vehicles as well—therefore, if the slowest vehicle was in front, the others did not have to worry about outrunning it.

Karnic slowed the beast of a truck and pulled in. Marks, which was in the passenger seat, jumped out and ran to the back of the truck and yelled to the people in the back to grab the bolt cutters from the gear. There was only room for the five-ton to pull onto the road before the gate, which caused the buses to wait on the main road. Luckily, few people traveled these roads. During times like these, though, minutes seemed like hours.

Marks was happy to see the cutters being lowered from the back of the truck—he really expected it to take much longer. As soon as his hands made contact, his feet began running with the cutters trailing behind as if they were trying to keep up. No sooner had he made it to the gate Marks had the lock cut with little effort, gate open, and everyone moving through. The three vehicles drove past him on down the road. The faster they were out of sight, the better, and Marks knew that. He closed the gate and replaced the cut lock making it look as if it had not been removed. He took a look around and could not believe how lucky they had been to not have been seen. He started running down the unpaved road to the rest of the militia.

Sawyer had to know what supplies they possessed and how much. He could not make any plans without it. "Platoon leaders, on me!" he said loudly, knowing the only thing that could hear them here would be the wildlife.

Even with the safety the 138th now felt by being away from civilian population, they still put their training to good use. Most of the men were on the perimeter, and the weapons they had taken from the MPs were divided along the perimeter. They were not going to be taking any chances at this point. Sawyer was proud to see that they did not need to be ordered to secure the area—his men were now fighting for their lives and country.

Then there were those with them who had not been not originally part of his company. Those who had saved the company. Darrian's group. With his platoon leaders gathered around, Sawyer looked over at the group standing together at the rear of the five-ton.

"Darrian," Sawyer said just loud enough for Darrian and those around him to hear then made a motion with his hand for them to come over. "Darrian, every one of us is very grateful for what the five of you have done," Sawyer said, taking the time to look each of the five standing before him separately in the eyes. He snapped to attention, and with a low, roaring voice, Sawyer issued the commands. "Group, attention!"

When all the platoon leaders were at attention, Sawyer continued, "Ready arms." They all saluted and held it perfectly, presenting the salute with thanks to the five standing in front of them.

"Order arms." The commander and his platoon sergeants brought their arms down simultaneously.

"Now I am sorry," Sawyer continued, "but we have to get to business. First I would like to know your plans." He was addressing the five standing before him. "None of you is obliged to stay, and—"

Before he could get another word out, Sawyer was cut off by one of the four standing with Darrian.

"Sir, my name is Kate, and I served as an MP in the army for eight years. With the exception of Darrian here, whom we only met this morning, all of us have served in the army or marines. When the shooting started, we met for the first time as we were drawing our concealed pistols and moving to the gunfire. Darrian here saw us moving in and gave us a very quick rundown of what was taking place. After giving Darrian my backup, we moved in, and you know the rest."

Kate then paused and checked the expressions on each person in her audience's face before she continued. "Sir, the men and I heard your speech. We took the same oath as you, and we agree there is no other path. If what happened in Saint Louis is a sign of what the government has become…" She paused before finishing and then gave the commander a stone-cold stare. "We, too, are traitors, sir."

Commander Sawyer could not help but stare with some amusement at the five of them. He found it amusing how all five of them were on the same page, even with the age differences. Hell, Darrian was only sixteen, and the oldest of the five was wearing a Vietnam veteran's cap. The new squad was truly one for a militia.

"OK," replied Sawyer. "Get a list of ranks, squad chain of command, and call signs to Sergeant Karnic. ASAP. For now, give me your platoon leader, and the rest are dismissed."

As Sawyer had figured, Kate remained behind, and it was now time for planning. His first need was to have a complete inventory, personal items included. The men were trained to never go anywhere without their rucksacks, so they were all stacked in the back of the buses—this provided Sawyer with some comfort, as he knew that his men at least had that portion of their gear. After addressing the need for inventory and all digital devices to be turned in and checked for the possibility that they were being tracked, Sawyer moved on to the next step of the meeting.

"OK, now one thing we know we are going to need but do not have is fuel." Sawyer looked at each man and woman standing in front of him to make sure they were all focused on him before beginning again.

"We cannot just stop and fuel up at a station or on a base, so where do we get it? Get back to me with options at, let's say, eighteen hundred hours." He put the question out there, but knowing that there would be no point in wasting daylight, he dismissed the group to complete their given tasks.

The number of men on the perimeter was reduced to fifty-fifty: half on the line and half doing inventory. When it came to the gear on the buses, the task took little time to complete. Each rucksack had been inventoried before leaving the armory, so a master sheet was derived from the individual sheets attached to each ruck. The five-ton was what interested Sawyer the most. He was concerned that after they had been taken into custody, their weapons and ammunition had become relocated.

Sawyer knew most of what should be in the truck—he always made it a good practice to watch the weapons and ammunition being loaded, especially when they were transporting M406 high explosive rounds for the M203 grenade launchers. Those, combined with the smoke grenades, opened up a great deal when it came to planning. They should also have 20,000 of 5.56 rounds for the M4 rifles, which was not nearly enough for each man to have even close to a full battle load of 240 rounds—instead, it would only be a little over half that. Sawyer's 128 men were mostly expert marksmen, so he had no doubt they could make due.

His main concern was that none of it would be in the truck and that their time would be cut short. Sawyer normally let the men do the tasks he assigned and waited for the report, but not today. He had to know if they had the weapons. Before he thought twice about interfering with the inventory, Sawyer had already walked to the rear of the truck. Sawyer set his eyes upon a miracle—they had everything, including cases of MREs.

It was now 1800 hours, and the platoon sergeants were already in the process of giving their reports to a very pleased commander. That was until the current fuel supply information was read. Both buses were down to a quarter tank, and the five-ton truck was just under that. They estimated that they had fewer than a hundred miles of travel before running out of fuel. After receiving the information, Sawyer was overcome with panic, although he certainly did not show it on the outside.

Rather than panic everyone, he said but one word. "Recommendations?"

"Sir," one of the platoon sergeants replied and then carried on, "Farms. Sure, most of the bigger ones have fuel delivered. We can find one and fill up."

"Sergeant, that is a great idea," said Sawyer. But everyone could feel a *but* coming on next, and it did. "But we have limited miles on the vehicles and no idea where the next farm with fuel is located."

You could almost hear a light sigh come from Sawyer before he spoke again. "Men, we are on our own—we do not even have the luxury of using the Internet."

Just then Sawyer remembered something. "You did check your men for all cell phones and electronics that could be tracked, correct?"

"Yes, sir," they all replied at once.

Then Sgt. Karnic spoke up. "Sir, I did not want to take any chances and had everyone with credit cards or IDs containing chips cut out the chips and destroy them. Sir, I would suggest checking your items for RFID chips."

Sawyer reached into his back pocket and pulled out his wallet. That method of tracking had never occurred to him. He thanked God that it had occurred to Karnic. As Sawyer opened his wallet in what was the fading light of day, he wondered if it might already be too late. While opening his wallet, he could hear Karnic opening his pocketknife. The first card Sawyer came to was his own military ID, and without looking, he handed it straight over to Karnic, who was ready to dispense with the tracking chip. Then Sawyer pulled out the new ID he had got just the month before, and there it was, another embedded chip.

Now it was all too clear why the government had required everyone to get the new REAL ID cards. The government had truly become scared of its own people. By the time Sawyer had completed the search of his wallet, he had five cards with the chips. Then he got a sick feeling in his stomach. "Distribute weapons, ammunition, and MREs to the men. Then load everyone and everything up. We are moving out." He suddenly felt like he had stepped on a land mine.

It only took fifteen minutes for the disbursement of supplies to the men and even less for everything to be loaded. In all, they were once again on the move within twenty minutes, but Sawyer had the fear that it was not fast enough. That fear eased just a little when they were back on the main road, but the ease did not last long before the new reality of running out of fuel hit him again. That problem still had not been solved.

It had been thirty minutes since they had begun traveling back down the main road, and fuel was nowhere in sight. The only things out here were trees. Sawyer was starting to have doubts that even a closed gas station would show soon.

"At least we are infantry—walking is our main source of transportation," Sawyer said and let out a visible smirk.

"Sir!" It was Spc. Marks. Sawyer received a rush of adrenaline from the sudden outburst. When he turned, Marks was walking quickly up the aisle toward him.

"Sir, I know where we can get the fuel we need. Back there, sir," Marks said with excitement hanging on every word.

"Where is 'back there,' Specialist? I saw nothing but trees."

"Sir, I saw a Highway Department maintenance garage. It was just off the road, and they have fuel tanks for all their equipment," Marks answered with less excitement and more of a self-confident tone.

Sawyer stared at Marks for a second and then up at his platoon sergeant standing right behind him. Sawyer knew that they had little room for error and could not waste any of the fuel they had by going on a wild goose chase. After seeing his sergeant's approval of the idea, Sawyer was put a little more at ease and picked up the radio.

"Ridge Runner, this is Cardinal. Over."

Karnic soon replied, "Go for Ridge Runner. Over."

"Ridge Runner, same as before—find us another area. Out."

Sawyer knew that he didn't need to go into details with Karnic. As he set down the mic to the radio, he turned back to Marks. "Let's find out, Specialist."

Chapter 21

DRIFTING THOUGHTS

Now they were on the move again, and Karnic's mind started drifting back to when he was small and he father told him about what had happened to his biological grandfather—how he had died with honor, fighting for his country, saving his men, and sacrificing himself for those in the village. Karnic also thought about how even though his grandfather had been a great man doing what was right, he and his men had been disgraced by the deeds of others. Karnic prayed that he and his men would not experience a similar fate.

He tried shrugging off the thoughts and focused on one of the stories his father loved to tell—one that was much more pleasant.

Karl's father served in the US Navy aboard the USS *Tutuila*. He never told Karl much about his time in Vietnam except a few of the more colorful adventures he'd had. When young Karl would ask, his father would start out by gazing at Karl, as if deep in thought, and then he would begin with, "This one time."

"This one time I was walking down a path along the banks of the Mekong. There was kind of a marketplace with dried fish and other things for sale. Well, one day I spotted the biggest bloated hog floating down the river—it looked like a hot-air balloon getting ready to pop." At that moment, he would pause and look at young Karl to see if he was still interested. Karl was always interested in the stories, even if he had heard them before.

After being satisfied that Karl was interested, his father would continue, "Then I saw something that changed the way I conducted myself for the rest of the time I was there." He would then shiver, like suddenly a cold chill was going through his body, and continue. "You would not believe it—I spotted four to five kids with sticks pull the hog over to the bank and drag it out. I then watched as they cut it up."

"Why did they do that?" Karl asked.

"Well, Son, I left at that point. I still had places to go and things to do and felt like I had seen enough."

Karl was puzzled and asked, "How did that change what you did there?"

His father looked at him, and based on the puzzled look on Karl's face, his father knew that he was ready for the punch line.

"Because..." he said, then paused for a moment. "Later, when I walked back down through the marketplace, little remained of the hog, and the boys had a stand in the marketplace where they were selling what they called Monkey on a Stick."

"Ewww!" Karl said. He ran off to the other room. He knew that he would be telling that story to his best friend the next day at school.

Chapter 22

THE RETURN

One thing nice about national forests: there are many fire roads cut through them, which are rarely used and rarely gated off. Now that they were once again off the main road and under the concealment of the trees above, the planning could begin. Once the perimeter had been secured, Sawyer called again for the platoon sergeants.

"Everything secure?" he asked once all five of them had arrived. After receiving the reply he was expecting from all of the sergeants, he began. "OK, this is how I see it. Not all of us are going on the fuel run. I am not going to jeopardize everything for this." Sawyer watched each of his platoon leaders and looked for how they all reacted to his plan as he laid it out.

"I will be taking the vehicles and two drivers," Sawyer said.

All five platoon sergeants said, "Sir!"

"As you were," Sawyer growled, bringing to the opposition to an end, at least for now. "When we break from this meeting, have your men remove everything from the buses and the five-ton. Leave nothing—take out the radios except for the one in the five-ton."

Sawyer could tell that this plan was not sitting well with the platoon sergeants—each one of them wanted to be the one to go on the mission in his place. "I will drive the five-ton and keep you apprised. Should we not return..." He paused, deep in thought. "Should we not return by twenty-two hundred hours or should we be compromised, you are to move on by foot. Keep to the woods. Each platoon will move in different directions. Gather men and supplies to continue the fight. Do NOT surrender. Any questions?"

No sooner had Sawyer asked this than he retracted it. "Hold it!" he said, as once again *Sir* had become a group word. "No questions—just break, and get your men moving."

Sgt. Karnic was standing at the door of the truck as Sawyer approached. Sawyer put up his hand to stave off any protest to his leading the mission. To his surprise, Karnic stood there and replied, "Have a smooth ride, sir."

"Damned Kraut," was all Karnic heard as Sawyer passed him to climb up in the truck.

Sawyer was ready—this would be the first of what he hoped would be many missions the UCM would embark upon. He shut the door, fired up the truck, and grabbed the radio mic. "Light Fighter, this is Cardinal. Over."

"Cardinal, this is Light Fighter. Over."

"Cardinal is moving out. Over."

"See you in a few, Cardinal. Over."

"Roger that. Cardinal out."

Now that they had notified his makeshift TOC (tactical operations command) that they were off and running. Marks was in the lead bus, followed by Kate in the second, and she was followed by Sawyer in the five-ton. Even though the trip was only twenty minutes, it seemed like they would never get there.

Marks pulled the bus up to a cable that was stretched across the entrance to the Highway Department maintenance shed. Marks's adrenaline had begun to pump the moment he came around the corner and set eyes on the place. It was time to find out if his hunch was correct. Slamming the emergency brake on and putting the bus in neutral all in one swift motion, Marks grabbed the bolt cutters and jumped up from his seat.

Marks's pulse was racing—since he had first caught sight of the place, he had fought to see the fuel tanks, but it was much too dark. As he cut a lock, he was a little amused by a thought. *Somebody is going to be buying a lot of locks tomorrow.* This would be his third one today and not even close to the last. Time was moving so fast now—everything he did seemed to be already done before he could even give it a thought. The bus even seemed like it was still rocking from the sudden stop by the time Marks had made it back to the seat and was moving forward once more.

Marks's eyes were moving everywhere, darting back and forth, searching every inch of retreating darkness as he drove around the building. The fuel tanks suddenly appeared as the lights above shined; much like one would illuminated an actor on a stage. High up, cradled on a concert stand was a thousand-gallon tank with the big, beautiful green label: *Diesel*. Marks was probably the happiest of everyone when the tanks were spotted—had they not been there, it would have been a long walk back with the others.

Marks did not want to waste any time, and he circled the convoy around to where they could all begin pumping as soon as he cut the lock. It took a very short time before the diesel was flowing. The fuel was gravity fed from the storage tanks to the fuel tanks of the vehicles, so it was taking twice as long. None of them complained—they were all just happy to see the needles on the gauge move up, not down.

Marks could never stand the smell of diesel, but tonight it smelled like the sweetest chocolate to him. He had already topped his bus up and moved it to the side and was almost done with Kate's and had signaled for Sawyer to prepare to move up. Marks was very proud of himself and enjoying being right.

"Move it over!" he yelled as he banged on the side of the bus. It came to life from its slumber and moved forward alongside the other bus, just behind the maintenance shed, out of sight from the road. Now it was time for the five-ton, and Sawyer slowly crept it forward until Marks gave him the signal to stop.

By the time Sawyer had climbed down from the truck, Marks had already begun fueling.

"This is taking much longer than I anticipated," Sawyer said to Marks.

Marks began to lose a little of the excitement he had been feeling from being right about the fuel being there. He slowly looked up at the commander to explain why when Sawyer spoke again. "It doesn't matter if it takes twice as much time—it was a great idea, Marks."

Upon receiving such praise from the commander, the wonderful feeling Marks had of a job well done returned instantly. He turned back to the pump with a smile. *This day at least is ending better than it started*, he thought. Then he looked down to his chest and fell limply to the ground.

Marks never heard the shot that sent the bullet through his heart.

Sawyer reached for his sidearm but he couldn't get to it before three men were on him and strapping zip cuffs around his wrist.

"Marks!" Sawyer yelled, even though from under the three men, he could tell there would be no reply.

"Get him UP!"

Sawyer's mind felt like it was going to short circuit. *It couldn't be*, he thought as the three men were bringing him to his knees.

"I AM GOING TO KILL YOU! YOU SON OF A—" Two punches to the stomach made it difficult for Sawyer to finish.

"Now, Commander, that is no way to speak to a superior officer."

"Womack, I—" At least he only received one to the gut that time.

"Bring the other driver over here!" No matter how hard he tried, Womack just could not find a commanding tone.

Womack had brought at least a dozen men with him; even if Sawyer's people had a chance to fight back, the odds were not even close to being in their favor. Sawyer was not about to give up, and he sure as hell was not going to tell Womack where his men were. He could make out the shape of one of Womack's men escorting Kate over from the buses. Sawyer watched as she seemed to not put up any resistance. "Could I have been wrong about her?" he asked himself.

Just as Kate and her escort were passing Womack, with ballerina grace, Kate planted her combat boot along the side of Womack's head. That in turn caused his many chins to begin a dance on their own. From seemingly nowhere, two more guards were on her, striking Kate with more blows than Sawyer had received so far. Sawyer began to protest, but as soon as his lips parted, the blows came down from above.

When it was over, he looked over at Kate. Seeing the smile on her face even after the beating she had just received, Sawyer knew he had not been wrong about her—she was indeed a soldier.

"You two think you are going to survive tonight?" Womack asked rhetorically.

"Well, after the events this morning, I now have total control over six counties—by tomorrow, it will be the state." Womack spoke like it had already happened. "See, it has all been planned out, and you did just what was expected of you. Granted, not quite as planned, but nevertheless things worked out."

"Why did you kill Marks?" Sawyer just had to know. The rage of Marks's killing was hard to take.

"Oh, you don't think you are leaving here, do you?" Womack asked sarcastically while letting out his pathetic laugh.

When Womack was through laughing, he said, "I am going to count down from ten, and if they do not say where the others are, kill 'em." Then he turned and began to walk away, counting as he walked. He really had no stomach for the gore.

Kate and Sawyer looked right into each other's eyes. They didn't want their executioners to be the last thing they saw before death—they wanted to see a fellow soldier. Staring intensely at each other and waiting for the bullets to strike, they heard two thuds. Very confused, both looked at each other and looked forward. Both of their would-be executioners were on the ground, motionless. *Thud, thud...thud, thud.*

"What the?" Kate said as the men holding them fell to the ground, almost landing on top of them.

Womack was also curious as to why he had not heard the kill shots and turned, saying, "I said kill——" Womack froze in place, mouth open and head tilted back. He was dead jut slow to fall.

Sawyer could not believe what was going on. None of his men could make it here—they didn't have any more vehicles. Then three figures moved quickly past and to the other side of the buses. This time, there was a great deal of noise before they moved back to Sawyer's and Kate's position.

"Sorry about your man there," one of the figures said. "We didn't want to get involved, but after seeing them shoot your guy and hearing they were going to execute one of you—well, it was pretty clear by then whose side to take."

"Who are you?" Sawyer asked, still puzzled by what just gone down.

"Oh, I am Robert. That over there——" he said and pointed at the figure of a young woman checking the dead, sporting what looked to Sawyer like a revolver on each hip and a ball cap on her head.

"That is my sister, Sierra." The man expressed great pride in calling her his sister. "Know the gentleman cutting you free? Well, he is a Texas Ranger, Carlos Sepulveda. Just call him Carlos. It's just easier."

Robert towered over them, even after Sawyer was able to get to his feet.

"Now," Robert started, "how about you explain just what the hell was going down here?" He stood waiting with his arms crossed as Carlos and Sierra joined him.

Sawyer looked down at Marks's body, motionless on the ground, in a pool of blood. "I will tell you everything after we take care of my man," Sawyer replied.

Without waiting for acknowledgment, he and Cartwright turned and moved to Marks's remains. Each of them took Marks under the arms and carried him to his bus, where they laid him down, his arms folded. Both bowed their heads, and Sawyer softly said, "Day is done. Gone the sun, from the hills from the sky. God bless you, Marks." He and Cartwright came to attention and saluted their fallen friend.

Once Sawyer had finished filling in the three who not twenty minutes ago had saved their lives, he realized to whom he was talking. "Now I have a question for you. You're the Squires family, right?" Knowing that he was right, Sawyer did not wait for a response before asking his next question. "How the hell did you end up here?"

"You are not going to believe it, but the same way these guys did. RFID locators."

Sawyer's gut feeling earlier has been right. After he and Karnic had gone through his wallet, it had given him a sick feeling. Now he knew why. He was even more sick that the thought had never occurred to him before today that everyone was voluntarily being tracked, granted without their knowledge, but the outcome was still the same.

"Wait. How were you able to use the chips?" Sawyer asked, puzzled that fugitives had that type of technology.

Robert looked at the other two in his group for their nonverbal approval before giving up the information, and he received the approval. "Well, it is not just the four of us. We have an ally in the FBI."

"Sam Crawford?" Sawyer asked a little too loudly.

"Hmm, so his last name is Crawford? Good to know," Robert said while turning to the rest of his group.

"He is your inside man, and you do not even know his last name? Plus you shot him, which almost caused him to lose his arm?"

"Yes," Robert said. He knew that it was time to move on—they could not stay here chatting all evening.

The question of how everyone had ended up here came to Sawyer. "We destroyed the RFID chips before moving from our first stop today. How did you find us here?"

Robert looked over at the bus that held Marks's body and signaled for Sawyer to follow as he began walking over to it. He opened the back door of the bus, and there was Marks with his arms folded—on his wrist was his new watch. The watch that had saved them that afternoon had almost been the end of them that night.

Robert reached in to remove the watch but was abruptly stopped by Sawyer. "I will get it," Sawyer said, looking Robert in the eye. Robert withdrew his arm and slowly stepped back.

"I understand—he is your guy," Robert said. "The watch puts out a signal, even if the phone is off or disabled. We simply followed it after the RFID chips were of no use. Your guy had no clue."

Chapter 23

BUG OUT

K arnic was beginning to worry—they had not heard from Sawyer in quite some time and they had only thirty minutes before bugging out, per the commander's orders. He had already addressed the other platoon leaders, and all the men were packed and ready to move out on his signal. He had all the bases covered and stood by the radio hoping for the call stating the all clear. Experience had taught him, though, that at this point with every second that ticked by, getting the call was less and less likely.

Karnic moved away from the area designated for the TOC and began to walk over to where the other platoon sergeants were located. "Everyone ready to move?" he asked the others as he looked down at his watch. Eight minutes to go.

"Yeah, the men are all ready to move out. You sure you do not want to know where each platoon is heading?" one of the sergeants asked Karnic.

Karnic replied, "No, and do not tell any of the others. If you're captured, you have no information to give about the others. Now get ready to move out on my signal, and good luck." All of them could feel how real the moment was. The feeling of splitting up had everyone stressed, even though they all knew it was the best for their survival.

Karnic looked down at his watch once more. Five minutes, and he would have to give the signal. He stood by the RTO as if attempting to will the call to come. All he heard was the howl of the wind getting louder and louder. Then he looked around and couldn't see anything moving from the wind—or feel it, for that matter. "Vehicles approaching," he said to himself, right before shouting orders throughout the area. "Take cover in the tree line. Three-hundred-sixty-degree perimeter. Push back one hundred yards. Prepare for attack."

Looks like we are going to have it out right here after all, Karnic thought, and he said out loud, "Nobody fires until I fire." He signaled for his platoon to split, two squads on each side of the entrance. He didn't want to give the approaching vehicles a way to retreat.

It seemed as if the vehicles he heard had been on their way for a half hour. It always amazed Karnic how far sound traveled in the forest when the night was calm and few creatures were out. His was the first to see the glow of light coming around the bend of the main road. As he watched, Karnic wondered what had become of Commander Sawyer, Cartwright, and Marks. They were late had it not been for hearing the vehicles coming from miles off, all five platoons would now be on their way in separate directions. Instead, it looked like they were going to fight it out here, and after counting five vehicles, Karnic could see that it was going to be a hell of a fight. When the convoy turned off the main road and onto theirs, Karnic hoped that he had trained his men well. He was about to find out.

Karnic gave out one last command to his men. "Let 'em pass, and stay down."

They were all hugging the ground so closely that there was no sight of them in the darkness. The first vehicle passed—it was a five-ton. Then two buses passed and then a Humvee, followed by a pickup pulling a horse trailer.

"What the hell? They brought horses to hunt us with?" Karnic was highly confused. The first three looked like theirs, but where would they have got a Humvee and truck with a horse trailer? Karnic had to get a closer look.

"Hold your positions," he ordered. "Smith, on me." Smith was one of Karnic's most reliable Platoon Sergeants and close friend, at least as close of a friend as anyone could become with Karnic.

Staying in a crouched position, Sgt. Smith rose to his feet. He and Karnic moved quickly at first until they were just behind the horse trailer—after it came to a stop, they dared not make another move.

Once all the motors had shut down, time seemed to just tick away with no movement. There was nothing but silence for a few minutes, and then things started popping, clicking, and squeaking. Karnic could hear two people talking but couldn't make out what they were saying. Then, suddenly, it was really clear.

"Where are they?" Roberts asked.

"They are definitely here for us. You're surrounded, asshole," Karnic expressed under his breath. Karnic flipped his rifle from safety to fire and gripped it tight—Smith followed his lead and was ready.

"We are late—I gave them orders to move out if we had not returned by twenty-two hundred."

"What the hell?" Karnic blurted out. "That you, sir?"

Karnic could hear the weapons being switched from their safe position as he stepped out from around the back of the trailer. To his surprise, he was met by the barrel of a revolver just a hair from his nose. As his eyes focused what was in his path, Karnic asked, "What the hell? Willie's Feed Sto?"

Sierra had moved in and was waiting there for them to make their move. She had caught their shadows from the brake lights when they had come to a stop.

"Almost two months on the run makes a person notice things, cowboy," she said as she withdrew the pistol from Karnic's face.

"Thanks. It was about to give me frostbite—you really should warm that thing up before putting it in someone's face. It's just polite," Karnic said—he couldn't believe she had got the drop on him.

"Oh, it was about to get really warmed up, darlin'."

Karnic could not tell if she was playing or not.

"Karnic, what are you doing here?" Sawyer asked. "I thought for sure you would have followed my orders."

"Sir, that is just what we were going to do until the sound of your convoy stopped us."

"Us?" About that time, Sgt. Smith stepped out, and then Karnic let out in his commanding voice that made the trees want to obey, "Bring it in, fifty-fifty security."

"I see you picked up a few new items while you were out. Did you get fuel?" That was Karnic's way of asking: Who the hell are these people and where the hell did they get a Humvee?

"Yes, the fuel was there, just like Marks said." Sawyer looked down at the ground, trying hard to control his emotions. "Sergeant, Marks was killed in action." Sawyer knew that it would not be the last time this would happen, but it never got easier.

Without asking who, where, or why, all Karnic wanted to know was one thing, and that was where his soldier and friend was now. As soon as the information had been relayed to him, Karnic called for one person. "Darrian!"

He did not have to call a second time. Darrian had turned into a soldier in a day.

Once Darrian stopped in front of him, Karnic spoke. "Son, you have given up a great deal today—the life you knew, the comforts of home, your innocence—and now I am afraid to say that you'll have to give up even more."

Darrian was frozen in place—having no idea what was going on. Then Karnic broke the bad news to him. "Darrian, Marks was killed in action."

Darrian had no clue how to handle the news—after today's events, he was on overload. Marks had been his mentor for years now—he'd been the one person Darrian could talk to about things happening in his life. Today was a day Darrian needed him the most, and he had tried all day to speak to Marks but never had the chance. Now Darrian never would have the chance to tell Marks how excited he was to be part of this with him.

"Darrian." Karnic paused. "You with us?"

"Hell, ya!" Darrian said while doing his best not to let others see him cry.

Karnic put his hand on Darrian's shoulder. "Come on, soldier—let's go bury our friend."

"Burial detail!" Sawyer cried out, and at that moment, the rumbling started. Those two words were the moment when they all felt the severity of the situation.

Chapter 24

NEW MISSION

After seeing that Marks received a proper burial, Sawyer filled Karnic and the other platoon sergeants in on what had happened. All of them were enraged by just how much they and everyone else in America were being tracked without their knowledge. They all wanted to strike back for their rights being violated, for being charged as traitors, for Marks, and for those who had lost their lives in Saint Louis. Sawyer wrapped it all up with the decision to go on radio silence for the trip back to base camp.

"Sir, you are sure the pissant is dead?" Karnic asked.

"Oh, he is dead. I saw to it that he had a silent night," Robert said as he patted the side of his Noreen .30-06 with the suppressor still attached.

Satisfied he would not be seeing Womack again, Karnic turned from Robert and back to Sawyer—he had only one question. "When do we leave for Arkansas, sir?"

"We will not be."

Karnic cocked his head ever so slightly and up, while both of his eyes slightly squinted, one more so than the other. It was a look that said: *Come again?*

"This last mission taught me something. I can—and WE can—no longer operate as members of the US Army." As Sawyer looked around, he could see that he had their complete attention.

"We were played today. We did just as our training taught us, and that was our mistake." Sawyer began to pace in front of the assembled leadership and thought of what to say. "We have to retrain our brains to think like the independent force this militia is, or we will fail. What are the things we need most? Give me the top three," he said and pointed at his men.

"Area of operation," said one of the sergeants.

"Yes. Next?"

"More supplies to fight with."

"Yes. Now one more."

"Intelligence," another sergeant said.

"Yes, but intel gathering should be a constant thing. I believe what we need as a rogue militia fighting against a tyrannical government is the people on our side."

"You are right, sir, and I know just how to do it." All eyes went to Karnic. This was what Sawyer had created this discussion for, hoping to tap into the tactical mind Karnic possessed, and it appeared he had been successful.

"Do we know what became of the rest of the 138th? If not, we need to find out, when we—"

"They were all arrested this morning before leaving the armory, " Robert blurted out, cutting Karnic off.

"Do you know where they are being held?" Karnic was soaking up the information like a cactus after a heavy desert rain. The gears were churning in his head now.

"Last I heard, before heading here, they were being taken to the National Guard Armory in Jefferson City. At least the enlisted men were. The senior NCO and officers were taken to Saint Louis." Robert wished he had more information to give, but they had limited cell coverage traveling to the area from northern Arkansas, when everything started breaking out in Saint Louis.

That was all the information Karnic needed. One side of his mouth rose ever so slowly, with the hint of a smile coming on. That was Karnic's happy face—he had his plan. "We take the capitol."

The others could not believe that was his plan—it seemed very ambitious for 134 men and 2 women, who were also poorly supplied.

"I am afraid you are thinking too big there, Sergeant." Sawyer couldn't keep from having a little hint of laughter in his voice. He thought to himself, *Karnic is only a mastermind at the smaller missions. This apparently is a little too much.*

"No, sir!" Karnic said, with a great deal of confidence.

Upon hearing those words, Sawyer, who was looking downward at the ground, brought his attention to Karnic very quickly. As Sawyer opened his mouth to address him, Karnic had already begun speaking.

"Sir, we have all the men we need trained and ready to fight. Our men are no fewer than five hundred, and those men are where the weapons and ammunition are located. All in one place, sir, and everyone believes we are running for Arkansas. The gratefully departed general is a testament to that."

Sawyer was disappointed in himself, disappointed that he hadn't made the same connections as Karnic. He prided himself on being able to create a reasonable battle plan, but Karnic seemed to put the best of them to shame.

"Do you have a suggestion for a jumping-off point for the assault?" Sawyer asked, knowing the answer.

Karnic said with complete confidence and a touch of nostalgia, "Yes, sir. Rock Town."

Chapter 25

GOING ON THE OFFENSIVE

I t only took a matter of minutes for the men of the United Constitutional Militia to load everything on the vehicles once the order came down. Sawyer had decided to leave most of the planning up to Karnic—it was a risky plan, but sound. After all, most of their plans had been created by Karnic. One thing they had going for them was that the men of the former 138th Bravo Company were from all over the state. Few maps would be required to get where they wanted to be. For Karnic's plan to work, they had to be there by morning, before the bodies were discovered at the Highway Department maintenance yard. Once the bodies were discovered, travel would be virtually impossible. They also could not take a chance on going back the way they had come. They had to move farther south, and by Karnic's thinking, it would put them almost to Springfield before they could go north again.

The atmosphere outside of Springfield at around three in the morning was calming for the men who were not lucky enough to get sleep. The men watched as the lights slowly passed and read street signs while thinking of home—a home that would never be the same to them; a home that many of them may never see again. Every so often, someone would let out a groan, one that expressed the person's disbelief of how the day was unfolding. Every one of them knew and important rule about being in the infantry, and that was: sleep when you can. Those who were still awake but not on security watch wished they could sleep.

Karnic was leading the pack, although this time he was not in the five-ton. This time he was in a Humvee. The others in the convoy really did not know where they were driving to, just that they had to stay with the Humvee. That became confusing when the Humvee kept getting closer to Springfield. Sawyer, who was in the five-ton just behind Karnic, wanted nothing more than to pick up the mic and ask why he was getting so close. Up to this point, the county roads had proven to be the safest for them. Picking up the mic would be just what Sawyer would have done had they not agreed on complete radio silence. Now Sawyer just had to trust that Karnic was leading them the best way.

Karnic had anticipated the need to make changes and to communicate those changes with the commander. Now that the time had come, he opened his notebook and began writing. He removed the sheet of paper and turned to the rear.

"Smith, attach this on one of the poles," Karnic said. Karnic had had Sgt. Smith cut a few long limbs at least two inchs wide and approximately five feet long before they had left camp—they were just for this purpose.

Smith placed the paper in a zip lock bag from his MRE and tied it to the end of the pole.

Karnic smacked his driver on the shoulder. "Turn here." After the turn, they were now riding on a three-lane road and traveling just outside of Springfield. "Passenger side and slow down!" Karnic screamed to his driver due to the noise coming from the Humvee, which was doing fifty-five miles per hour. The driver just nodded and began executing Karnic's orders while Smith prepared to send the message by unzipping his window.

"What are they doing?" Sawyer asked his driver, knowing he also had no clue. It didn't take long to figure it out, though—the stick poking out of the back window was quite the giveaway. Quickly rolling down his window, Sawyer was eager to receive the intelligence.

"Leave it up to Karnic to find a way," Sawyer said and chuckled.

"What was that, sir?" the driver yelled.

"I said hold it steady." The five-ton was not as loud in the cab as the Humvee, but with the window down, everything combined made it difficult to hear. Sawyer was finally close enough to reach out and grab the pole It was relatively easier than he had thought it would be at first glance. Pulling the pole in and taking the note off the end, Sawyer looked like a child unwrapping birthday gifts—full of excitement. Smith had done a great job with securing the note, and when Sawyer finally made it to the message, he began reading immediately.

"Going to use most direct route to the north, I-44, making exit in after fifty-six miles." At that point, Sawyer felt that Karnic had lost it for sure. He said softly to himself, "They'll be watching the interstate." Sawyer continued reading.

"They know we are heading south. Nobody will be checking the interstates for us traveling north or for a convoy lead by a Humvee. I feel it is worth the risk. One honk, yes. Two, no. Do we proceed?"

Sawyer was in deep thought; Karnic's plan was very risky—one that could cost them everything and put bystanders' lives at risk. It was not a move he would have considered two days ago, but now was a time for taking chance.

"Honk one time," Sawyer called out, addressing the driver loud and clearly so that there were no mistakes.

The driver did as he was ordered, and the Humvee speed up.

The miles clicked off one by one. Each mile marker sign brought them closer to their destination, Rock Town. No man in the convoy was happier to see the exit for mile marker 131 than Sawyer. He had faith in Karnic, but he was ultimately the one to blame if things did not work out. Karnic traveled the back roads once again, and few in the convoy knew where they were. All the men could see out the windows were trees, hills, and drop-offs.

They drove for another hour before turning down what appeared to be a deserted gravel road. Karnic's driver looked at him, awaiting directions.

"Drive until I tell you to stop, Private," Karnic said nonchalantly as he marveled how much things had changed since he had been here as a little boy. They passed a road sign with rusted bullet holes in it that read "Four Mile Road."

Memories of the place came rushing back to Karnic—they mostly consisted of Angelique. She was his childhood love, his first and only, for that matter.

That was a time long ago, he thought to himself. Yet even more came to him as he passed her house—or what once had been her house. He couldn't believe his eyes as they passed by—he could have sworn that he saw Angelique's parents sitting on a swing in the front yard. All the other houses had become vacant— most likely due to the poor condition of the road, Karnic assumed. It had always been a problem. It was an ideal place to set up camp and plan their attack. There were freshwater springs and deer, and it was far enough in the woods, Karnic knew from experience, that they would hear somebody coming from miles off.

Chapter 26

ANGELIQUE

A ngelique lay awake in bed with her eyes closed and wondered what time it was—with her mind racing, she opened her eyes ever so slightly to look at the clock sitting on her mirror-topped nightstand. Like every other time she had looked at the clock, only ten minutes had passed since she had checked last. It almost seemed like the clock was teasing her, if not haunting her, with the mirror top showing the time to her also at each glance.

Sleep had been something hard to come by over the last few months—it was something difficult to achieve when she did not feel like the day had been fulfilled. For the last few months, there had been less and less to do at the office, due to the current state of the Union. In fact for the last few weeks, she had spent very few work hours in the office and most of them at the gym. Little was helping with the sleeplessness; the nights just ticked by for her, with sometimes thirty to forty minutes passing before she had to look at the time.

Finally, she thought as she rose from her bed. It was four thirty. She normally woke at five. Angelique started her day wanting a hot cup of black coffee in her hand. That was what she always wanted first thing but never had. Her day started with brushing her teeth, using the toilet, and dressing for her morning run. Her total time from bed until she was out the front door averaged ten minutes. It wasn't that she was excited to get out and run five miles as much as it was that she wanted to have her morning coffee.

Once she returned to her apartment and before the door had fully closed, she had pressed the on button on the coffeemaker many times. Lately the run was what she looked forward to as much as the coffee. It was the one thing that shook off the long, restless nights, even though it did not take much time before she began to feel despair—despair over the thought of going into an office that once had swarmed with agents hard at work but now barely had janitorial staff.

Angelique stood outside the building, looked it over, and remembered the excitement she had once felt when arriving at work—never knowing what the day was going to bring and not being able to wait to find out. She let out a sigh and all but forced herself to walk in.

"SHIT!" she exclaimed upon seeing Johnathan heading her way.

Johnathan had been positioning himself to get her job, yet he held back in the hopes that she would one day accept one of his many invitations to dinner, concerts, rides, and vacations. It never seemed to end with him, not since the day she had made the mistake of meeting him for dinner one night to discuss work. Now the guy literally had nothing better to do than make passes at her. Angelique was much taller, and lately she had used it to make him uncomfortable, not for fun but for him to leave without her having to turn down another one of his advances.

"Miss Carringer!"

Well, here we go again, she thought to herself before addressing him.

"Yes, Johnathan. Good morning." Angelique was doing her best to be polite. After all, she was still his boss and wanted to keep a good working relationship with what staff she had left.

"Great, were you able to get a good night's sleep? You are looking really spry this morning." As he spoke, he ran his eyes up and down her body, and Angelique could feel her skin crawling a little—almost like it was trying to run away without her.

"It was OK. What do you have going on this morning, Johnathan?" Angelique thought it best to get him focused on work and not on her. She knew it would not be good to fold him up like a pretzel, even though deep down she wanted very much to hurt him.

"Oh, this job just keeps a person moving. Just checking to see if you have received any information on the events taking place in Missouri."

Angelique just stood there, holding her coffee in one hand, her other placed atop the Colt 1911 riding her hip. It was her relaxed posture when conversing with others—every so often, people would swear she was caressing the thing, soothing it as if to keep it calm. After a minute of thinking, *What the hell is wrong with this guy? He knows there has been no intel on anything coming through this office in weeks*, she gave him a crooked smile and started moving for her office.

She said, "I saw that last night on the news—it is quite the mess. I will let you know if there is any intel, and you do the same, OK?"

"Sure thing. You're originally from Missouri, right?" he asked in a manner she was not sure about. It was just off.

Angelique shrugged it off and replied, "Yes, up to the point I left for the army." Now she was finally to her office door and wanted to make damn sure he did not follow her in. "Hey, could you bring me the security logs for the last week by ten hundred hours? We may not have much happening around her, but some things we need to stay on top of. Thanks." She was so proud of herself as she closed her door.

Angelique sat behind her desk and stared at the door—she had absolutely nothing to work on. The secure lines to the Internet were down, and she could not use most of the systems for DHS. Any information she received was during her morning calls to Washington. It was little surprise at this point that phone calls provided less intel than watching the nightly news feeds.

Then Angelique's thoughts turned to what she had seen on the news yesterday and then to how this morning's conversation with Johnathan had gone.

"Am I from Missouri?" she said out loud to herself. Since Johnathan had asked that question, she'd had the thought of home bouncing around in her thoughts. Then she thought of the last time she had taken a vacation, which was not in many years. It was not long before Angelique came to the conclusion this would be the perfect time. The thought of seeing her parents put a smile upon Angelique's face.

She made up her mind, picked up the phone, and called in the request. It was something that normally would not be approved on short notice, but with the current circumstances, she had no problem. She was a little surprised when there was no pushback over her request for three weeks of leave. Anxiety even set in a little after the approval. Her mind was already set, and her mood began to change—she could feel it deep within herself.

Only one thing left to do, she thought while picking up the phone on her desk and dialing. "Johnathan, can you come to my office? Thanks." It was not really a question, and she didn't even allow time for him to reply. She often phrased her orders in the form of a question and found people that responded to the illusion of a question much better than a direct order.

The triple knock was a sure signal to her that Johnathan was just outside. He was the only one who did not use the two-strong-loud-strikes method. Angelique just figured it was due to his never being in or around the military. Often she wondered how he had been able to get the position he held. There was nothing special about the guy—she just chalked it up to knowing all the right people.

"Enter."

"Here are the security logs you requested. I was just finishing them up," Johnathan said straitening the logs up as he walked through the door to lay them on her desk.

"Great, I will go over them while I am gone."

"Taking an early lunch?" Johnathan was puzzled by what she had just said. He knew Angelique's schedule, beginning to end, and she never took an early lunch.

"No, I am taking a three-week leave, and if there are any issues while I am gone, feel free to call."

Excitement ran through Johnathan at the thought of being in charge. Thoughts of what he could do during those three weeks began racing through his mind.

"I am confident you will be able to handle whatever comes up," Angelique said. "Just keep me in the loop with anything major. I know this is sudden, but the caseload for this office has become pretty much nonexistent since the Squires farm." To ensure that he was listening, she paused from the organizing of papers and other items on her desk. Not to her surprise, Johnathan almost looked like a salivating dog only inches from a fresh steak.

After a few minutes, Angelique was walking out the office door and almost gliding down the hall. The thought of taking a vacation had not even crossed her mind over the last five or so years since her last vacation. Had things not come to a standstill around the office, it would still be the case. Now she felt like a new person. With a smile on her face and one hand on her .45-caliber weapon, she all but danced to the exit. Angelique knew that in less than twelve hours she would be back home in Rock Town, Missouri.

Chapter 27

ANGELIQUE ON VACATION

Angelique found herself becoming more excited with every mile that she drove closer to her parents' house. Packing hadn't taken her long—she kept a bag packed just in case her job took her out of town for a few weeks. The pre-packed bag was a time-saver, and with this trip, Angelique only had to change out the formal wear for casual clothing. Then she was off. The Texas border was nothing like she had figured it would be. For most of the ride, there were few signs anything was happening—that was, until the Missouri state line. Angelique was still fifty miles from the state line, and traffic was at a crawl. It was not going to move any faster.

After moving two miles in an hour, Angelique decided to get off and take back roads—even if it took longer, she would rather be moving than sitting on the interstate and waiting in a fifty-mile line. It was another hour before she reached the next exit, again two miles farther down. Many of the other travelers seemed to have had the same idea, but at least this long line was moving. Having traveled extensively around the Central United States, Angelique had no need for a map or even the use of her GPS. Being on vacation didn't hurt, either, and taking the back roads, she figured, would help restrain the explorer within.

As the traffic began to thin out and the miles started to click by once again, Angelique could not help letting her mind wander. "How have they not been able to capture an entire National Guard company within twenty-four hours?" she asked herself, mused at the idea that two white buses and a five-ton truck would not stand out. Also: how tight of a border crossing was there at the state line if I-44 was backed up for fifty or more miles? With a little snicker, Angelique shook her head and decided to not think about it and to instead focus on her vacation.

She ran over in her mind the first time she had gone home after joining the army. With the three days of leave between basic training and her military police training at Fort Leonard Wood, Missouri, a mere forty miles from her home, she had wanted nothing more than to see her parents. She had already accepted that they would not be at her graduation from basic—the idea of her joining the military had created quite the rift between her and her peace-loving parents.

When she had returned home after being gone for ten weeks of basic training, things had not improved. Neither parent would say much to her, except to blame Old Jerry and his stories for her joining. Those feelings had run deep, until she had returned from her second tour overseas, just in time to spend a few days with Old Jerry in the hospital.

Angelique had started receiving letters from her mother after a month into her second deployment, and soon after that, her father had written. She hadn't understood why or what had changed. She had always sent letters and gifts to them and got nothing in return, not even one letter, through her whole first deployment. None of that mattered, though—when it came to her parents, she didn't hold a grudge.

When her tour had been over, the first place Angelique had gone after being dismissed for R & R was home to Rock Town, Missouri. It was the one place that had always been home, the place where she had first gone to school and met her first love, Karnic. It hadn't been quite the return Angelique had dreamed about, though. After her welcome-home party and after asking where Old Jerry was for the tenth time, she had received the depressing news. Jerry had had a very short time to live—cancer had moved throughout his body, and his fight had been nearing its end. Not minutes after the news, they had all headed with her to the hospital to see Jerry.

The idea of losing Old Jerry had scared Angelique more than both deployments. Jerry had taught her most everything she knew about fighting and had helped her to become the woman she was now. Once at his room, she had rushed in and had thrown her arms around him. Tears had been dripping down her cheeks.

"You trying to strangle me, girl?" Jerry had said in the strongest voice he could. The last thing he had wanted was to look weak in front of a fellow soldier, even if he still saw her as the stubborn little girl kicking truck tires.

"Why didn't you tell me sooner?" she had asked while letting up on his neck and sitting alongside him on his bed.

"The last thing you needed on your mind when going to a place like the Middle East was an old man here. Besides, your parents and I haven't been this close in years, and that was a great feeling. Now can you do something for me?"

She had looked him directly in the eyes and had taken his hand in both of hers. "You do not have to ask me for anything; just tell me what you want, you old grunt."

"Great, then get off my catheter hose—the pain pills don't help with that." Jerry smiled in agony, unable to take the added discomfort any longer.

She had leaped up like a cat sprayed with a fire hose and had apologized over and over.

Jerry had begun laughing so hard that the pain from it almost caused him to lose consciousness. Then Angelique and the others had joined him. Even with the pain, he had been so happy to laugh that hard one last time.

After things began settling down, Jerry had asked for a moment alone with Angelique. Once they had been alone, Jerry had begun talking quickly—he could feel his time was running short. "Ange, I knew when you were a very little girl that you were a warrior. I tried to obey your parents' wishes and not encourage those traits. It did not take long for you to show me that was no use." Jerry's lips had gone to what Angelique recognized as his beautiful smile in the making—he was just too weak to get all the way there.

"You have proved my belief in you—you make me so very proud. I need you to do one thing for me." She had waited, eager to do what her best friend and dearest friend had asked. "We both have taken the same oath—never forget it. Live by it. We may die, but we few keep this nation under our protection until death relieves us from that duty."

Tears had filled Angelique's eyes, and as if a dam had broken, they had all come pouring out at once. She could tell he was fading away.

"Give an old soldier a hug now." Angelique could tell that Jerry was barely able to get it out, and as she had her arms wrapped around him, she had felt him marching off into the distance.

At this rate, Angelique might as well have stayed on the interstate. The thoughts of Jerry had taken her over to the point where she found herself on the side of the road, her tears rolling once more. "This is no way to start a vacation, damn it!" Angelique scolded herself for crying. The thoughts of Jerry were the only thing that ever brought tears to her eyes. She began thinking of other times during her youth—not times with Jerry, but times with her first true love, Karnic.

Angelique went over in her mind how they had met and just how horrific that day had been. Her most pleasurable times had been throwing him on the ground. She had really enjoyed that. Even though he had been tall and lanky, he had still been better than the straw dummies and stick men she'd trained with. Karnic never could put her down—then again, she had been the one training him. That was up until the day he and his family had just moved away, out of the blue. These days moving wasn't that big of a deal—you could still stay in touch very easily, through text and hundreds of different ways, thanks to the Internet. But not back then. Many people then were lucky to own a phone—Angelique mused about how alien that concept was to her now.

Angelique had been so lost in her thoughts that she had passed through the four Humvee checkpoints and halfway across the state without even noticing. She was only an hour away from her parents' house.

"At this point, they are most likely sitting out front waiting to greet me pulling down the drive," Angelique told herself. She had already made up her mind that nothing was going to disturb her vacation at home with the parents.

As the familiar gravel road came into sight, her pulse sped up—she was minutes from seeing her parents. Turning onto the gravel took Angelique back to the days of riding the bus to school and all the great memories. Then her investigative-agent side took over, and she noticed the fresh vehicle tracks on the road. She wondered what could have made them—as far as she knew, her family members were the last people living on Four Mile Hill.

Then again, she thought, *when we talk on the phone, they mostly ask me about my life and if I have a boyfriend yet.* It was a touchy subject with her, since most of the men she had contact with were either scared of her or outranked by her. Then there were men like Johnathan—it would make her happy to transfer Johnathan to Alaska. Angelique was prepared for the relationship aspect of the visit and knew that the same old questions would be asked.

As she was cresting the hill, her parents were sitting in the swing, smiling and waving, just as she pictured they would. But they were not there long. Before Angelique knew it, her mother was opening her car door—while she was sliding the car in park, her mother reached out to give her a hug. With that hug, Angelique felt like her vacation had finally begun.

Chapter 28

ANGELIQUE'S HAPPY PLACE

The atmosphere around the Carringer house was calming, and Angelique had not felt this at home since before telling her parents she was joining the army. It was a great feeling, and as she crawled under the same bedcover, in the same bed, in the same room, as she had done all through her childhood, she finally fell fast asleep.

"I thought you military types awaken early to seize the day," her father said, waking her from a peaceful deep sleep.

"I am not in the army anymore. Yes, I still do," she replied while wondering just what time it was. She didn't have to wonder for long.

With a slight sarcasm in his voice, her father said, "Eight in the morning is late in my book, but then again that is farm time, not military." As he turned to leave the room, he let out a little laugh when he saw her jump up from her bed.

Angelique could not believe it was that late; mostly she couldn't believe that she had slept through the night without once waking to check the time. She now remembered what it felt like to be fully rested, and with the smell of coffee in the air, she looked around for her running shoes. Fully dressed and ready for her morning run but still drowsy from her deep sleep, Angelique opened her bedroom door. On this morning, she didn't make it past the kitchen. By the time Angelique realized what was happening, her mother had put a large cup in her hand, and she was drinking. The run Angelique was about to go on never crossed her mind again.

After breakfast was over, the three of them sat chatting and drinking coffee. Her parents caught Angelique up on what she had missed on the farm, and Angelique tried her best to seem interested. She felt it would be the same if she told them stories about her life, only they would most likely tune her out altogether. Her parents believed that what she did for work was sit behind a desk and nothing more.

During the conversation, Angelique remembered her drive down the gravel and the fresh tracks. "Did you finally get some neighbors out here? I saw a lot of tracks on my way in." She was curious and hoped that if her parents had new neighbors, they were good neighbors—people her parents would get along with.

"Oh, no, dear. We assumed you knew them, since they drove by a few hours after you called to say you were on your way," her mother replied, with confusion in her voice.

Angelique was puzzled by such a response and was even more curious now. "Why would I know them?"

"Because they were in military vehicles."

"We don't all know each other, Mom." At that point, Angelique had to learn more, but she didn't want her mother to feel like she was interrogating her. "Can you describe them for me? How many?"

Her mother thought for just a second and then began. "Your father and I watched as they passed by, so yes. The first one was a truck, really big and tall. It looked loaded with a lot of stuff. Behind that were two white buses full of men."

At that point, Angelique's heart started pumping at double its speed. She could not believe what she had just stumbled onto. Her mother had just described the rogue company. But then her mother went on.

"Then behind that was one of those Jeep-like things with four doors, and then—"

"Hold it. There were others?" Angelique asked her mother as the excitement she was feeling drained from her. She figured it must have been a unit out looking or training in the area. It wasn't unheard of for the military to rent land for training.

"Yes, there were——"

"That's OK, Mom. I'll ride down later and check it out. Where did Dad get off to?" Angelique asked, no longer excited about the prospect of finding the rogue company. She felt that the idea of their being in Rock Town was a little unbelievable since they had been last seen heading south for Arkansas.

The morning flew by, as Angelique helped her father with the chores. She could tell that age was beginning to catch up with him. When she was little, he would have these same chores completed in half the time, with her help. This caused Angelique to feel a bit sad that she was not closer to help them more, but knowing her father, Angelique was sure that he wouldn't allow her to do so. After all, that was where she got her stubborn streak.

Now Angelique wanted to take a walk—she just had to see the area she had spent so much of her childhood in: her training area in the woods. As she laced up her boots, the memories started flooding back, and even though most of them were good, she remembered that it was also the spot where Karnic had informed her that they would be moving.

The moment Angelique went through the gate leading out to the back fields, she had a strange feeling, one she had felt many times before. Knowing that she was not in a combat zone or out on a case, she attempted to dismiss the feeling. It was to no avail—the feeling persisted. Her body was on alert, and Angelique didn't understand why.

The feeling started to relax once her old training area appeared, or what was left of it. Since most of it had been made of straw, sticks, logs, and dirt, little remained. Nevertheless, Angelique could tell it was the right spot. As she stood in the center of the area and pictured the way it once had been, the only thing Angelique could make out clearly was the log she would run on and walk down for balance and shrunken mounds of dirt. It looked to her like some animals must have been walking around out here this morning—the weeds were noticeably disturbed.

Goose bumps rose instantly as Angelique heard the ever-so-soft rustling of vines and weeds behind her. She instinctively reduced her center of gravity, squatted, and spun in one fluid motion. Striking out with her leg, Angelique made contact with what she realized was another human. There was no stopping until she had dominance over whoever was now on the ground. Every motion was a reflex to her; she rarely had to think about what moves to make. After knocking the legs out from under the person who was now about to be lying on the ground, her leg came free. Her spin continued until she had come around once more, only this time there were a few more feet and her Colt between her and her attacker.

"What the HELL!" a man's voice cried out as he thumped against the ground.

"Don't move an inch," Angelique commanded, in a stance ready to strike once more.

"Where in the world did you pull that from?"

Angelique felt there was something very familiar about the man she had just put on the ground, but she couldn't place it. That would have to wait. She could tell instantly that he was a soldier—and a staff sergeant, at that.

"Never mind that. What are you doing here?" she again commanded.

Angelique knew that he had to be with the guys her mom had seen pass yesterday and the very same group she planned on visiting later. What she didn't understand was why he was in this spot at this time.

"Damn, you think you could let me win for once?" the soldier asked.

A flood of memories came rushing back to her, memories of sparring with Karl. Then it hit her like a pile of bricks.

Squinted as if staring at something unbelievable, Angelique saw the name tag on his uniform. "Karnic? Karl Karnic?"

Angelique began lowering her Colt slowly in disbelief. It was unbelievable to her and hard to wrap her thoughts around. Angelique was frozen, standing there and just staring at him. She knew that he was saying something—she just couldn't make it out. She visualized shaking her head to clear the thoughts racing around inside.

"Angelique," he repeated, trying to get her attention. "You going to let me up?"

She stood up straight and reached out her hand.

"Only if you don't make me put you back down," she replied as they gave each other a huge hug. Right off, she noticed that he was no longer the lanky boy she had once been in love with.

The next hour was spent sitting on the rotten makeshift balance beam, talking about the past—where Karl had gone to live and how his Opa had given him service tags belonging to his biological grandfather and how his Opa had been a sergeant under his command during the war. Karl told Angelique things that he never spoke of, like how he felt the day they moved away, deployments he had been on, and many other experiences he'd had, with the exception of the last few days. In return, she told him all about her life from the time they departed until that moment.

Karnic was startled to hear that Angelique headed up the DHS office in Dallas. He was glad that he hadn't told her what had transpired recently. Angelique seemed to be satisfied with her own assumption that they were in the area for training, nothing more.

Angelique could tell that her feelings from all those years ago were coming back. She thought it had to be due to how abruptly their relationship had ended. She remembered the day even more vividly when Karnic stood up, looked at his watch, and said, "I have to be getting back. We have a big day tomorrow and much planning to iron out. You remember what it's like."

"Oh, I sure do. My days ran like that up until that gunfight at Squires Ranch." She shrugged it off. "Had things not gone the same, I may not have ever seen you again, so at least one good thing came from it." Angelique was beginning to feel like a schoolgirl again, and she liked it. "What is your phone number? I'll call or text you later."

Karnic almost panicked but then replied, "I made everyone leave them at the armory. Didn't want the distraction while in the field. Let me take yours down, and I will most definitely call sometime soon."

After he took down her number, they hugged good-bye, and then she watched as he disappeared into the woods.

Chapter 29

CAMP

Being back on Four Mile Road brought back memories for Karnic of "the girl who dances in the woods," whose name he later found to be Angelique. His thoughts drifted back as he moved around the encampment checking security and seeing to the needs of the men. He knew that at times like this, morale was very important. Karnic's thoughts often drifted back to the year he and Angelique spent together in their youth, up to the point when he and his family had suddenly moved away.

They had spent every minute with each other, at school and after. It had been much more difficult for them to spend time together outside of school, as Angelique's parents forbade her to date before she was sixteen. As with most other teenagers, being forbidden had not stopped them. Since Angelique had spent a great deal of time at the far end of the field along the woods, they would meet there often.

It had worked out really well for Angelique, more than for Karl. Often Karl felt as if he had just been there to be her punching bag but those were only the times when he was not looking up at her from the ground, after being flipped, thrown, pushed, or pulled to it by her. Angelique had really enjoyed having someone not just to practice on but also to train. Many hours after school and on weekends had been spent running through the woods or sparring with each other. On many occasions, they had practiced hiding and camouflaging skills when Angelique's parents had happened to almost catch them.

Karnic moved from one guard position to the next. It turned out to be an even better area to occupy than he had first imagined. High ground was almost always preferable, but they were in a valley. Well, at least their vehicles were. The men were mostly all on the perimeter pulling security, and Karnic had made sure that the perimeter ran along the ridge of the valley.

One great advantage of the area was Raven Bluff—the bluff overlooked the major road in the area yet was a good mile and a half away. This provided a great tactical advantage on the east side of camp—anyone coming for them from the south would be easily spotted. South of camp ran a creek filled with fresh spring water, water the men desperately needed. To the north and west were nothing but woods for miles, with the exception of the gravel road running northwest.

As Karnic moved along the perimeter, he put the men on a rest cycle of two up, two down. It was the first chance they'd had to get some real rest. At this point, they were happy to sleep on the ground under the shade of the trees above. At almost every security point Karnic came to, they asked the same question: "What's next, Sergeant?" The problem was that Karnic really did not know at this point, but that wasn't what he told his men.

"Just gathering some intel to put the final touches on the operation." It wasn't a lie; they were waiting for intel now that they had a secure way of obtaining it through Robert's connection with Sam. They also had an operation to plan—it just had not been started. Each time he answered his men, Karnic hoped that there would be useful intelligence when he returned to the TOC.

After completing his rounds of the perimeter, he ensured that those in the camp were given an opportunity to also get some rest. Those who were not in the camp worked endlessly to ensure that the equipment was ready to go on a moment's notice. Everyone in the militia was dedicated to the task ahead. Karnic always felt that he was serving with great soldiers. Now he felt that they were much more than great—they were historic men. They were the kind of men who were written about in history books, and he was proud to lead them.

Karnic's visit to the tent that held the TOC was not what he hoped it would be. It was frustrating. Karnic and Commander Sawyer started the same rest cycle they had the men on, even though neither wanted to rest. Each time Karnic relieved Commander Sawyer, there was still no intel, and that was the way it went the rest of the day and all night. By the next morning with no intel coming in, Karnic let being back in the area get the better of him. He decided to chase some old memories, although that wasn't how he described it to Commander Sawyer.

"Commander, I am going out on foot to do some reconnaissance of the area. I want to check out the house we passed," he said with confidence, attempting to hide his real motive.

"Check out if they have fuel tanks while you're out." Sawyer looked up slowly with a who-you-trying-to-fool expression.

"Will do, sir."

And he was off. Moving through the woods would take a great deal less time than traveling on the gravel.

Chapter 30

RETURN TO CAMP

On his way back to the TOC, Karnic made another round to each security point around the camp. When he made it to the overwatch position at the top of Raven Bluff, he could tell by the body language of the men on watch that nothing good was heading their way. Also there were only three of them, the fourth had undoubtedly been sent as a runner. He moved up to the overwatch position and squatted behind a large black oak before saying anything to them.

"Find something interesting?"

Upon hearing Karnic's voice, they almost jumped up from lying on their chests to their feet.

"What the?" they replied, rolling over on one side to make eye contact with him.

"Sergeant, we just sent Crawford for you. How did you get here so fast?" They were puzzled by the quick response to the runner they had sent not two minutes ago.

"I was out for a stroll. What do you have?"

"Sergeant, we have been seeing what appears to be black government SUVs and other heavy transport vehicles. They were with a convoy of..." The man began running through the list of observations they had made. Karnic sent one of them to inform the perimeter to be on alert, with everyone on the line.

"I am heading to the TOC. When Crawford gets back, send him if you observe movement this direction. Copy?" Karnic wondered if they were already under surveillance from above. The drones used today were very quiet, but even they could be heard way out here if they were not at a high elevation. All Karnic knew was that he couldn't hear them at the moment.

As he moved back down the hill, he wondered about the intel—most importantly if they had received any. Things could get heated around here quick, and the only plan they had was to move deeper in the forest at this point and last as long as possible. That was one plan he hoped they would not have to fall back on. He had hoped that with the proper intelligence, they could move in a few days to free the rest of the men and take the capitol.

As the TOC came into view, Karnic could see Crawford exiting the tent and heading his way.

"Sergeant, I was looking for you." Crawford picked up his pace and closed the gap between them. Even though he had informed the commander of what they had observed, he felt he just had to inform Karnic as well.

"Just came from overwatch," said Karnic. "Black SUVs, Humvees, got it. Let them know we made contact when you get back there. Thanks."

Crawford lost his motivation at that point—it felt like Karnic had taken a needle and popped his balloon. With a nod of his head, he replied, "Yes, Sergeant," before charging up the steep hill.

When Karnic walked into the TOC, he could tell by the atmosphere that something was happening. He could also tell by the fact that Robert was on the phone, either writing down information from Sam or planning a date for the weekend. Karnic was amused by the thought and wished he could plan a date with Angelique for the weekend instead of planning an attack on the state capitol.

Robert ended the call he was on and tore the paper from its pad before turning to the commander and Karnic. "Sam came through big."

Karnic and Sawyer were so glad to hear Robert say that. They had been waiting for Sam's information in order to plan the mission that would take place in just a few days. Robert walked over to them, and before he could relay the information, he was hit with questions.

"Was there anything on our current position? Are we secure here?" Karnic wanted that information up-front. Every second counted if they were about to be attacked.

Robert looked down at the notes he had taken and replied, "No, the traffic they have seen on the highway isn't for us." Karnic could feel a *but* coming, and it did. "But it isn't good. They are preparing to declare the state of Missouri under martial law at eight tomorrow morning." Robert looked up to gauge their reaction to the new intelligence, and it was just what he expected, calm. From what he had noticed in his very short time with the group, they did not react to things with their feelings. Most of what the two men did was gather intelligence and work out solutions. Robert knew that their gears would really be cranking by the time he was through giving them the intelligence he had just received.

"Then we must move tonight," Karnic stated, knowing that movement would be impossible after the declaration of martial law.

Sawyer gave him a nod to show he agreed, and then he looked back at Robert and asked, "What is the other problem?" Sawyer knew from watching Robert's expressions while he was getting the information from Sam that there must be more. He was correct.

"The rest of your unit is being moved in the morning by zero-six-thirty hours."

"Well, looks like we will be moving out early. Doesn't leave us with much time to plan—it looks like things are going to be by the seat of our pants for a while, gentlemen," Sawyer replied, then made eye contact with each Karnic and Robert separately while stating "We are going to succeed tomorrow, and this militia will be stronger when we are done."

"Yes, sir," Karnic replied.

Robert looked at his notes once more. "Sam also said that they just arrested the lieutenant governor for treason. Apparently he had become very publicly verbal about the current situation of your arrests, the other companies, the massacre in Saint Louis, and the buildup of troops in the state. He is being held at the Jefferson City police department until transport arrives in the morning."

The three of them stared at one another until one said what the others were already thinking. Sawyer looked at Karnic, as he began to speak, knowing that he was the best at quick tactical strategies.

"We have three clear objectives," said Sawyer. "First, the armory, where the men are being held; second, the police station; third, the capitol. We all in agreement?"

Karnic and Robert both saw those three objectives as the main goals and nodded their heads in agreement with Sawyer.

"Great. Now how do we take control of all three places with the very limited manpower?" Sawyer again looked at Karnic, with a strong social cue to lay out the ideas Sawyer knew were running through Karnic's mind already. Sawyer thought to himself as he gave the cue, *I bet he sits at home at night playing chess against himself.*

Karnic didn't say anything—he just stood in deep thought.

"I do not know about you guys, but I have never been to Jefferson City. Does anyone have a map?" Robert asked, knowing that the answer was going to be no. He wasn't sure if gas stations even carried maps anymore.

Then Karnic began. "You're right, Robert." Karnic turned to one of the runners they kept in the TOC to use for communicating with the men. "Bring me Crawford, Jackson, and Sergeant Smith," he ordered the runner before giving him a hand signal to be on his way.

Karnic continued, "The three of them have lived in that area all their lives and know it well. They can tell us what they know about the police station and the capitol building. The armory we have all been to many times over the years—we will just need to survey any changes before entering. It might be a rushed plan, but we have the element of surprise on our side. After all, they probably believe we made it to Arkansas by now." Karnic was visibly happy over the thought.

"I feel like we might be getting a little ambitious with attempting to take all three positions," Sawyer said. "We are too limited on manpower, and we will have nothing in reserve." Sawyer's concern was going through the minds of all three men.

Sawyer then continued: "I am making the armory our main objective. That will be the only hope we have if the other two objectives get into trouble. I am sure with all the movement spotted by those on the bluff, it will not be easy to take."

Karnic might have the strategic mind, but Sawyer was not far behind. Karnic agreed with the commander's assessment.

"You are correct, sir—it will be. The greatest number of our troops will hit the armory. I think it is time to take a page from history. Patton, to be more to the point." Karnic had always known that his interest in history would pay off one day, and today was the day.

He looked over to another runner, who was listening intently to their discussion. "Pull all but two men from each position and have them stuff one set of uniforms with sticks and grass and then place it in one of the seats of the buses. Move!"

Karnic looked back and filled the others in. "During World War Two, Patton had a ghost army in Britain to fool the Germans. Well, we are going to create one to fool the Jefferson City police force."

Sawyer could see the usefulness of this tactic, but he did not quite get how he was going to use it. "What objective do you suggest using it on?"

"Sir." Even in a relaxed social environment, Karnic always used proper military courtesies. That they were fugitives and planning the takeover of a state capitol did not change that fact.

"We are going to need three men to drive both buses and the five-ton. Then we are going to report their location to the authorities." Karnic was waiting for pushback.

"Great plan. I like it," Sawyer replied, to Karnic's surprise. "That early in the morning there will be few people in the station, making it easier to take."

Robert nodded his liking for the plan. "This is a tough-enough mission we are all undertaking here. Carlos, Sierra, and I are with you, but we just have one thing that we feel your men should be reminded of." Robert did not wait for them to ask what it was he wanted. He just said, "We all need to remember that we are not in another country fighting the enemy. The people we are going up against are Americans, and we must do everything we can to limit the number of casualties whenever possible."

Karnic reached out with his left hand and placed it upon Robert's shoulder. With his right, he reached out to shake Robert's hand. The two of them looked eye to eye as Karnic replied, "We are going to be great friends."

Robert's contribution to the militia was highly thought of from the first thud he had created with his rifle. That contribution was greatly appreciated by Sawyer and Kate, both of whom would be dead by now instead of the pathetic officer, Womack. Everyone felt that he brought great insight, an intelligence network, and his skills with a long rifle to the team.

"That will be the first address before the mission briefing. We are all on the same page when it comes to preserving American lives," Sawyer replied, thankful for the man standing before him.

"Now back to it," Karnic said as he gave Robert a pat on the shoulder. "There is not much we can do about planning for the armory. I say we wing it—drive right up to the front gate."

The others looked at Karnic as if he had just had the worst idea of his life. Sawyer could not resist. "Wing it, Sergeant? How are we going to even get close to the place if our buses are being chased by the police?"

As Karnic gave what they assumed was a smile and pointed out the window of the tent, he began. "I bet the men remember riding in a cattle trailer to their first day of basic. I know I do."

"That is true, but as soon as they spot it, red flags are going to be sent up." Sawyer felt that he had found the flaw in Karnic's plan.

"Sir, not if a sweet-looking, light-brown-haired, green-eyed girl like the one standing by the truck right now is driving." Karnic was now pointing at Sierra. "That girl will make putty of the guard at the gate long enough for us to make our move around to subdue him. From that point, it will be time to wing it, sir."

Robert began to protest out of instinct as his sister was to be put in danger. But by the time Karnic had finished speaking, Robert had changed his mind. Sierra was no longer the little sister who needed protecting. The way he saw it now, they were the ones who needed protection from her. Robert struggled with their new relationship, born from the death of a great deal of their family, but he was proud of the way she had not let it destroy her. He just hoped that if they survived it all, Sierra would be able to let go of the fight and anger.

"As far as the capitol building goes, Sergeant Smith will take twenty men, along with Kate and her squad—that should be able to secure it as long as the police station is secure with those out on patrol chasing our buses. That is where I feel you come in, sir."

Karnic looked up from his notepad, where he had been making notes for the plan. Karnic knew that the commander would want to be in on the assault of the armory to free the men, but Karnic had other plans.

Sawyer gave Karnic his full attention and had a sense of what he was going to suggest.

"Sir, with the order coming out tomorrow for the establishment of martial law..." Karnic fell silent for just a second at the thought that martial law was really happing here. "You will be the best person to go into the police station with no more than ten men. Use the implementation of martial law and the fact they are chasing our vehicles to get in and then take it over."

Karnic waited for Sawyer to overrule him, just as he had done with the refueling a few days ago. Only this time Karnic was not going to roll over and accept it. This time he was prepared to argue this point to the end.

Silently rubbing the back of his neck, Sawyer walked around the TOC before he spoke. It was a walk that didn't take that long to complete. On his second trip around, he began speaking. " I want to be on the assault of the armory. I feel the men there need to see the face of leadership when they are freed."

Karnic knew it was coming to this and began his argument. "Sir, I..."

Sawyer threw up his right hand to silence Karnic, and it did. "So, Karnic, your ugly mug will have to suffice. Have a safe trip, Sergeant." Sawyer knew that Karnic was prepared to argue his point, just like he had been when climbing up in the truck to leave on the refueling mission. Only this time it was Sawyer taking all the air out of Karnic's lungs. That made Sawyer feel just as good as if he had come up with the idea himself.

Karnic just grinned at Sawyer—he understood that even the commander needed to have his fun.

"All right. Now we know how it is going to go down—if there is nothing else, let's disseminate the information to the platoon sergeants so that they can prepare. I believe we came in undetected yesterday, and we've seen no signs of surveillance. Have the men keep one on watch at all times in their current position. I want the rest to get all the rest they can. Tomorrow is going to be a long day." Sawyer had a good feeling about the upcoming mission.

"One last thing: we will move out at zero three hundred hours. I want all the cover of night we can get. Everyone agree? Great. Dismissed." Sawyer didn't wait for a response to the question.

"Karnic." Sawyer mildly addressed the man while moving closer to Karnic on his way out the tent.

"Yes, sir."

"Karnic, I will brief Kate and her squad on the mission tomorrow." Karnic could tell from the moment Sawyer and Kate had returned from the refueling that something had happened between them to create an unbreakable bond. The two had only known each other now for less than four days but it might as well have been four years. Karnic had only two words for his commander.

"Yes, sir." Upon those words, his mind turned to Angelique and how beautiful she looked after all these years.

Chapter 31

ZERO HOUR

K arnic awakened from what was now considered sleep, real sleep had become a thing of the past days ago. He looked at his watch. It was one in the
morning—two hours before they would move out. He wanted to assure himself
that everything had been addressed that needed to be before the mission began.
After tending to his own gear and stowing his assault pack and vest by the horse
trailer, Karnic made his rounds to the locations of the platoon sergeants. As he
expected, they, too, were up and moving. He went to each one and checked for
updates that might affect the mission—he felt relieved to discover none. Karnic
also verified with each one that one man should be left on post and the rest
should gather at the rally point thirty minutes prior to moving out.

After doing so, Karnic made his way over to the commander's tent, and to
his surprise, Sawyer was not in it. The places Sawyer would be were limited,
and with the illumination of the almost-full moon, the search would not take
long. After checking the TOC with no success and after telling men to begin
taking it down for transport, Karnic moved on. He then thought that Sawyer
might be inspecting the vehicles and began walking that way.

As Karnic approached, he began hearing a noise that almost sounded like an
animal eating something, and the way it was smacking, it had to be large. This
was one fear Karnic had: that a black bear would stumble into their camp—it
would create one hell of an issue and would affect the entire mission. Karnic

brought his M4 up slowly from the low ready as he slowly rounded the front of the five-ton. The five-ton held the MREs, and Karnic could already picture the bear leaning up against the truck with his snout buried in a box.

With the stealth Karnic had become known for, he crept around and there up against the truck like he had imagined, stood the bear. When Karnic began to raise his rifle to his shoulder, the strangest thing happened: the bear began to split into two separate forms from the bottom up. Karnic was puzzled by what he saw. Everything became clear as he watched two of the bears legs stay in one place and the other two stepping back. Then Karnic realized what the smacking sound really had been.

As he lowered his rifle, Karnic spoke.

"Good morning, sir, Kate." And he walked on passed the two hiding in the shadows of the five-ton truck.

"Sergeant," Sawyer replied without missing a beat as if nothing had been going on.

"The men will be gathering up over by the TOC in thirty minutes. I'll have them there then, sir," Karnic said without breaking stride. As he listened for a reply, he was surprised when one did not come his way.

Karnic went on with preparations for the mission, and to his surprise, he didn't see Sawyer or Kate until the leaders' meeting, when the two of them appeared, wide awake.

As Kate walked by Karnic, she said softly so that only he could hear, "Being in a militia does have its perks."

During the leaders' meeting, Sawyer stressed Robert's concerns about casualties once again. They were not just Robert's concerns but everyone else's concerns as well. They all talked through their portions of the mission.

"Who will we be driving the buses and five-ton?"

"Three of my guys, sir. They know the area well enough to keep it going for a while. They also know their job is to surrender, not fight, when it comes down to it," said Sgt. Smith. With every beat, the confidence he had in the men he had chosen showed in his voice. He continued, "After they have the police chasing them, they will radio for the next stage to begin with 'RED, RED, RED.' That is when your part takes place, sir." Sgt. Smith turned it over to Sawyer at that point.

"After receiving your signal, I reply, 'RED, RED, RED,' in response. This lets everyone know that my team and I are on the move. When I have the police station secure, I will give the single 'WHITE, WHITE, WHITE.' That is when you move on the capitol building." Sawyer ended by pointing at Sgt. Smith, who began once more.

"I will then respond with 'WHITE, WHITE, WHITE,' signaling acknowledgment and the movement of my and Kate's teams on the capitol."

Karnic picked up from there. "Once I hear that I have received your movements, I will signal 'BLUE, BLUE, BLUE.' From that point, Sierra will pull up to the gate and charm the guard, and we will come out the back and subdue him. After that, there is no need for radio silence. Give sitreps every fifteen minutes when possible."

"OK, everyone has a mission. Any questions?" Sawyer looked at each of them, and they all appeared good with what was asked of them. "OK, if things go to hell in a handbasket, disperse in all directions and attempt to make your way back here. Let's move out," Sawyer said with great confidence and energy. Upon breaking, the sergeants took their team members aside to go over the mission once more. It would not be the last time before the mission kicked off.

Sawyer and Karnic looked at their watches—it was time. Everyone was loaded, and after one more check of the area, they began what would become a major part of American history, whether or not they prevailed.

Chapter 32

UCM GOES ON THE OFFENSE

Adrenaline and fear ran through every man and woman of the UCM as they all made their way to the Missouri state capitol building in Jefferson City. Everyone took a different path and knew where to be at the appropriate times to meet mission time hacks. Hardly anyone said a word during the journey, but everyone ran through different scenarios of what might happen when the mission kicked off. Each knew that no matter how much planning one did, it never survived the first shot.

As the capitol building came within sight, Sgt. Smith moved from his seat to the front of the bus. He signaled for Kate, and she in turn got the men up and ready to move. "Get ready to move—we will only be stopping for a thirty seconds," Kate informed them, and each was set to go.

The driver pulled down a road only a block from the capitol, with plenty of cover to conceal the men as they disembarked. "Stopping in five," the driver called out. Everyone's pulse began to race, and each could almost hear his or her own heartbeat.

The driver didn't need to count down—he could see a stop sign coming up. Each person was pressed against the person in front, waiting to move. The door opened with Sgt. Smith standing behind it, and before they even came to a stop, the first four had already jumped. Smith didn't waste time getting out of sight and moved quickly to darkness, away from the streetlights. By the time he crossed the freshly cut grass, everyone had exited the bus. The early morning was quiet, and they were all now on the move to the capitol building through the dark, just out of the reach of the streetlights. Once close enough to see their entry point, they settled in and waited for the signal to move, checking one another's gear.

The driver headed for the other end of town, where he would meet up with the other bus and the five-ton. As he drove, Rodger thought about the events to come as he took in the sights of the city and how, thankfully, there was little traffic on the streets since it was early morning. The anticipation of what was about to take place filling his thoughts. He was going to intentionally get the cops to chase after him while trying to outrun them in what basically amounted to a school bus. He yelled back to the fake soldiers seated on the bus, "Hold on, men—we are going to have some fun!"

As soon as the other two vehicles spotted him approaching, they began to move from the woods just outside of the city. It was time—the plan was to drive right down Missouri Boulevard, the heart of the city. Everyone agreed it was the best place to kick their plan off—they were certain to pass at least one cop. Little did they know how soon they'd pass a cop. Just as the boulevard came into sight, so did the lights from a cop car, and with those lights, the mission was a go. Rodgers who had just let off Sgt. Smith and Kate picked up the mic.

"RED! RED! RED!" he called out, setting the chain of events into action. Now it was Cdr. Sawyer's turn to move.

"RED! RED! RED!" Sawyer confirmed, and he watched from down the street as three squad cars left with lights and sirens breaking the darkness and silence of the night. Sawyer waited a few minutes before having his driver start their part of the mission. Once he was sure no others were going to be joining the pursuit of the convoy, they moved.

There were eight of them in the Humvee, so things were more than a little tight, though it was not noticed by the speed in which they exited. Sawyer was the first to walk through the door, his team following close behind. He held up official papers to the man behind the glass of the front desk. "Open the door—this is an order from the president of the United States declaring martial law over the state of Missouri!" Sawyer said it with such authority and power that the officer behind the glass didn't even notice that the paper was a supply request form from the mess hall.

As soon as Sawyer stopped speaking, the door came open, and his men entered. The officer behind the glass approached with more than confusion on his face. "Can I see the orders?" he asked, unsure of himself.

Sawyer did not even acknowledge his question but asked one of his own. "How many officers are on duty, and how many are in the building?" Sawyer asked from the commanding position of parade rest.

"Just myself, the jailer, and dispatch. The other officers went in pursuit of the rogue military company spotted in town." The man had obviously never been in the military—otherwise, he wouldn't be so nervous.

Sawyer could not help from grinning as he looked around the room. "After the rogue company, you say?"

"Yes, sir, we spotted them just five minutes ago," the man replied, with a little more perkiness in his voice.

Sawyer's grin became even larger. "Well, isn't that interesting?"

Sawyer gave a nod to his man who had come up behind the officer. With little effort, he slid his right arm under the officer's chin and locked it into the left on the other side, putting him into a hold, from which he would be unconscious within a matter of seconds. "Looks like you spotted others from the rogue company."

Sawyer then turned and ordered his RTO to make the call beginning the next and most dangerous stage of the mission. "WHITE! WHITE! WHITE!" he called out over the radio, knowing what was about to happen.

Smith heard the transmission loud and clear. Looking over to Kate, he could see that she had heard it as well and had already given their RTO the signal to respond, and he did. "WHITE! WHITE! WHITE!"

Then only two seconds later they heard Karnic's team at the armory come over the radio. "BLUE! BLUE! BLUE!"

Everything was now in motion, and what the next few hours were to bring, nobody knew. For now, Sgt. Smith knew one thing, and that was his ultimate goal: take the capitol building and free the lieutenant governor.

Smith gave Kate a pat on her shoulder to signal that they were moving—she in turn did the same to the next, and so forth. Smith was amazed at the lack of security around the place. Then again it was not as if state capitols were frequently assaulted. He, like the rest, still had a hard time with the way things had escalated, but he understood the part he, Kate, and the rest of the squad were now taking in the events. Keeping to the shadow was about to become much more difficult, and Kate could see the look Smith gave her, the look saying, "Let's talk." She held her hand up for them to stay before moving over to Smith.

"You see the parking entrance over there?" Smith was pointing to a paved road leading to the back just past a manned guard post. "That guard looks a lot like Mack, doesn't he? Even close to the same build." Mack was on Kate's team, the oldest man in the UCM. He had served in Vietnam.

"I think I see where you are going," Kate replied, with a hint of excitement in her voice.

"I have an idea." Kate turned to her team and signaled to Darrian to come closer. Darrian was the youngest in the UCM and also was on Kate's team. Darrian stayed low and moved in close to Kate and Smith in order to keep the volume of their voices down. He unhooked his M4 from his gear, which had previously belonged to his best friend and mentor, Marks. Karnic had passed Marks's gear over to Darrian after the burial and he treasured nothing more in the world than that gear. Settled in close to the two others, he waited to hear what they had in store for him, and it was not a long wait.

"Drop all your gear and look like a kid again." Those were not the words Darrian had expected to come from Kate. He followed her orders, though, all the while hoping they would become much clearer soon. As he began the transformation, she continued.

"I need you to wander up to the guard post looking for your dog. Lure him out, and then we will take him down. Can you do it?" Her plan was crystal clear to Darrian now, and he was more than willing to accept the mission.

As soon as Darrian had finished wiping the black camo paint from his face, he was ready to begin. Backtracking through the shadows, he came to and stepped out on the street about a block down from the capitol building. He then started walking down the street, whistling and calling out for Fido, and then, he laughed a little—he was using the most common dog name ever, but why not?

"Here, Fido! Where are you, Fido?" he called out all the way down the street and even sprinted after the imaginary dog a few times, as if to catch him. Darrian was so believable that Kate even caught herself looking for the dog in the direction he sprinted.

"The kid is good," Kate said while shaking her head in disbelief that she had even looked for the lost dog.

As Darrian got closer to the guard, his acting became even better. Everyone could hear the concern in his voice over his imaginary lost dog.

The guard leaned out of his shack to get a better idea of what was going on. He had heard someone coming but had not been able to make out what the person had been saying. Then it became clear once he took a step outside his booth.

"Here, Fido! Where are you, Fido?"

"Who the hell names a dog Fido anymore?" the guard asked himself. He saw the boy sprint to the side of the drive. *Well, at least he sees him,* he thought, and then began to walk over to give the kid assistance. It never dawned on him that it was almost five in the morning and some kid was out here looking for his lost dog.

"What's he look like, son?" the guard called out, happy to assist.

Darrian jumped back a little as if the guard had startled him. With a little touch of fake fear in his voice, Darrian spoke. "We parked up the road to let the dumb dog use the bathroom, and it ran off. I just saw it, too." He pointed up into the dark area of the shrubs.

The guard looked and could not see anything but darkness.

"You sure he is in there?" the guard asked as he pulled a flashlight from his belt and shined it just beyond the shrubs. Instantly the guard knew from the five rifle barrels pointing at him that there was no Fido to find.

Chapter 33

BATTLE AT THE ARMORY

Seated a few miles away from the armory, where the men of 138th Bravo Company were being held, Karnic could not help but find a little humor in the situation and start laughing from the back of the cattle trailer he and seventy men were now smashed into. Some of them were asleep standing, held up by the bodies of those around them. Karnic's laughter made men who knew him uneasy—this was due to the fact that they had never heard him laugh aloud. Where they were parked, there was no fear of others hearing, so Karnic decide to let the men in on what was so funny to him.

"Who are we, men?" he called out.

"United Constitutional Militia!" the men called back as one.

Once again Karnic asked, "Who are we?"

Then the men replied even louder than before, "United Constitutional Militia!"

"WE ARE THE MILITIA, CORRECT?" Karnic asked.

The men replied with, "HOOAH! HOOAH!"

Karnic felt it was time to let them in on the gag. "Yes, we are the militia. Now look at the sign to your left."

Each of them looked out through the horizontal steel panels of the trailer and saw nothing.

"Keep watching," Karnic said.

Then it happened: the headlights from a passing car lit up a street sign—it read "Militia Drive."

As the men saw the sign, they all started to laugh, they were a militia attacking an army armory on Militia Drive. To many, it would not be funny, but to a trailer full of men who'd had the crazy last four days they'd had, it was downright hysterical.

Robert called out for silence just in time to hear the last of the message coming over the radio. *White* was all he heard, but he knew it was their time to move. Robert looked at Karnic standing by his side and waited for him to give the go-ahead for him to reply.

"WHO ARE WE?" Karnic called out.

"UCM. WE STRIKE LIKE LIGHTNING, STRIKE LIKE LIGHTNING. BOOM! BOOM!"

That was not the response Karnic was expecting, but it was even better. Karnic looked at Robert.

"Send it," Karnic said with vigor. Then Karnic yelled through the slats of steel to Sierra, "Let's move it, darlin'." He knew that would eat at her.

As the wheels began to roll, everything became very quiet in the trailer. Karnic and Robert stood with one hand on their weapons and the other on the door latch to the trailer. They knew that once they stopped and the guard got a look at Sierra, they would only have a few seconds to make their move while he was distracted. The closer they came, the faster their pulse rate became. The moment was close—they could feel the truck coming to a stop.

Sierra was very calm, as she sat in the cab of the truck just off the road and waited for the signal to move forward. She was ready to kick this thing off, and this was the point she hated the most, being so close to starting and not being able to. Sierra reached for her revolvers and checked them like she had many times before to ensure that they were loaded and ready. The two .357 Magnum revolvers made her feel as safe as she did with Robert by her side.

"What the hell are they doing back there, having a pep rally?" she asked the person in the mirror looking back at her. Then she heard it: Karnic's voice and "Darlin'."

"I'll show him *darlin'*!" Sierra exclaimed, and then she turned the key and hit the gas.

She could see the guard in his booth at the gate—past him on down the drive, she could see many others out patrolling the area. As Sierra moved her foot from the escalator to the brake, her hand slowly dropped down to her revolver. Driving with her knees, she put on a big, toothy smile and began rolling down the window with her other hand.

As the cab came into view, the guard was stunned by a sight he had not counted on seeing this early in the morning—or at any time of the day, for that matter. Sucking in his middle-aged stomach and puffing out his chest, he then cleared his throat to speak with the beauty. As she stepped into the lights above the gate, her beauty captivated him even more. Within a second she was there, stopping at his gate just inches away with the smile of a beauty queen—a beauty queen whose finger was motioning him to come closer as she brought the truck to a complete stop, and he did step closer, right before stars appeared in his vision and everything blurred into darkness.

The two soldiers in the back of the truck lay there, ready to jump into action as soon as Sierra had the guard talking and distracted. As the truck came to a stop, instead of talking, all they heard was a *thunk, thunk,* much more like the sound made when checking a watermelon in the grocery store than the sound of something big hitting the side of the truck. As the men slowly pushed themselves up over the side of the truck bed, all they could see was Sierra.

Sierra was looking back at them with the barrel of a revolver in one hand and a mischievous look on her face. The two soldiers looked at each other, and then leaped out of the truck and grabbed the guard and threw him into the bed of the truck. While they did so, Sierra stepped out, took a step closer to the guard building, and pushed the button for the gate. The whole thing only lasted about twenty seconds before they were once again moving.

Karnic and Robert, who were all pumped up and ready to leap out and kick things off, were very confused when the truck began to move. Confusion didn't even begin to explain their feelings when they saw the guard post pass by the rear of the trailer.

Chapter 34

———◦❀◦———

VACATION'S END

Angelique awakened the next morning and still could not get Karnic out of her mind. She could not believe in such a coincidence much like what had just happened. Karnic had joined the army and just happened to be training down the road from where they had been children? Over and over, thoughts of him ping-ponged through her mind, but these thoughts were set aside when her mother entered her room. The information that her mother provided brought a start to Angelique's morning that she had not experienced since before her last deployment.

With saddened features, her mother stared down at Angelique and just let it out, like ripping off a Band-Aid. "We are out of coffee, sweetie." Three words Angelique never wanted to hear in the mornings were *out of coffee*. She reached back with both arms and jerked the pillow from under her head, and as she thought about letting out an overly exaggerated moan, Angelique had an epiphany. Just down the road was an army infantry unit. *I know they have coffee*, she thought.

Angelique slithered out of her bed, much like a snake on a chilly spring morning. The more she thought about the coffee and running into Karnic once again, the faster she put on her sweats. Army coffee always tasted bad, but since she hadn't started drinking coffee until her first year in the army, it tasted great to her. Had it not been for the army, she may never have started drinking it, but in the military, if you wanted a break from working or training, you either smoked or drank coffee. Since Angelique didn't want to destroy her lungs from smoking, she chose coffee. At first she had just held it, but it had not been long before the little sips she took became bigger, and then she was hooked.

Once dressed, Angelique stepped out of the back door of the house, stretched, and took deep breaths of the fresh Ozark morning air. After a few stretches to loosen up her muscles and joints, she was off. Keeping at a slow jog rather than her usual fast-paced run, Angelique took in the sights. Running down an old gravel road was something she missed greatly—the closest she had been to the feeling was running through a park, but it was not even close to the same experience. As she ran, she checked her pocket to make sure that she had grabbed her identification from Homeland Security, just in case they tried throwing obstacles between her and the coffee.

After a mile and a half, Angelique knew, from years of living on the road, that she was coming to the end. With every step, she waited to see men training or at least having breakfast. *Then again if they are training, they may be staying out of sight*, she thought as she looked even harder while jogging. Her memory of where the road ended was spot on. She could see the hillside of Raven Bluff and hear the creek in the distance. She knew that this was the end of the road because the county had stopped repairing the concert slab through the creek years ago—it had washed out too many times.

Coming to a stop and looking for any signs of the soldiers' presence, Angelique became even more curious as to what they had been doing here. It was clear from her observations that they were no longer in the area, and all thoughts of coffee were replaced with the possibility this was somehow the unit everyone had assumed made it to Arkansas. With that thought, she reached for her cell phone out of instinct even though she knew it was back on her nightstand. She turned back the way she had come, and this time she ran back at a faster pace. She had phone calls that needed to be made. For the first time in months, Angelique felt like there was work to be done.

As she ran, one thought kept coming to her. How the hell had Karl become part of this? Trying to work the thoughts out, she ran and ran. Other than how Karl became wrapped up in this, she tried to figure out just how the hell they had ended up here. Then like a two powerful magnets slapping together, it came to her. *Karl Eugene Karnic. He brought them here to stay on familiar ground, but where are they now?*

Angelique looked over to her right and was amazed at how run down the house Karl once lived in had become. Angelique was deep in her thoughts when the sound of voices pulled her back to the here and now, and she slowed to almost full stop. Listening for the voices once again, she could tell one was her father's.

"I don't know where she is!" he was saying emphatically. Angelique had now completely stopped.

Then she heard another very familiar voice. Johnathan. "We know she is here, and if you tell us, things will go much smoother. Now where is Angelique?"

"That little weasel of a man," Angelique mumbled while attempting to figure out just what he was doing at her parents' house. From where she stood at the bottom of the hill on the gravel, Angelique could see that there was more than one black SUV. Down deep, she knew something was not right, and with that thought, she moved off the gravel into the woods. She moved slowly among the tall grass and between the trees to the backside of her parents' house.

With the distance between Angelique and her parents being reduced with every step, she could hear much clearer the conversation Johnathan was having with her parents. What she heard caused her heart to pound in her ribs like a robber attempting to get out of a jail cell.

"Put them in the car—we'll take them with us. They will tell us what we want to know," Johnathan instructed one of the many other Homeland Security officers.

After hearing Johnathan's orders to the men holding her parents, Angelique wanted nothing more than to run over and demand an explanation, but the number of personnel they had brought told her it was not a social call. Moving quickly and swiftly through the woods, she could see her parents being place in the back of the SUV. Her first thought about something other than her parents was of her .45s—both were lying on her nightstand just beside her bed.

From behind a big oak tree, Angelique bolted. She could hear men inside— she assumed they were looking for her. The oak tree was just a few feet from the back door and big enough for her to hide behind, and from there, she listened for any information she could gather. It took only a few minutes for Angelique to get antsy, although she had already put her plan into motion. As soon as she made it to the tree undetected, the first thing she did was grab a limb lying on the ground and began scratching the back of the house with it. *Ah, I have a nibble,* she thought as a slight smile appeared on her face.

The footsteps of an agent grew louder and louder, and Angelique could tell by what boards were squeaking just where he was located. That was the advantage of home turf. As she heard the screen door's spring stretching, Angelique moved into a stance for pouncing on her prey—she was the lioness, and the unwitting agent exiting the back door was going to be her prey.

"We're moving out!" a voice called from the front of the house, and her prey stopped in his tracks, turned, and followed his orders. Angelique, on the other hand, could not tell if she was relieved or disappointed in the sudden turn of events.

As the agent moved back to the front of the house, she used the stick to her advantage once more. The back door was almost fully opened by the agent when Angelique heard the call. She knew her plan had to change, and so it did. As he turned to head back to the front of the house, Angelique grabbed the limb jutting from the tree just above her head. Using the limb, she pulled herself up, while with her other hand, she placed the stick in the top of the door, close to the hinges.

Once she was back sure-footed on the ground, she listened. She listened for the squeaks and boots hitting the wood floor and wondered how far the agent would get before realizing the door didn't close. She did not have to wait long, for there were no squeaks or boots connecting with wood. The agent wasn't moving. Angelique once again positioned herself ready to strike. Then came the sound of boots: he was moving to the front of the house. Her body relaxed, and she listened to the sound, judged his position in the house, and waited for her moment to move.

Angelique did not waste time—once the agent passed the bedroom that contained her pistols, she moved. Again with the characteristics of a lioness, she moved ever so stealthily. Not one board squeaked, and not one foot touching the floor could be heard. Even the drawer that held her .45-caliber Colt 1911s, which always created a great deal of noise when opening, seemed to bow to her and remain silent.

Angelique had no illusion about what was going to take place next. The men out front had her parents, and she had her .45s. She felt that was enough, but one thing stood in her way. The men out front were her agents, and the last thing she wanted was to get into a shooting match with fellow agents. She needed intel. At this point, even though she did not want to, she had to let them take her parents.

Angelique moved quickly to the front of the house in the hopes of gathering a little more information about what Johnathan was doing here with so many men. She opened the front door ever so slightly and pressed her ear up to the opening. The first words she heard were *taken the capitol, sir.* Angelique was greatly confused now.

Johnathan's voice sounded like he was in disbelief as he spoke. "What do you mean they have taken the capitol?"

"Sir, the reports coming in say it was a three-stage attack on the state capitol of Jefferson City—"

"By whom?" Johnathan asked, cutting off the agent giving the report.

"It's believed to be the rogue unit thought to be in Arkansas, sir." The agent closed his notebook, signifying to his superior that he had given him all the information he had received.

"OK. Let's load up and move out. Our information about the chief having a connection to the unit was spot on—she is probably there with them now," Johnathan said to the agent as they climbed into the SUV.

Upon hearing the conversation, Angelique's jaw dropped, and an audible gasp came out. She slowly closed the door and started walking through the house while attempting to make sense of what she had just heard. Halfway through, Angelique stopped suddenly and said aloud, "Karl Eugene Karnic!"

Chapter 35

CAPITOL

Sgt. Smith look intently through the glass of his optics at the microscopic red dot he held positioned at the center of the security guard's chest. He waited for the guard to go for his weapon and prayed at the same time that he would not—with this many rifles trained on him and only three feet away, it would be certain death.

Darrian felt a little sorrow for tricking the guard, who only wanted to help a kid find his dog. Once he concluded that the guard was not going to do anything stupid, he turned to him.

"I am going to remove your sidearm, and then we can have a little talk, OK?" Darrian asked in a confident but otherwise-soothing tone.

Not wanting to make any excessive moves or noise, the guard merely nodded in compliance. Few people would want to do either of those when at this end of what he could only assume were loaded rifles. He could feel his revolver being drawn from its holster and his radio being detached from his belt. That wasn't all he felt—other than the items being removed from his person, he started feeling pressure building in his ears and a tingling sensation moving throughout his body. He then found himself very curious as to how they were slowly turning out all the lights from all around him till it was as if he was looking down a tunnel.

With her weapon trained on the guard, Kate watched closely for any aggressive movement. She knew from experience that things could get quickly out of hand. Then she saw aggressive movement and tightened up on her rifle, pulling it just a little more snug into her shoulder. His upstretched arms were ever so slowly moving downward. She could not believe somebody would be so stupid to go for a gun with so many firearms already pointed at him, especially after his had already been removed. She centered the red dot on his chest, and her finger began to exert more pressure upon the trigger. The lower his arms became, the more pressure she put on the trigger. Then she heard him speak.

"How are you turning out the l…"

That was as far as the guard made it before Kate, with her rifle in hand and an expression of disbelief on her face, watched him land in the bushes directly between them. She then looked to Smith, who to had the same expression—it could even be seen through his camouflage face paint.

"Did he just faint?" Smith asked while attempting to hold back the laughter. He then looked back down at the man lying in the bushes.

"Let's get him on over here and awake," Smith said as he reached down to grab the unconscious guard's arms to drag him over. "Put him up against the tree," he told Kate. Both of them still could not believe what had just happened.

"Lights…lights."

"What the hell is he talking about?" Darrian asked as he watched Kate splash more water on the guard's face.

"Stop," the guard said as he came back to a state of awareness. "What did you do to me? I was cooperating!" he exclaimed as if somebody had rendered him unconscious.

"You fainted," Mack said to him from the darkness.

"The hell I did! You…"

"We did nothing. I saw it many of times in 'Nam. Hell, even did it myself once— that is how I know. It happens. Now let's move on." Mack, being the oldest of them, had seen enough in his life that somebody fainting was no longer that funny to him.

"Who are you guys?" the guard asked.

"We are the ones asking questions. Where are they keeping the lieutenant governor?" Smith asked with composure and a commanding tone.

The reply in return was one mixed with sarcasm and confusion.

"The lieutenant governor? He isn't here."

Chapter 36

BUILDING THE RANKS

S ierra calmly drove up the drive of the armory—she was heading for the
upper parking area positioned above the armory. As she was driving up and
around the loop, she had her arm hanging out the driver window and her head
out just enough for her hair to be carried by the cool, crisp morning air. She
concentrated hard to keep her teeth from chattering together since she was no
longer wearing her flannel shirt or her ratty old cap. No, all that could be seen
was her white and very thin spaghetti-strap undershirt. Since the armory was
built with the Missouri River a few hundred feet away, the moisture in the air
made it that much colder.

To the guards whose attention she captivated as she drove by, she was a sight
of pure beauty. It was for that reason alone that she was now freezing. Sierra
figured that the best way not to have a gunfight all the way to the armory was to
draw attention to her and away from the very crowded cattle trailer full of heavily armed soldiers. For that reason, she waved at each individual along the drive.

Once the parking lot came into view, she could feel the adrenaline rushing through her body at the anticipation of what was to come. The parking
lot was large and was only at half-capacity—she knew that had to be due to
the five buses and other military vehicles sitting and waiting to transport their
prisoners. She drove around all the vehicles and headed for the end closest to
the armory—the less open area everyone had to run across, the better. Sierra

didn't know a great deal about the military but what she did know told her that the uniforms the soldiers were wearing looked a little strange.

Karnic was twenty ways of confused, and Robert was right there with him. The two of them stood at the back of the trailer, pressed in tight with the rest of the men, ready to burst through the rear gate into action. That was something they had planned on having to do by this point, not just coursing up to the front doors of the armory. Karnic wondered how it was possible they had not been stopped or shot at by one of the many groups of soldiers he could make out from the darkness of the trailer. Once they came to a full stop, the two men threw open the latches and exited while scanning for any resistance. As Karnic was scanning, Sierra came into sight, and he then knew how they had been able to make it to the high ground. Karnic gave directions to the men who followed, as did Robert did the same to those following his lead.

Robert moved to overwhelm the personnel of the prisoner transport in the hopes of capturing their vehicles. The vehicles were not far away, thanks to Sierra parking the truck and trailer between the men of the U.C.M. and the building and providing both Robert and Karnic a tactical advantage. Robert, with a dozen men following closely behind, raced for the first vehicle—he was only a few yards from the rear when he saw a rifle containing what was most likely a bullet with his name on it, for the rifle was pointed directly at him. Knowing the rifle he carried was going to take much more time to swing in position to fire first, Robert's instinct took over. Before he had his rifle anywhere close enough to send a round in the man's direction, he heard the shot. At that instant, his heart stopped.

Heading for the armory, Karnic was followed by sixty-plus men of the UCM, all hoping that they could keep the element of surprise just a little longer. It was a hope that ended when they were only half the distance to the building. There it was: the shot that let everyone on post know it was time to fight. Karnic hoped that one of his men had fired the shot and was not getting fired at. The element of surprise was over. In the back of his mind, Karnic knew they were in a much better place, thanks to the quick thinking of the vengeful, brown-haired, green-eyed beauty driving.

It all seemed like a dream, and his body was going through the motions. Robert was in a state of utter confusion—he knew that he was good as dead. Yet he was up against the rear of the bus, and his heart had started beating once more. He stared down at his would-be executioner, whose heart struggled to pump blood to a brain that was no longer contained within the confines of his skull—it merely pumped in ever-shorter streams upon the asphalt.

Snapping his head up, Robert realized just why he was still among the living. There was the one-time high school journalist and documentary filmmaker. Sierra was running right at him, with both revolvers outstretched as if they were dragging her along—one was smoking. Robert had never felt so much love for his sister as he did in that moment.

With the shock of the last few seconds wearing off, Robert was back in the fight.

"Thanks," Robert said as Sierra positioned herself alongside him at the back of the bus.

"When are you going to start taking care of yourself, soldier boy?" Sierra asked with strong sarcasm in her voice.

Shaking his head in response as if to say, "Whatever," Robert began assessing where his men were. With surprise, he saw them closing in on a group of people whose hands were stretched high above their heads and who were screaming, "Don't shoot! We're Americans!"

Just feet from the wall, Karnic gave a signal for his men to stack on him. As they were trained to do, one after another fell in behind him on the wall. Many had their M4s pointed up high to the roof, while others were pointing their M4s to the far end of the building, and the rest were pointing in every other direction from their new location. Eyes and rifles had every direction covered, yet Karnic knew that one grenade or rocket-propelled grenade (RPG) landing close could kill half of his men.

It was never good to have so many bunched up in one area, and from here, he had to strategize quickly. Looking back at the line of men, Karnic had it, and he set off for the middle of the line of soldiers along the wall. Stopping only for a second, he tapped two men on their shoulders.

"On my command, you are last man for this group, and you are last man this group. Roger?" Karnic asked.

Acknowledging the orders Karnic had just given them, both men in unison responded, "Roger."

Without delay, Karnic turned and swiftly moved to the other end of the line, where Sgt. Lee Platoon Sergeant of first platoon was positioned.

"Lee," Karnic said with a strong, commanding voice.

Without taking his eyes off his area of fire, Lee acknowledged, "Sergeant."

"You are going through the front entrance with half the men—move on the tap!"

"Roger," Sgt. Lee once again replied.

The last man in Sgt. Lee's group had his eyes trained on Karnic and understood what it meant when he saw Karnic's left arm wave in the direction his line was facing. Without hesitation, he kept one hand on the trigger and, with the other, tapped the man in front of him. That tap reverberated all the way down the line until at last it reached Lee. Upon feeling the pressure on his shoulder, Lee quickly rounded the corner of the building, closing the fifty yards between his group and the front entrance. With each man keeping his weapons trained in every direction, they followed closely behind.

Karnic was almost back to the head of his group when he heard shots from around the corner where he had just sent the men. As he turned to look back, he saw the last two men moving around. Now it was his turn. The men behind him were ready to go, and he knew there would be no need for a signal to move, but he sent one back anyhow, not only to ensure that they all moved but also to give Lee time to draw guards in his direction. Once Karnic felt the return of the signal, which told him that everyone was aware it was time to move, he was off and moving.

Chapter 37

———— ∞ ————

LIEUTENANT GOVERNOR

Sawyer and his men wasted no time moving through the police station. At the same time that the front desk officer was being immobilized, men of the UCM were already at the dispatcher's desk.

With rifles pointed in his direction, the dispatcher was calm and slowly removed his headgear as he spoke. "Listen, guys, you are going to want me on this radio. If the officers in pursuit call in, they—" Sawyer cut him off, not by raising an overpowering voice, but by calmly raising his hand and signaling his desire for the man to stop speaking. The man did so.

"We have an RTO," Sawyer said. "Your assistance will not be necessary. Now if you will join the other officer." He pointed at the front-desk officer slumped over in a chair on the other side of the room.

"Sir, this is not that big of a city, and these guys know my voice. If they hear your guy's voice, one they do not recognize, they will know something is wrong." The dispatcher spoke calmly and with respect.

Sawyer moved very little as he looked at the man and assessed him. "Where did you serve?" Sawyer finally asked.

"I served with the Sixteenth Military Police Brigade out of Fort Bragg," he said with confidence.

"Stay where you are—however, Specialist Hall here will be listening. Can you call the jailer out?"

The dispatcher replied with a nod and picked up the phone. "Gary, can you come out her for a minute? We have a drunk and disorderly."

Within seconds, Taylor opened the door to the jail cell area, and to his surprise, he was met with the barrels of more rifles than he wanted pointed at the space he was currently occupying.

"Things look pretty orderly out her to me, Buck," Taylor said to the dispatcher while placing his hands slowly on the back of his head.

"Set him over by the other guy." Sawyer gestured to the slowly awakening front desk officer.

"How many in your cells?" Sawyer asked.

"Only one." Taylor was a little hesitant to continue and that piqued Sawyer's interest.

"This city isn't that small."

"You're right. Everyone was cleared out for one guy." Buck was still hesitant to speak, but he knew that they would find out whether or not he spoke. "It is Lieutenant Governor Bristol."

Every UCM man in the room looked at one another with absolute astonishment. Sawyer could not believe his fortune.

Chapter 38

FIGHT OF THEIR LIVES

Moving with focus and desire—focus on his objective and the desire to not catch a bullet—Karnic, with his men close behind, jogged toward the back entrance of the armory, his M4 at the ready. With the entrance directly ahead, it was not the ideal situation, and Karnic knew it. *Could be worse*, he thought, feeling fortunate that they had not been spotted. Hearing the firefight still raging in the direction of Sgt. Lee's team, Karnic began to feel that he had taken the easy way, although there was no way of knowing that with the little intelligence they'd had.

The feeling that he had it easy passed quickly with an explosion of glass where a door had once stood. Things began moving so slowly that Karnic wondered how the shards of glass kept moving in his direction and didn't fall to the ground. Then almost as if he were unaware, his weapon fired, and he could see it was on target. Five feet within the door, the man fell to the ground, but two more took his place.

With him and his squad still moving forward, Karnic could feel the pressure created from rifle fire to his left and right. The men had fanned out as much as they could, making Karnic the tip of the spear-shaped formation. As they approached the double door, Karnic wanted nothing more than to kick it open—he even prepared to do so until he remembered that they opened to the outside, then readjusted a second from striking out.

While keeping his trigger finger in its place, with his other hand, Karnic reached out and grabbed the door handle, jerking it open with enough strength to break the glass (had it not already been shot out). The man on his right did the same with his door, and they passed through with eyes on the adjacent hall, where the three men with multiple bullet wounds lay on the floor. Karnic could tell that they were no threat in their current state. He signaled four men to train their weapons on down the hall that the dead men had come from. The rest passed by and followed Karnic forward to the gym, which held the men.

Karnic had known he might have to fire upon American soldiers, but now that he had, he could feel a sickness coming from deep in his gut, one that he knew would be there for a while. Although he didn't have time to stop and investigate, he wondered why the men were in such strange-looking uniforms.

As Karnic came near the doors to the gym, he could see five men standing in front of them with weapons in their hands. Two men stood on either side of a man standing in front of the secured doors. Karnic and his men knew there was no way of knowing who would be hit on the other side of the doors if they opened fire. They all felt sick from the killings that had just taken place, but accidently killing the men they were here to free would be much worse.

With all their fingers at the ready, each of them demanded, "LAY DOWN YOUR WEAPONS!"

Sgt. Lee made it to the top step leading up to the entrance of the armory. He glanced back and down at the path he and his men had taken—the sight was horrifying to him. Lee had trained for years and had yet to see combat. Now he looked back and could see that many of his men had been wounded or killed. The wounded lay screaming in agony, some pulling out their first aid kits and tending to their own wounds. No matter how much they cried out, nobody would be coming to treat them until the mission was complete. That was what every man in the infantry knew and understood. Mission first.

Lee's hypnotized state at the horrific sight was broken with a sudden force that pulled him and another soldier just off to his left down the steps—men who were lying face down on the steps reached up and grabbed hold of his gear and pulled him out of the line of fire. To Lee, everything was happening fast. *This must be what clothes feel like in a washer*, he thought as he slid down the steps. On the way down he tried to take a deep breath but found none.

The lack of oxygen was beginning to take its toll—everything was going dark as Lee struggled to take in air. He began to feel sorrow at not ever asking his girlfriend's hand in marriage or telling her how much he loved her the day he left for what was supposed to be training, not the beginning of the next American Revolution. Then it happened. One very short gasp of air made it in and then another slightly longer than the last, continuing on until Lee was able to take in a full breath.

Lee's thoughts went to how great the sulfur- and cordite-filled air smelled moving through his nostrils. Bringing up his hand to his chest, he could feel the wetness of blood, yet it was not his. Both the rounds he had been in the path of had been caught by the ballistic plate in his vest, which had then pushed all the air from his lungs.

Making his way back to his feet, Lee could hear nothing but the ringing in his ears from the rifle fire. *Funny how it doesn't hurt your ears when you are fighting for your life*, he thought as he slowly slid to the grass along the left side of the steps. Making his way up the incline, he could see that the doors were so shot to hell that the latches would most certainly be damaged. That was a real problem—the glass was shot out at the top and bottom of the door, yet due to the wire between the glass, only jagged teeth remained.

Now that he was back at the top, Lee could see clearly that this would be a problem. Lee wondered how many of his men were going to be lost making it past the doors—it was a thought that he wished he had not started. He looked all around for another way in and noticed that most of the windows along the front of the building were out. They were tall and just over a foot wide, not near the size a soldier could move through quickly covered in gear. No, the doors were the only foreseeable way into the armory.

Lee raised his rifle and took aim at the hinges, thinking about how many shots it would take to free them from the door and the frame. Seconds later he had his answer: a full thirty-round magazine to ensure they were separated. With the emptying of the second full magazine into the second hinge, Lee could not help but feel that he was wasting precious ammunition.

Reaching into his pouch, he could feel there were only two full magazines left. To be sure, he glanced down at the other pouches, and as he did, he caught a glimpse of a baseball-size object drop from above. Instantly Lee was hit with a burst of adrenaline, which he felt was unbelievable given the amount already running through his system. Frantically Lee searched for the grenade, and no sooner had he spotted it than it vanished—it had been punted like a football by the man beside him on the wall while the next guy down fired up at the rooftop. The grenade was landed in a parking area and exploded, destroying a Silverado.

Lee turned to the man beside him who had just made the kick and said, "Score!" Then his focus was back on the door.

With the last round fired into the hinge, Lee prayed for his plan to work. Looking down to the men firing just over the top step, he signaled for them to stay—he motioned for the men behind them to stack on him. Filled with anxiety and adrenaline, they quickly moved and gathered to his rear. They were ready to go.

Lee reached out to the door with his KA-BAR knife in hand. Slowly he put it in the space between the door and its frame. Working the blade just a little at a time so as not to break it, he pried the door away little by little. As he pried, Lee could feel the tip of his blade snap. Little by little, it dug in, and the door moved free from its frame. His idea was working, and in a few seconds, the door would be free.

Bullets passed through the doors from the inside, and his men sent them back in response. Lee swore he could feel the heat as the hot lead screamed past. Now it was time—there was enough separation to pull the door the rest of the way. Looking back and using his peripheral vision, Lee gave the man to his rear a nudge with his elbow, letting him know it was time, and he in turn sent the nudge on down the line.

It was not long before his nudge was returned, and at that moment, Lee could feel fear coming on strong—not for his own life, but for the lives of the men who were about to die entering the doorway. With his fingers quickly pressed between the door and the frame, with all his strength, Lee pulled, and the door came free. As the door hit the concrete Lee was already on his way through the opening, all the others inches behind him. Now he didn't just think he could feel the heat from the bullets—he was certain.

Chapter 39

THE NEW GOVERNOR

"A ttention!" Sawyer called as the jailer came into the room with the lieutenant governor. The look on the governor's face was of confusion. He recognized Sawyer's face from the reports prior to his arrest. No, the confusion was not from wondering who the men were but why they were here. The last report he had received suggested that the unit was moving into Arkansas, yet here they were in the police station. Now he was returning a salute to the commander.

"What are you doing here, Commander?" the lieutenant governor asked as his hand returned to his side.

"Sir, we have come for you. We feel that you have the support of most Missourians. My men need somebody who will speak for them. We were set up, sir." Sawyer felt it was no time to beat around the bush.

"Well, Commander, I guess we are in the same boat now," the governor replied as he shook his head in disbelief. "Commander, I hate to inform you of this, but the rest of your men are being held at the armory and in Saint Louis."

Sawyer moved from the position of attention to parade rest and began to speak with a little smirk on his face. "Sir, since the government decided to frame us as traitors, we no longer have any allegiance to the government. We are now the United Constitutional Militia." He paused to study the governor's reaction. It didn't take long for Sawyer to see that he had made the right decision about breaking him out. Sawyer continued.

"Secondly, sir, the freeing of our men at the armory is already under way."

At that moment, Sawyer felt like kicking his own ass—he couldn't believe he had forgotten about the group going for the lieutenant governor at the capital. "Radio!" he blurted out, followed by, "Excuse me, sir."

"White One, White One, this is Cardinal. Over." He waited and then repeated, "White One, White One, this is Cardinal. Over." Once again he waited.

Moments like this—not knowing—were always the hardest for Sawyer, and these days it was much worse. Then he heard it, the sweet bark of static right before a transmission made its way through.

"Cardinal, this is White One. Over."

Sawyer felt a little relief at hearing Sgt. Smith's voice. "White One, what is your sitrep? Over."

"Cardinal, lieutenant not at location. All members accounted for. Plus one guard. How to proceed? Over."

"White One, keep safe and hold for instruction. Over."

Sawyer thought hard about the turn of events. He found it a bit interesting how things had worked out. Still standing alongside the RTO, Sawyer took the radio once again. "Red One, Red One, this is Cardinal. Over."

Without delay, he got a response. Sawyer had a good idea of what the buses were doing. Ever since they had taken control of the police station, his RTO had been forwarding information from the police dispatch to his drivers. So much so that the law enforcement following him had started thinking they had real-time satellite coverage feeding them information.

"Cardinal, Red One, things are getting tight out here."

Sawyer could hear tires screeching and gunfire as the driver maneuvered the large vehicle around what he could only assume were very tight streets.

"Red One, when you get clear, pick up White One at the drop-off point. Copy?"

Red One, with confusion in his voice—undoubtedly due to the light parade following closely behind him for the last half hour and the occasional breaking glass from bullets sticking all around him at a high rate of speed—replied, "Copy, Cardinal," while wondering how he was going to get free.

"Cardinal out."

Sawyer looked directly at the dispatcher. "What can you send out to get my men free?"

"Well, sir, it is easy to pull back state and city, but they are not the only ones in pursuit."

"Who the hell else is there? FBI? DEA? Marshals?" Sawyer hated playing guessing games and wished people would stop making him.

"No, sir, SCN."

Before he could ask who the hell the SCN was, a call came over the radio. "Cardinal, this is White One. Over."

Quickly Sawyer raised the mic to speak. "Go for Cardinal."

"Cardinal, we have movement. Frank here says it is the governor preparing to move. Please advise. Over."

Sawyer didn't show it. But this was what he loved, conducting multiple missions simultaneously, and he was great at it. "White One, hold, gather intelligence only. Over."

"Dispatch, send out the call." Sawyer then focused on the governor. "Sir, are you with us?" he asked, confident of what the reply would be.

"From the beginning, Commander. These are the times when great men no longer stand by, but make themselves heard."

Very satisfied with the lieutenant governor's response, Sawyer picked up his mic once again. "White One. Over."

This time only a few seconds passed before Sawyer received a reply.

"Cardinal, this is White One. Over."

"White One, pickup will be at drop point. Copy."

"Copy, Cardinal." Sawyer heard the break in communication and knew more was to follow since Sgt. Smith and Kate were both seasoned soldiers and always properly ended the transmissions with the word *over*.

"Cardinal, we have intel, will brief after extraction. Over."

"White One, copy. Cardinal out."

Chapter 40

———— ❧ ————

TIME TO MOVE

Karnic held his weapon tightly at the ready—with both eyes open, he peered through his ACOG and placed the red reticle in the center of what was apparently the commanding officer's chest. More precisely, the reticle was on the shiny brass-buttoned center of his chest. Somehow even with emotions and adrenaline flowing, Karnic's men were able to restrain from firing. The officer and his men were obviously outgunned, but it didn't seem to bother them—they stood their ground as if they had superior strength in numbers.

"I say again, put down your weapons!" Karnic's command was said with such power that his own men felt they needed to put down theirs.

Knowing there were a great many rifles aimed at him and that they all had fingers on their triggers, the commanding officer replied, making direct eye contact with Karnic and never breaking it.

"Sorry, Sergeant, but I will not give that order to my men," the commanding officer said.

After a second, he continued, as he knew that there was no time to waste. "I am Colonel William Marks. We are on the same side, Sergeant."

Karnic felt a burst of emotion run through his body as the colonel stated his name. "Marks?"

Karnic knew that Marks had family in the service, but Marks had never said what rank they were or where they were serving. Karnic never imagined that he would run into one.

"That's right, Sergeant. If you are not in the believing state of mind, just bring up my boy. He has spoken highly about you, Sergeant."

Karnic couldn't believe what was happening. He slowly lowered his rifle and began to stand up straight. One thing he didn't want to do in this situation was let this guy know that his son had died.

Hearing the firefight out raging on the other side of the building, Karnic addressed the colonel. "Where do we go from here, sir?"

"Sergeant." Col. Marks signaled for his four men to lower their weapons, and they did with a little relief. "We are with you, Sergeant."

Surprised, Karnic had one concern to address first. "Then order your men to cease fire."

"Sergeant, my men were ordered by me not to fire upon you the second I spotted the young lady knock out my guard at the front gate," the colonel replied, while his body language said, "Don't think I didn't know you were coming."

"I guess your guys back there lying dead didn't get the memo, and..."

"Those are not my men, Sergeant!" The colonel sharply spoke with distress in his voice as he continued. "They are with those out front. The men yours are fighting now, the SCN."

"Well, order them down. I don't give a damn who they are with." Karnic knew that every second wasted could mean the life of another one of his men currently engaged in battle. Frustration was starting to take over, and Marks could read it in Karnic's body language.

"Sergeant, they do not take orders from me, only the United Nations." Just that sentence coming from his mouth gave Marks the need to wash out his mouth.

"What kind of shit is that?" Karnic couldn't believe what he was hearing, but he decided to wait until later for questions.

"Sergeant, we can go through the gym and attack them from the rear. There are four walking the catwalk. My men and I will take them, and you can move on through."

Without waiting for acknowledgment of his plan, the colonel and his men turned and entered the gym.

With what passed as a stunned expression for Karnic, he looked left and then right at his men.

"Make a hole!" announced the men with the colonel as they moved through the doors—all the men knew that meant they should make a path for them to walk. The colonel disappeared into hundreds of men packed in the gymnasium, with two men in front and two behind.

Twenty seconds later rifle fire erupted. Without delay, Karnic sprang forward through the doors of the gym to find Marks standing in the middle of his four men with their rifles pointing upward. Up above, Karnic could see clearly two men on the catwalk with their blood raining over the edge.

"Move it, Sergeant, through that door—you can flank them!" said the colonel as he pointed to the door at the far corner of the gym. "We will keep the men covered here! So move!"

Even though space was limited, those in the gym managed to make it look like Moses parting the Red Sea for Karnic and the men following close behind. Karnic slowed down when he reached the doors—in his mind, he pictured hitting them so hard that they would embed themselves in brick before stopping. Once again everything seemed to move in slow motion as the doors opened. Before the doors had touched brick the M4 in his hands had started to warm up and sent multiple rounds into the body of a man thrown back by the violent opening of the doors.

Karnic could see that his plan to draw most of the personnel to the front was successful—the hallway through which they had just entered brought an entirely new meaning to the phrase *like shooting fish in a barrel*. Karnic and the men to his left and right dropped to one knee and continued to fire. Things moved so slowly for Karnic that he swore he was seeing the rounds being sent up and down the hall, though he wondered why he didn't see the one that caused the burning sensation in his torso. Karnic marveled at how warm his blood was as it exited the wound, yet he kept firing. Fire he did until a great weight took him to the floor.

Sgt. Lee took a deep breath and pushed the door with all his might as he shoved it from his path, then entered and fired down the hall. Lee understood that being the first man through the door in this situation did not hold a high percentage of survival. With that understanding, he was not going down without firing a shot. As soon as his rifle's muzzle passed the door and aimed down the hall, his finger tightened on the trigger, and he began sending rounds to the other end. He was surprised when his rifle bolt locked open due to firing all the rounds in the magazine. Along side him others stood with the bolt locked open due to empty magazines also when they fully expected to have been gunned down upon entering. With a quick raise of his hand, the firing ceased from those who still had rounds in their weapons. At the far end of the hall gunfire was being exchanged by those in the hallway crossing the one they now stood in, it was not long before that weapons fire slowed to a stop.

Dropping his spent magazine and slapping in a full one, Lee released the bolt, loading a round in the chamber. Crouching down and pulling their weapons up to the ready, those around him followed suit, and at a steady pace, they moved forward. Nearing the end of the hall, they slowly moved around—with men on both sides of the hall facing one another. Sgt Lee watched the corner across from him as one of his men watched the corner coming up on his side. With each step the men took revealing more of what was down the adjoining hall. While they exposed more and more of themselves to those who might be in the adjacent hall, the first thing they noticed was how shiny and reflective the floors were. But they knew that it was not from floor wax.

The firefight was over, and Lee could hear the sweet sound of men calling out, "UCM! UCM!" Lee lowered his weapon as a few moved past to the other end of their hallway and secured any personnel who might be alive. Lee got a lump in his throat when he saw Karnic lying on the floor. He rushed over to the help the others with the casualties. Lee had thought that Karnic could never be killed. As Lee watched the others removing the wounded and the dead, he saw movement come from Karnic.

"Secure the compound! We are not done yet!" Karnic ordered as the body of a fellow comrade was lifted from on top of him. Gun fire could still be heard in the distance, and even though the men in the gym were without weapons, they were ready to fight. A few of them had secured weapons and gear from those who had already fallen.

With the burning pain in his side, Karnic attempted to stand up straight. "Let's get these men weapons. Get with Colonel Marks in the gym, and find out where the supply sergeant is located. Send Colonel Marks my way when you are through—we have to have a talk."

As men began exiting the front of the armory to engage those who still intended them harm, many followed close behind to treat the wounded. When they looked out over the grounds for targets, they were amazed at the sight. Many were dead on the low-cut, grassy field, but the amazing sight was of men with their hands on the back of their heads and weapons far out in front of them. Every so often a shot rang out from the parking lot where Robert's team was located. Many of the men chuckled at the sight before making their way down.

As the men from the U.C.M. approached the men lying on the ground, they commented, "Looks like you have met the squire."

Chapter 41

<hr>

ANGELIQUE'S STAND

S tanding in her childhood bedroom with her mind racing and attempting to make sense of what had just happened, Angelique let out a deep breath. This was not the first time those she cared about had been in danger, but it was the first time that those who were in danger were her own family, her own flesh and blood. And Angelique didn't know why. For her, the worst part was that her own agency was posing the threat and holding her parents. From what she could make of the situation, it was due to some connection she might or might not have with the rogue military unit.

Even with her heart pumping adrenaline through her veins, Angelique knew a few things had to be done quickly. She had to get out of her exercise clothes and put on something that was easy to move in. Within seconds, she threw open her closet doors and began to change. Stripping off her sweaty clothing, she scanned for the clothing inside. She knew what she was looking for, even though it had been many years since she last had seen them, and there they were. A pair of old olive drab green fatigues that Old Jerry had given her for a birthday long ago. Angelique almost felt like he had known that this day would come.

She slid on the fatigues from a bygone age and then reached for a black sports top. She felt lucky that footwear was not an issue. She had brought her black tactical boots with her, and she quickly laced them. Without missing a step, Angelique reached for her Colt 1911 pistols. As she slid them into their holsters, one on each hourglass hip, a calming feeling followed. Grabbing three rubber bands from her dresser, Angelique put her long, blond hair back into a ponytail and then covered the rest with a plain black cap. The process would have taken most people some time, but due to her years in the military, it took Angelique mere minutes.

Catching a glimpse of herself in the mirror on the way out her bedroom door, Angelique marveled at how much her outfit reminded her of *Tomb Raider*. With an emotionless face, she said to no one, "Lara Croft doesn't have shit on me," and she continued out the back door.

Angelique conjured a mental image of the vehicle that held her parents and tried to picture where they might be. She knew the top speed of the vehicle and the condition of the gravel road. Then with her knowledge of where they would most likely be taken, Angelique could only assume that they would make a left on the pavement once they came to the end of the gravel road. She ran beyond any speed she had before in the direction of her father's work truck, where she grabbed a pair of wire cutters from his toolbox. Then she changed direction to the four-wheeler parked nearby. Intercepting the vehicle was a possibility—she thought it might be on a stretch of highway that ran just a mile behind her parents' house.

At a full run and with the back of the ATV in front of her, Angelique went airborne like a cowboy mounting his trusty steed. Almost before her rear had touched the seat, she was off, cutting a path through the open field at full speed.

With the wire cutters in hand, Angelique skidded to a stop and next to a stretch of fencing, which put her in position to cut without having to leave the seat. After cutting a hole in the fence, she drove through the opening and was off. She shifted back into gear and thumbed the throttle forward, pushing the ATV to its max as she bobbed and wove through the forest and over the hill that lay on the other side.

As Angelique crested the last hill, the trees began to thin. She pressed her thumb harder on the throttle only to find there was no more to give. It took just a minute to cross the field with the highway bordering its far edge. Crossing the ditch between the field and the pavement, she let off the gas and could see a great distance in both directions.

Since there were no vehicles in sight, Angelique flew from the ditch and parked the ATV across the center strip of the highway. With almost acrobatic skill, she spun up and off the seat and landed with both boots firmly planted, then rested her hands on her Colts, which were cradled by her thumbs. Staring down the highway at the hill in the distance, Angelique waited with the image in her head placing them in sight. Yet there was nothing.

After a minute or two passed, panic began to creep up. *Have I missed them?* she thought. With the worry that she may never see her parents again and still confused about what was happening, a question remained in her mind: What had Karnic got her into?

Even thought she was a seasoned veteran of many combat and law enforcement operations, Angelique still could not answer the question of what to do if the SUV did show.

"Time to find out," Angelique said as she saw the vehicle crest the hill in the distance. A plan was not formulated, but the only acceptable result was clear: the retrieval of her parents. As the black SUV grew closer, Angelique felt something that she had not felt since her first tour in the Middle East: anxiety over what was about to occur. It was common for a person to feel anxiety in a time of high stress, but the creeping anxiety was not helpful. It could only hinder her reactions and thoughts.

Taking in a deep breath and exhaling, Angelique then took another deep breath, slowly felt her lungs expand, and slowly exhaled. Almost instantly her nerves begin to settle, washing the anxiety from her mind and body. Angelique standing in front of her ATV with her thumbs placed atop each Colt was quite the menacing sight. That was evident from the reaction of the vehicle coming up behind her. As she heard the SUV's brakes engage and its tires screech on the pavement, not a muscle moved in Angelique's athletic body. She knew that the objective was coming right at her, and slowing down whoever had stopped was of no concern.

As the SUV came to a stop, men began disembarking from every door. It reminded her of a packed clown car, only these clowns were packing a great deal of hardware. The driver sat staring with the most unusual expression on his face—he was not quite able to figure out exactly what was happening. As she stood there almost statuesquely, Johnathan's SUV closed in behind them, and once again agents with weapons drawn exited the vehicle.

There he was, the man who made her skin crawl. Johnathan. Slowly walking forward, Johnathan did not take his eyes off Angelique. For some time, he had lusted for this woman, and there she was now. She was five foot ten, with blond hair, blue eyes, and a strong athletic body that a gymnast would be jealous of. Then again, gymnasts were not sporting two Colt 1911s on their sides and probably could not wipe a fly's ass at fifty yards with them.

When he approached the left front tire of the vehicle he was almost standing directly in front of Angelique, Johnathan stopped with little emotion. At the same time, he heard, "That is far enough." As she spoke those words in an authoritative tone, Angelique could hear grips being tightened up on all the rifles pointing in her direction. At that point, Angelique almost let out a chuckle, thinking, *So this is what they mean by biting off more than you can chew.*

Johnathan spoke with a slight hint of sarcasm in his voice. "Well, there you are. We've been looking for you."

Angelique quickly responded, "Yes, here I am. How about you explain to me what is going on and why you have my parents."

Now devoid of any emotion, Johnathan unbuttoned his jacket, and with his thumb pulling one side of his jacket back, he placed his thumb in his belt keeping the jacket pulled to the rear. Leaning against the SUV, he seemed casual, like things were just business as usual. But that was not the case with the others present. Every man felt like Angelique's eyes were staring right at him as she spoke.

"Why are you here?" she asked once more, already tired of his game.

Cocking his head just a few degrees to one side, Johnathan responded, "Did you think you could go against DHS and help your boyfriend? Did you really think there would be no consequences?"

Angelique could not believe what she was hearing, but then she thought of how her situation might look to the DHS. She had just happened to take a vacation at the same time that a rogue military unit was camped out in her backyard. And she did have a connection with one of the leading men in the unit.

"You've got it wrong," she replied with authority and emphasis. "I am on v—"

"Don't try feeding me that bullshit! We have orders to bring you in and your family."

"Orders from whom?"

"From the head of the SCN." Johnathan spoke as if the SCN were the ruling power.

Angelique was stunned by what she had just heard. When the SCN program had been first implemented, she had known that it would be bad—she just hadn't thought it would happen this quickly. With a touch of laughter, she said, "What? Are we governed by the United Nations now? Not our own government?" Angelique laughed a little more just to get under his skin.

"Lay down your arms and come with us!"

Angelique knew at that point that she had Johnathan off balance, and she understood that there was no talking to somebody who had made up his mind.

"Drop the act!" Johnathan yelled. "Your boyfriend will be surrounded within the hour, and all of them will be brought in, dead or alive. My preference is of the nonbreathing sort."

Angelique heard a touch of jealousy in Johnathan's voice when he'd said the word *boyfriend*. She pretended like he had said nothing, but she did have a question. She looked at the man closest to her and ensured that she had eye contact before speaking.

"Cameron, you served under me and trained with me. You know I would never do what this son of a bitch is saying. Yet you stand here with a rifle aimed right at me, ready to pull the trigger for him."

Then she turned to the man on the other side of the vehicle. "Ken, we fought many battles side by side in the sandbox. Do you really believe that I am capable of turning against my country? Jeff, how about it? Do you believe? I should not have to stand here and explain myself."

Angelique let her head hang down and shook it a little.

"So you know I was simply on vacation," she said slowly.

Johnathan saw that she was getting to the men and that their rifles were beginning to slightly lower as if they had lost faith in what they were doing. Angelique was beginning to get to them.

"Kill her!" Johnathan shouted out.

The first two men she had addressed lowered their weapons and spun on the balls of their feet until they were facing those behind them. Their weapons again came back up and trained on those behind them, with one exception. Cameron now had his close enough to Johnathan's nose that Johnathan could smell the gun oil.

Stunned by the turn of events, Johnathan stood with both hands down at his side. He looked over at Angelique—who was carrying both Colts, with one pointed in his direction—and had a thought: *When the hell did she draw those?*

Chapter 42

COMING HOME
TO ROOST

"Cardinal, this is Red One. Over."

Hearing the transmission, Sawyer hoped for some good news. News that meant they were on their way to pick up White One, but that was not to be the case.

"White One, Cardinal here. What's your situation?"

"Cardinal, the police have broken off their pursuit, yet we still have others who are a bit more feisty. Request further instructions. Over."

Karnic could hear the radio chatter and came to the conclusion that they were no longer on radio silence. After the call had ended, he grabbed the mic from his RTO. "Cardinal, this is Blue One. Over," he called and instantly received a response.

"Blue One, Cardinal. Sitrep. Over." Sawyer had a little eagerness in his voice. This first opportunity to get an update from the progress at the armory excited him.

Karnic understood, for he felt much the same—not knowing how the others were prevailing could take its toll. This was one radio call he enjoyed making, although he did not show it.

"Cardinal, we have the dugout. I repeat, the dugout is ours."

"Excellent, Blue One. Can you afford some visitors? Over."

Karnic marveled at how he and Sawyer were on the same page.

"Affirmative, Cardinal. I'll be waiting—will give them a great reception. Over."

"Ridge Runner, I have one more request. Over." Karnic knew it would be something Sawyer felt was difficult since he had changed from Karnic's mission call sign to his personal one.

"Send it, Cardinal," he said, and then Karnic listened intently.

"Ridge Runner, are you capable of picking up White One? Over."

Karnic thought about the request and about the increased difficulty now that the whole city was awake and somewhat aware. Then, as he looked up toward the top of the hill, he cracked what was Karnic's patented I-have-a-plan smile. In the parking area, protruding out of a truck window, were cowboy boots. At that moment, he knew how to retrieve the fighters safely.

"Cardinal, pickup will be in ten. Copy?"

"Copy, Ridge Runner. Cardinal out."

Seconds later Karnic heard the call go out to White One and then to Red One as he began walking up the hill to the truck, where Sierra seemed to be relaxing with her feet propped up on driver's-side window.

As he approached the driver's door of the pickup truck, he heard noises that he thought were impossible coming from the truck.

"Snoring? How the hell are you able to sleep?" Karnic asked, just feet from the door, and then he received a response he wasn't planning on: the clicking of the hammer on Sierra's pistols and then the sight of a muzzle.

"I get it where I can, never know when the next time will be, cowboy." Then to Karnic's relief, the pistol disappeared, and he heard the sound of it being uncocked.

"I have a run for you if you're up to it," said Karnic.

"I don't have time to make a run for your needs," Sierra said, closing her eyes once again.

Taken aback by Sierra's response, Karnic didn't know whether to drag her out of the truck or laugh. Since he wasn't really the laughing type and dragging her from the truck would probably only get him another good look at her pistols, he choose the only thing left. "Well, I need you to pick up Smith, Kate, and the others. While you are out, maybe you can stop for a lollipop."

Commander Sawyer handed the radio mic back to his RTO and then looked around the room at the police officers.

"Gentlemen," Sawyer began, "the events of this week have changed the lives of many men. All have been forced to take actions they most likely would have never dreamed of. These men have been betrayed by their government and are now hunted in the country they pledged to defend."

He paused for a second to allow the words he had just spoken to set in, for the question to follow would be a hard one to answer.

"We have all heard the quote: 'From time to time, the tree of liberty must be cleansed with the blood of patriots and tyrants.' Well, gentlemen, I am here to tell you that time has come. My men and I have had this forced upon us—you will not at this time. For now, it is our fight, but don't think for a second that tomorrow, next month, or next year it will not become yours."

Again Sawyer paused from pacing from one side of the room to the next and chose his words carefully. "I have to ask this now and want to give you a choice. Change cannot come by just us few. Who among you will join us in this burden set before us?"

At first, not one person spoke or made any movement. This was a hard decision to make, one that would change life as they knew it forever. Each man had to decide for himself.

"You already know where I stand, Commander," spoke the lieutenant governor as he crossed the room to stand by Sawyer.

Buck was the first to stand. "I am already part of this—I took the same oath you did, sir."

"I am in also," Taylor replied as he took the outstretched hand of the lieutenant governor.

The front desk officer hung his head and avoided looking at the chair where he had been sitting. "Sorry, I cannot get involved."

"That is your decision," Sawyer replied, understanding. Then he moved his attention to those who had just volunteered. "Will be glad to have both you men. I just have one more thing to ask." He focused his attention on Buck, the dispatcher. "Do you have family? A wife, children?" Buck shook his head no.

"Taylor, same question." Sawyer felt no need to repeat the question. Taylor smiled a little at the thought, and then the smile slowly went away as he answered, "Yes, sir, I have a daughter and a beautiful wife."

Hearing the speech, Sawyer knew he was conflicted. After over to Taylor, Sawyer placed his hand on Taylor's shoulder and spoke. "Then go home to them," he said, removing his hand turning to walk away. Even though Sawyer needed every man he could get, he did not want to see families torn apart if he could prevent it.

"Sir!" Taylor replied. His courage could be heard in that one word.

Sawyer turned back and looked the man in the eyes. He could see the soldier within, and then he spoke. "Taylor," Sawyer said, taking him to one side away from the hearing range of the front desk officer. "You may play one of the most important roles. You can support us another way: get the word out. Send us recruits—go to the VFW, the American Legion, anywhere able-bodied men may be, and be heard. Can you do that for us?"

"Yes, I can, sir." Taylor spoke with confidence.

"You can start with the officers heading back this way and anyone else you can find—they are needed today." Sawyer knew it was a long shot that Taylor would be able to convince anyone, but it gave the man something meaningful to do.

"Sir, how do they find you?" Taylor asked.

"Send them to the armory on Militia Boulevard. It is now our base of command." A smile spread across Sawyer's face as he said those words. A few hours ago, he hadn't thought it was possible for them to have it.

Turning back to the room, he said, "OK, let's load up and move out! Take any weapons you can find—we are going to need them. We are moving out in two minutes!"

This was not the way Sawyer pictured the morning going, but he could not have prayed for a better outcome.

Chapter 43

NEW BASE OF COMMAND

"Hey, Sergeant, great job looking after your men," Colonel Marks said to Karnic with admiration. "Now if you don't mind, could you call up my son if he isn't busy. It seems like months since I last saw him." Marks said this with excitement and anticipation in his eyes.

Karnic's face grew slightly pale as he spoke the words. "Sir," Karnic struggled to speak. This was the first time in all his years he'd had to tell a parent his or her son had died, and he feared it would become commonplace. "Sir, I regret to inform you that I cannot."

Colonel Marks unfortunately had done notifications in his career and recognized the implications of Karnic's words, yet held out hope that he was wrong. "Well, then, perhaps later when he is not busy." He spoke with a mild quaver in his voice and feared what would be spoken next.

Karnic swallowed down his emotions, straightened his stance, removed his hat and placed it in his left armpit, and he then spoke with clarity. "Sir, I regret to inform you that your son, Specialist Marks, was lost on a vital mission. He was killed in action while securing greatly needed resources. Resources that made it possible to be here today."

The busy compound, with men moving in all directions and shouting orders, vanished in Colonel Marks's world. All that existed were flashes of memories: the first time he'd held his son after his wife gave birth, birthdays, Christmases, his son's first day of school, and his son's graduation from basic training. That day he had watched as his son marched across the parade ground in his dress uniform for the first time at Fort Benning in Georgia. The memories turned to anger and rage as the reality of what had been taken from him took over.

"Was it one of these Strong City Network bastards?" the colonel asked Karnic. Marks was visibly attempting to control himself and maintain his composure as a superior officer.

"I am not sure—we didn't know about the SCN before today. However, that would explain quite a bit. He was with Commander Sawyer on a fuel run when it happened."

"Well, Sergeant, I would like to speak with Commander Sawyer. ASAP."

"Sir, with all due respect, I know you are grieving for your son, but we are no longer part of the US Army. Therefore, we are no longer under your command."

"Well, Sergeant, in that case, I request to have a talk with your commander. Sergeant, just in case you have not realized it yet, neither am I or my men." The words exited Marks's lips with a great deal of distain.

"Sir, the commander is in route. For now, though, I can introduce you to the man who put the bullet through the head of the man who killed your son."

"Thank you, Sergeant. One other thing. Where is my son now?" Marks asked, a little more at ease knowing his son's killer no longer drew breath.

"He was buried with respect in a beautiful spot on a hilltop in the Mark Twain National Forest."

"When this madness is over, you will have to show me one day, Sergeant," the colonel replied, knowing that the day might never come.

Karnic turned to one of his men. "Ask the Squires to the colonel's office." Turning back to Marks's father, Karnic said, "Sir, I have preparations to attend to. I hope you understand."

"Before we go, Sergeant, what is this UCM your men were hollering?"

Karnic took a few minutes to explain the name of the militia, and when he finished, it brought a little bit of spirit back to the colonel's eyes.

"Thanks, Sergeant," Colonel Marks replied when Karnic was finished with his explanation of the UCM. As Karnic turned and began walking away, Marks called out to one of his men who worked in supply, and they began walking to his office.

Karnic looked out over the front lawn of the armory, where men were preparing for a fight that none of them had ever imagined just a week ago. Reaching back, he pulled his wallet from its pocket. Opening it, he pulled out an oval disk, which was not shiny but more of a polished rust—at the top were two small holes, and running the length were cutouts with only a few spots holding the two halves together. Both halves were mirror images of the other. On them, he rubbed his thumb over the lettering stamped into the steel—some of it was in German, but the lettering in the part his thumb passed over was clear to everyone. *Karl E. Karnic.*

Karnic had heard the stories about his grandfather all his life—they had been told to him by the man who had been his grandfather's best friend and sergeant. The man he grew up knowing as Grandfather. Karnic had never felt very close to the grandfather whose last name he carried, not even when his father had given him his grandfather's dog tag after he had finished basic.

Now looking out over the field where his fate loomed, Karnic looked upon the rusted piece of metal with new eyes. He felt a connection that spanned decades, as he imagined what his grandfather must have felt and thought during his final hours. Looking over at the wounded being cared for and moving to the gymnasium, Karl, too, wondered if he shouldn't send the healthy away to fight another day.

After a few minutes, he said to himself, "No, Grandfather was saving a village. We are saving a nation."

Taking one last look at the dog tag, Karnic felt part of his grandfather with him. "Sergeant Lee!" he called out, and within seconds, Lee appeared by his side.

"Yes, Sergeant?"

"Are we prepared to pluck the ticks off the backs of our dogs?"

"Yes, they will not make it past the tracks crossing the road a hundred yards before the gate. We have men on either side to disable their vehicles."

Satisfied with his answer, Karnic nodded. "Great, they will be coming in last."

"Let's pick any the commander and the prom queen bring with them as well. Make sure the path is clear for the buses—those men have been out there for too long."

With a nod, Karnic signaled to Lee that his orders were complete and turned and began walking to the area holding the wounded. Karnic felt it was time to find out just what kind of casualties they had taken.

Chapter 44

THE PICKUP

Riding down the divided highway, Sierra and Carlos could sit quietly and enjoy the calm, soothing sounds of the road. Though one could not tell, both were physically drained after the events of the early morning. They marveled at all the traffic, as if nothing had changed. Everyone was fully aware of the enactment of martial law. How could they not be? It was announced regularly over the radio.

Sierra and Carlos could not understand how the people could go on with their days believing that the government knew best. The one hope they both shared was that others would wake from their sleep and open their eyes to the reality of the world around them. For now, they traveled among the sleepwalkers.

Carlos tensed up where he sat in the passenger seat as his eyes locked on a white vehicle pulling alongside of them. On the door of the white vehicle in bold blue print were two letters in blue: *UN*. He looked over at Sierra, who had already taken notice of his sudden change.

"What?" she asked as she looked in the mirrors and expected to see a cop car—but there was none.

"I have heard stories about it—even seen videos online—but only thought of them as conspiracy nut jobs. Now I am not so sure," Carlos replied.

"Again, what?" she asked with curiosity.

"They were videos of trains carrying hundreds of UN vehicles throughout the country. Nobody ever said where they were going or why—it was believed that they were being staged for something." Then Carlos paused, rested his elbow on the door, and stroked his newly grown beard as if in deep thought.

"Staged for what?"

"For this," he replied calmly as the UN vehicle slowly passed them in the right lane.

Sierra watched as the vehicle pulled ahead and thought about what the former ranger had just said. *Has this all been orchestrated?* she wondered. The thoughts of her family being used for this purpose made her sick, and with tears beginning to form in her eyes, she quickly shook the image from her mind and chose to focus only on the here and now before any tears had the chance of pouring from her eyes.

"In about three miles, we will see the exit," Carlos reminded her, seeing that she could use a distraction.

As he spoke, Sierra's finger tripped the blinker, and she began moving over to the right lane of traffic. Thinking she was just preparing, Carlos sat quietly until she began to move over onto the exit ramp.

"The next exit is ours," he said while watching the UN vehicle making its way down the exit.

Still, Sierra continued following the vehicle. After spending the last few months with her, Carlos knew that there was nothing more he could say, and he sat back and wondered what Sierra hoped to gain. That all changed once his eyes saw where the UN vehicle was heading—he hoped Sierra wasn't going to follow. Just off the exit sat a gas station parking lot and more than a dozen white cars with blue lettering. As he looked over at Sierra, Carlos could tell that the excitement of the morning was not over.

Carlos thought to himself that this was a very bad idea, but he calmly looked over at Sierra and asked, "You are not pulling in there, right?" As he asked his question, he was answered by the turn signal. It was clear that she was. Readying his pistol, Carlos could see that there was going to be a fight.

"We are just locals to them, ranger boy," Sierra said. She still had somewhat of a smile on her face, and that worried him.

Following right behind the UN vehicle, they pulled into the gas station. The UN men went right to meet the others, who were apparently waiting for their arrival, and Sierra went straight for the gas station, where many of the soldiers were entering. Removing her sidearm as if it were just another day, she looked at Carlos as she opened her door and said, "I'll be right back. You want anything?"

"No, I'm good," Carlos replied, looking at her questioningly as she closed the door behind her and began walking into the store like just another girl on the block. Sitting in the truck surrounded by what he now considered the enemy made Carlos feel as if it were the end. Trying to not watch them, he could hear them talking from the distance, but he was unable to understand what they were saying. The thing he did understand was that they were not here on vacation.

Watching the gas station doors and straining to hear the conversation between the UN men, Carlos could not help but feel a little jealousy toward those who still slept and didn't yet understand what was happening. Carlos thought about how nice it would have been if he had only come in late for work and had never taken the phone call that changed his life. That wasn't the case, though, and he had already hit the bottom of the rabbit hole. Now he only felt sorrow. Sorrow for the millions of lives that were going to change and be lost, due to a government controlled by people out for power.

Carlos's heart thumped hard and fast in his chest, and his grip tightened around his pistol as Sierra exited the gas station doors with two UN soldiers, one on each side. Moving for the door handle, ready to exit, Carlos took in a deep breath and exhaled. He enjoyed and savored the breath it as if it would be his last. As the last of the breath crossed his lips, his muscles tightened, ready to make his move.

Then he heard it, laughter. "She's laughing?" Without realizing it, hearing Sierra laugh relaxed Carlos's tense muscles, and he sank back in his seat. Sierra was the only person he knew who could make a man beg for a moment of her time or fear for his life.

"Dad, look what I found. Can I keep them?" she giggled.

"Dad?" Carlos said under his breath. "I'm thirty-five." Mentally shaking his head, he replied, "No, we have horses to pick up. Let's go!" He raised his hand to say hi to the two men.

"Sorry, boys, I have to run," Sierra said with a hint of sadness in her voice as she gave each of them a pouty face and began to walk backward to the driver's door.

"How will we meet you again, madam?" one of the soldiers asked, enchanted by her beauty.

"I told you boys. Tonight. Hope you can make it," she said and then slowly pulled the sucker from her lips and gave them a wink.

"We have to go, Daughter," Carlos said, lightly growling the last part.

Jumping in the truck, Sierra waved the sucker at the two men before placing it back in her mouth. The two soldiers slowly walked over to their companions, occasionally looking back in the hopes of getting just one more glimpse of Sierra as she began to drive away.

"Dad? Dad?" Carlos asked as they were once again on their way.

"Relax. They bought it."

"Next exit, Daughter," he said sarcastically as she let out a little snicker. "You know I am only thirty-five, right?" Carlos said as they turned on to the exit to pick up Smith, Kate, and the rest of the team.

Reluctantly dropping the topic, Carlos asked, "Where to now?" There was a hint of hurt in his voice.

"Karnic said to drive to the end. It will stop at the river. After that, we sit and wait—they will find us."

Once at the end of the street, Sierra looped the truck around so that the back gate of the trailer was to the river. This put them facing in the proper direction for a quick exit. Once set, she reached down and retrieved a radio taken from the supply room at the armory. "White One, this is Goldilocks with back to the river."

"Goldilocks?" Carlos asked. "Couldn't have come up with a better call sign?"

"White One, copy."

"Did it not work?" Sierra asked as she adjusted her hat and watched for any signs of trouble. Carlos did the same.

After a few minutes, Sierra could sense that Carlos was watching for something, something she must have missed—what, she could not put a finger on. She watched as cars crossed the street they planned to exit on. Something had definitely caught Carlos's attention. Sierra felt the change in him. The ability to judge others' emotions had always been something Sierra possessed, and it was something she had come to rely on. In all her life, she had only met one person whose emotions she could not read and who drove her crazy. Karnic.

"There!" Carlos blurted out. "That SUV has crossed at least four times now. They must be looking for White One." Years of law enforcement had trained Carlos to see patterns, and this was an easy one to track. At the same time, the two of them felt a shift in the truck and directed their eyes to the mirrors. They watched as figures passed from the shrubs to the back of the trailer, and moments later they heard the gate of the trailer closing.

Understanding just what had taken place, Sierra once again grabbed the mic on the radio. "Goldilocks has the bear tucked away."

Military radio etiquette was not something Sierra had learned, but for those at the other end, the message was still loud and clear.

Chapter 45

THE RUN

Waking up early in the morning had become a natural occurrence for Todd. After fifteen years of service in the military, sleeping past five was something his body just would not allow, no matter how hard Todd tried. The morning started like any with stretching in bed, working the stiff muscles and joints. Military life was not easy for a soldier who had put his all into it. Whenever the opportunity for training schools had become available, he had been the first to request, and with his military record, he had always been approved without question.

The military had been his life, and now it was over. Nothing in all the training he had prepared him for this—waking with no purpose or goals set for the day. Civilian life was something Todd was not cut out for. Service to his country was what he lived for. Unfortunately due to the recent cuts, he had been let go, and something about it did not sit right. Each morning over the last six months, he had thought about what had happened and about the day he had reported to his commanding officer and received the news of his pending discharge.

"With all my training and experience, why me?" Todd asked the silent room around him, even though he knew there would be no reply.

Within a few minutes, as Todd turned his body to begin the day, the question repeated itself in his mind like a scratched record. Standing in front of the toilet and relieving the pressure from his bladder, Todd peered through a small window into the darkness concealing the forest beyond—he imagined troops marching by on their way to morning physical training, calling out cadences as they marched in step. He could almost hear it as if it were real. "Mama, Mama. Can't you see what the army has done to me? They took away my faded jeans. Now I'm wearing army greens..." Once he flushed, the daydream ended, and it was back to civilian life. To Todd, there was nothing sadder than a soldier without a mission.

Slipping into his military PT uniform each morning provided Todd with the sense of belonging that he craved. It was the only part of his former life that he felt comfortable wearing now that he was discharged. Once properly dressed, with his reflective belt secured around his waist, Todd liked what he saw standing in front of the mirror over the sink. As he observed the man staring back at him, Todd could find no fault, except for the two-inch facial hair that now covered a once-chiseled chin. The idea was to help make the transition easier—even now, Todd wanted to cut it from his face. Like every other morning, he reached up, ran his fingers through the facial hair, turned away, and let out a sigh.

Looking down at his uniform as he made his way into the kitchen provided Todd with a little encouragement. He felt that he was still in the same great shape, if not better, mostly from the longer workouts. When the workout was over, he would not be putting on his uniform for the day—rather, he'd be wearing jeans and a T-shirt.

As he readied the coffeemaker, the same thought brightened his morning as it did every other. *At least the coffee was better.* With the timer set, he began his workout with stretching in the living room. This was the only part he disliked, although had learned long ago that he needed it as the years passed.

After ten minutes, his body was ready for his morning run to begin, and Todd was looking forward to it. With his new home located in the Ozarks, the run provided him with hills to conquer, great scenery, animals, and fresh air. Now that it was springtime, Todd hoped the scenery would be even better with dogwoods blooming and birds chirping.

On his way through the house to the back door, Todd always made the same stop. The one thing he couldn't have on all the military facilities he had traveled to were his weapons, and now that he could, he had many. Todd peered into his ultimate man cave just to ensure that everything was as it should be. As with every other day, this was going to be his next activity: reloading brass he had picked up from the range the night before to ensure that it was cleaned and ready. Todd flipped the switch of the new tumbler system, which had arrived the day before. With everything in its place, he high-stepped to begin the run.

As Todd went through the door and jogged down the driveway, the cool valley air hit his skin, creating goose bumps and standing his hair up like little rockets preparing for takeoff. The scent of spring rushed through his nostrils with every breath and filled him with its soothing aroma. In the distance, light was breaking over the horizon, creating a carnival of colors. This is what he had hoped for; with Todd's eyes focused on the brilliant lights, a rush of energy filled him. Every step brought more speed, as if he were chasing the light before it was gone. Soon the colors would fade away as the sun struggled to overtake the darkness.

As the sun won its battle against the night, Todd could now see the beautiful dogwood blooms all through the forests on either side of the road. He looked at how they stood out from the still seemingly lifeless trees around them. Every mile brought more beauty, and it saddened him to know that the beauty would end in only a few days' time, as petals would fall to the ground, one by one, only to be reclaimed by the earth for yet another long year.

Enjoying the morning air, Todd ran and ran, sweat soaking his shirt to the point that it could not hold another drop. Watching as morning commuters passed on their way to work, he placed one foot after the other, thinking only of the cool air rushing across his skin. With just over a mile left before home this was the point of the run that he felt the most and pushed his body the most, all focus was on gaining more speed.

The serenity was abruptly violated by the rush of vehicles traveling in a tight convoy. Startled by the instant change, Todd directed his focus to them. Deep down, he felt a twinge in his gut and came to a full stop as the tail of the convoy slowed. As he watched the three white Hummers pull quickly into his neighbor's drive, Todd noticed the two bold blue letters, *UN*, upon a side door. Truly puzzled as to why the Conway's would be getting a visit from anyone in the

United Nations or as to what the United Nations was even doing in the United States, Todd once again began running.

The closer he came to the Conway's' drive, the stronger the twinge in his gut became. Without warning, Todd could hear the unmistakable sound of Roy Conway's scream: "I'LL BE DAMNED!" It was then followed by the report of shotgun fire. The shot was followed by automatic fire, which was clearly not Roy's.

As he watched, Todd realized that he was no longer on his feet but had taken cover in the ditch running along the highway. From that position, he watched as soldiers in blue and black uniforms rushed into the Conway's' home. Then once again he heard a short burst of automatic fire. Focusing on what remained of Roy's body, Todd could not register what he had just witnessed.

Todd watched as the soldiers carried the few firearms the Conway's owned out to their Hummers. Before they placed the firearms inside the vehicles, Todd watched as one held up the weapons while another seemed to be looking at a clipboard.

"My God," Todd said to himself. "It's a checklist!"

Todd quickly turned on his belly and low crawled to the woods in hopes of not being seen; the only thing on his mind was getting back home. As he crawled deeper into the woods, the image of what had just occurred kept playing in his thoughts. Todd had stopped watching TV and listening to the news months ago. None of it made sense to the way he saw the world, so his solution had been to not play the game. Crawling on his belly through the woods with rocks cutting and bruising his body, Todd wished he had.

Now deep into the woodland, Todd quickly leaped to his feet and ran, moving through the forest as if returning a game-winning kick in the Super Bowl— moving around a tree here, dodging a limb there, and running with every bit of energy and muscle strength that could be summoned. Then a thought struck him. *Am I next?* The thought commanded his body to move faster, but it failed— there was simply no more speed to be had.

With glimpses of his home in sight from between the trees, Todd's speed began to reduce to a jog. His eyes focused on the driveway as more of it came into view. Todd watched for the slightest sign of the UN vehicles and felt lucky that they were not there. His speed was once again restored. Bursting from the forest, Todd ran for the back sliding doors located at the rear of his home. Leaping upon the deck and sliding it to one side before a second foot was planted, he was home. But his home no longer felt as a home should.

Now standing where he had been stretching just thirty minutes ago, the one thought Todd had was to get moving. Once again he moved with all the speed he had left to his man cave. Normally, entering the room brought him ease—now, there was only concern: concern that he might not be able to get everything loaded in his truck before they showed. Todd grabbed his rifles, pistols, and ammunition, making trip after trip to his truck—it seemed to have no end.

Get moving, Todd thought as he looked at what was left in the room, but he knew there would not be time. *One last thing.* Todd reached out and grabbed his body armor and sprinted from the room and out through the door leading into the garage where his truck was waiting. He entered his truck. Seated behind the steering wheel, he placed the pistol in his hand on the cup holder next to him and took a breath, wondering if he was overreacting. After a few seconds, Todd thought, *If I am, then this will just be a nice drive.* Reaching up to the visor and striking the button of the garage door remote, Todd started the truck while he waited for the garage door to open.

Inch by slow inch, the garage door opened, and then Todd's question was answered as the door opened to reveal boots. Grabbing the pistol to his side with one hand and opening his driver's door with the other, Todd felt instinct take over. After witnessing what had happened to the Conway family, Todd had already concluded there would be no talking to the soldiers, so he went limp and dropped to the concrete floor, rolling and firing.

Rounds from his Glock 17 flew true and struck the first two men in the legs. As the two fell, Todd directed his fire to the others who were advancing from the second vehicle. As the bullets struck home and as others struck the concrete where he once had been, Todd was on his feet, moving and firing more rounds into the two who were holding their legs. After dropping his pistol, Todd began sending rounds from a now-deceased man's rifle before the pistol made contact with the ground. Todd placed rounds in the neck of one man just above his vest. As Todd's last round made contact, he pointed his weapon to what he hoped was the last of them.

With his hands going up and his rifle falling to the ground, the man yelled with a thick French accent, "Don't shoot! Don't shoot!"

"Then don't move." The threat was made that much more believable by the tone in which it was delivered—not as a yell but in a calm, cool, gruff voice, which made all three words sound as one. The messaged was received. *Now what am I going to do with this guy?* Todd thought to himself.

"In the garage," Todd ordered and signaled with the rifle the direction he wanted the man to move just in case the man's English was not up for the challenge. Walking slowly to ensure that he made no sudden movement, the UN soldier neared the entrance of the garage with Todd directly behind him. As soon as the first of the soldier's boots passed the threshold, the man felt a blinding pain in the back of his skull. Quickly his world darkened as he felt himself falling forward. Behind him Todd whipped off the rifles buttstock where it had made contact with the back of the man's head.

As the man's forehead bounced up from the concrete floor with a strong bass tone, Todd puckered his face. *Ew, wow, I am going to remember that*, Todd thought and shook his head as he walked over to the Humvees. Grabbing radios, weapons, notebooks, and IDs, Todd went quickly through everything in the truck and moved the corpse from his path. One last glance at the area, and he had his answer to the question he had asked of himself not five minutes ago.

"No, you are definitely NOT overreacting," Todd said to himself, using the same gruff voice as earlier. Walking back to the truck, Todd looked down at the blood covering the concrete and felt laughter coming. *I am not cleaning that up*, Todd thought.

Then Todd jumped in and started the four-by-four, only to look down and realize he was still wearing his PT uniform. Without wasting any more time, he exited the truck, ran through to the far end of his closet, and ripped his uniform from its hanger. Todd didn't choose his most recent uniform—he hated the digital gray with a passion. Rather, he chose his old BDUs from his first years in the service.

Todd didn't take time to change—instead, he took off the way he was. Driving down to the road, Todd had no destination in mind. After an hour of driving, his eyes spotted an object in the road up ahead. As he closed the distance, Todd wondered what kind of shit he was driving up on. There, in the middle of the road, stood one of the hottest women he had ever laid his eyes on, and she was packing .45s.

Chapter 46

INCOMING

Tired and drained from a long morning and little sleep, Robert walked into the room where Karnic was busy relaying transmissions over the radio. Catching only the last of the transmissions, his body filled with anger.

"Goldilocks has the bears tucked away."

Robert raced over to a window facing the upper parking lot and peered out, praying to see the truck and trailer sitting where Sierra had parked it, but where it once had been contained nothing but empty space.

Karnic lowered the mic to the table beside the RTO. Seeing Robert's movement and knowing that the protective nature of Sierra's brother was about to surface, Karnic prepared himself as Robert turned with his fist clenched and slowly walked across the room in his direction.

"Where did you send her, you son of a bitch?" The words rumbled through Robert's teeth as he swung a powerful blow and made contact with Karnic's left cheekbone. Those present in the room stood as still as statues as Karnic raised his hand and signaled them to freeze. Karnic looked Robert in the eye and knew that he would have reacted the same had the roles been reversed.

"That is the only one you get," Karnic said calmly, rubbing the soreness away.

"Where is she?" asked Robert, barely able to control himself as all his muscles tightened and his fists got ready to inflict justice on the person who had placed his sister in danger. Not that she had been selling cookies the last few months, but at least he had been there to watch her back.

"I understand, Robert. I do. She is safe. Carlos is with her—they were the least conspicuous, and that is what was needed for the pickup of White One. She just checked in and reported that they have them and are on the way back. Nothing to be alarmed about." Karnic relayed the information with ease in his voice. Karnic was relieved that Robert had not found out earlier.

"Nothing to be alarmed about?" Robert asked. "You don't know my sister." He shook his head.

"Ridge Runner, this is Red One. We are two minutes out. Over."

"Can we put this on hold?" Karnic asked as if it was a question, but Robert understood it to be more. "They're coming in, and I could use you for overwatch."

"We will be picking this up again later, and you had better hope nothing happens to her," Robert replied. He stopped in the doorway with his rifle strapped to his back for Karnic to see as a silent reminder that Robert had the means to enforce this clear threat.

Exiting, Robert moved quickly to higher ground while pushing the thought of Sierra from his mind the best he could. Now focusing on the here and now, Robert reaching an area overlooking the front gates and lay in the morning dew that was sprinkled upon the green grass. Readying himself, he checked and flipped the scope covers open as he drew the weapon tightly into his shoulder. Robert took deep breaths as he positioned his left hand under the rear of the stock, watched over the road, and waited for the new arrivals. The wait was not long—he could see the two buses full of straw soldiers rolling for the safety of the gates.

Through the magnified scope mounted above his Noreen .30-06, Robert could see that those men had had a difficult morning. Countless holes pierced the steel; little glass remained, same with the paint. From closer observation, Robert could see just how lucky they were to be close to the gates as segments of rear tires spun violently around and flew off one section at a time. Had it not been for the two tires on each side at the rear, they would have ended their run long ago. Now they were closing in on a point near the railroad tracks.

Beyond the two buses, Robert could see those who had done much of the damage: four SUVs with the letters *SCN* stenciled across the hood. The sight of them agitated Robert a great deal. Knowing that they were not Americans eased his feelings about raining lead down upon them. With the last of the two buses nearing the tracks and Robert's crosshairs placed upon the chest of the first driver, it was time.

As he exhaled the air from his lungs, Robert's trigger finger began applying pressure to the trigger. The power of the rifle was unleashed simultaneously with the last of the air contained in his lungs passing from his body. Cutting with ease through the morning air, the bullet struck as Robert had desired, piercing the glass windshield, moving on to its final destination, and then painting the inside of the windshield red.

Robert watched as the lead car swerved sideways and skidded toward the tracks. As both tires on the passenger side made contact with the steel, he could see the occupant being ejected and clinging to nothing but air as the car began its roll. Robert watched as it tumbled round and round—by the second flip, the former occupant was no longer hanging out the window, and in his place was only red.

Before the first car had stopped rolling, those who followed were too distracted by the vision of the car's demise to notice the flashes of fire as bullets exited muzzles. From both sides of the road where the lead car had once been, two 240 Bravo machine guns unleashed their fury upon the car's companions. Unarmored, the SUVs resisted little—instead, they veered off the road or came to a slow, rolling stop in the road. Within a matter of seconds, their pursuit had ended, with few of them having time to realize that it had.

Thanks to the magnification of his scope, it seemed to Robert that he had watched everything unfold from the front row seat. Robert felt little for those who didn't belong here and only sought to do harm to his country. With the first of the groups now safe inside the gates, Robert's thoughts returned to Sierra.

Chapter 47

SIERRA'S RETURN TO BASE

Even though she had a full load in the trailer attached to the back of her truck, Sierra waited. With the engine running, she sat while the truck idled. Carlos looked over and wondered what she could be waiting for—he knew that the black SUV they had seen cross the street a few blocks down would soon close in on their position. Watching for the vehicle, he could see how busy the streets and sidewalks had become within a few minutes. *All the people just going about their day*, Carlos thought.

Just as he opened his mouth to ask why they were still sitting there when they were apparently being hunted, the black SUV appeared around the corner of the next block. Making the turn, with tires screeching, the SUV headed straight for the truck where they still sat idling.

"You think it might be a good time to move now?" The SUV was now only yards away—smoke rose from between its tires and the pavement as the three tons of steel and men came to a halt.

"Now we are really screwed," Carlos said as he checked his weapon and reached for the door handle to exit and begin the fight.

"Not yet, ranger boy!" Drawing her pistols from their beaten black leather holster, Sierra swiftly took aim at the grill, now only a few car lengths away.

Almost sounding as one, two shots rang out. Sierra had placed the shots not at the driver or the passenger but into the grill, which ensured that no matter the number of people in the car, it would not be following them. As engine coolant began pouring at a fast rate onto the pavement, Sierra dropped the shifter into drive and hit the gas, launching the truck forward around the SUV. Unlike in the movies, cars in the real world cannot take numerous bullets and still stay mobile. The vehicle was moving nowhere with two slugs deeply embedded into the radiator.

Their teeth chattering as the truck tires rumbled over cobblestone streets, Sierra's cargo watched those who still slept as they barreled down the narrow streets. As she approached the end of the street, Sierra could see traffic lights in the distance turning red, yet it seemed to not bother her as she listened to Carlos inform her of their situation—a situation she was well aware of. As Sierra let up on the accelerator a hundred feet from the light, the passengers trapped in the trailer relaxed, thinking the wild ride was close to its end. The feeling only lasted a few seconds—then, they were all thrown to one side of the trailer.

As Sierra spun the steering wheel to the left as if she were playing *Wheel of Fortune*, Carlos screamed at her, "Why does it have to be all or nothing with you?" Tires screeched, and brakes locked up all around them. The sound of breaking glass, horns, and twisting metal came from all around. Sierra felt a little relief as her foot pressed on the accelerator and she took them down the road. The trailer was fighting to get free, and the men inside were holding on with all their might. Soon, they were barreling down the highway they had come on, and Carlos felt more at ease.

As they lay on the trailer floor, Sgt. Smith and Kate looked at each other— they both had expressions on their faces that seemed to ask the other what had just happened. Shaking off the turmoil that just occurred, they began checking on the other men and found only bruises and sprains. Sgt. Smith and Kate got on their feet and then looked out through the spaces of the rails over the highway, where they saw only commuters.

"Looks like we are clear. Anything on your side, Kate?" Smith asked as the air rushed in from all sides with a thunderous, howling roar.

"All clear here," Kate replied while turning away from the trailer's side and letting her body slide down to the floor once again. Laying her head back against the side wall, she looked up at Sgt. Smith as he kept watch. "You know I was discharged from service only nine months ago."

Smith turned his head slightly to acknowledge that he was listening. Seeing his actions, Kate continued, "During that time, I have not exercised. Had I known I would be sitting in the middle of a revolution against my own government, I would have doubled my workout." Kate closed her eyes and laughed at the thought.

After a few seconds of reflection, she began once again. "You know, back in Saint Louis, right before things turned, I was telling myself over and over that it's not my problem." The anguish in Kate's voice could be felt by all. "I was still repeating that in my mind as I drew and fired again and again."

Smith turned to face her. "Do you wish you would have stayed home now?" he asked with empathy.

Looking up at him with a straight face devoid of any emotion, Kate replied, "NO. Didn't you listen to what I just said? I wish I would have exercised."

Throughout the trailer, laughter erupted.

Then Mack spoke. "How do you think I feel? I was discharged in 1973."

Once again, laughter rang out, even louder than before.

Carlos sat silently as they drove down the highway. He reflected on the recent events and now understood why Sierra had chosen to sit waiting for the SUV to get so close. Feeling as if he should say something to Sierra, he said, "I had my doubts about you back there, but you did the right thing."

Sierra could see the exit where the UN vehicles sat swiftly approaching. She turned to Carlos. "Well, you might not like this." And she raised her revolver and fired the remaining four shots contained within. Three of the four flew harmlessly through the air and struck the side of the gas station. The fourth shattered the glass from a UN vehicle.

"What the hell!" Carlos screamed in reply while readying his rifle. "Do you have a death wish?" The logic of what Sierra had just done was lost upon him.

Looking out the back glass, he could see only a long, white snake with blue spots heading down the exit ramp. Carlos even imagined the head hissing at him. "Well, to answer your question, HELL, NO!" Sierra answered Carlos's question.

Carlos's continued "Well I do not think it was right! And it looks like many more have showed up since we stopped."

Looking over at her driver's-side mirror and watching as the UN vehicles crossed the median, Sierra felt that she might have made a bad call for the first time since leaving the ranch.

With the ear-piercing gunfire, all the laughter in the trailer drew to an abrupt end. The trailer's inhabitants looked at one another, puzzled, as they all made their way to an opening in the trailer's wall.

"Holy shit!" Darrian shouted as he spotted the white vehicles giving chase.

Kate looked up at the inexperienced young man who had just spoken and grabbed him by his gear to drag him down.

"Stay low!" Kate shouted out to the others as they prepared for what was to come.

As Sgt. Smith watched the white UN vehicles closing in, he could not believe what his eyes where telling him. "We are being chased by the United Nations?" he said to himself. "This just keeps getting better and better." He slapped the bottom of the magazine in his M4 rifle to ensure it was seated and ready, and then he checked his ammo pouches for easy access.

"Keep your weapons inside and do not fire until I give the order!" Carlos ordered. He was focused—he knew that a firefight was at hand. A firefight he could have not have imagined. A firefight from a horse trailer doing sixty-five and accelerating.

"Sergeant, they are on us!" one soldier let out, with panic in his voice.

"Hold, hold. Let them get alongside. On my command, aim for the driver!"

Seconds passed as they grew ever closer and began maneuvering along both sides of the truck.

"Ready! FIRE! FIRE!"

Carlos watched as the UN vehicles closed in. Two hundred, one hundred, fifty yards, and still nothing from those in the trailer. The closer the snake came, the faster his heart beat. He just kept thinking about the ten miles they needed to cover and could not see a way to do so with so many coming to stop them.

"If they will not fire, I will," Carlos said as he grabbed the window crank and began lowering the window.

"Wait."

That one soft-spoken word, accompanied by a tender squeeze of an angel's hand upon his shoulder, instantly slowed Carlos's heartbeat. As he was led back into his seat by the subtle pressure Sierra applied, he relaxed.

"Just wait."

He listened as Sierra spoke softly.

Looking over at his mirror, he watched as the white snake wrapped itself around them.

Chapter 48

ANGELIQUE DIVIDED

E verything went very quiet, yet Angelique heard everything. With both pistols drawn, Angelique watched as those she had served with and trusted for years turned on one another. Cameron and Ken decided quickly where they stood. Believing Angelique, they faced down those that they, too, had trained and served with. Jeff held his weapon low. Angelique looked over the chaos taking place before her and watched as orders were shouted and demands made.

"How far is this going to go?" she asked herself, not wanting to get into a firefight with those she once served beside.

Struggling with the situation, Jeff's mind raced, and his emotions ran high. Visions of his past service with Angelique swirled and mixed with visions of the practical consequences of turning against the agency. Then it became clear to him that there were only two real choices. Be hunted as a criminal or praised as a hero. Suddenly a hatred for Angelique for putting him in this position bubbled up inside him.

The hatred grew faster and faster as the seconds ticked by until Jeff's path became clear to him. Raising his weapon once more, he watched through the optics as the red dot moved across the pavement. With his finger planted firmly on the trigger, by the time the dot reached Angelique's boot, Jeff was ready to fire. He watched as the red dot ran the length of her leg and across her finely tuned abs and settled between her breasts. With his trigger already in motion to send its fury upon her, Jeff knew it would all be over within a second.

Stunned by the rifle fire, the agents stopped demanding that the others drop their weapons. Each looked to see where the shot had come from and who had been hit by it. All eyes turned toward Angelique.

Chapter 49

CATCHING UP

" Fire! Fire!"
The moment all in the trailer had been waiting for had come. The wait seemed almost too much for most to endure as the UN vehicles closed in and wrapped around them. It was now time. Before the second order to fire had been spoken, rifles slid through the slits all around the trailer, giving it the look of a porcupine.

Sgt. Smith focused on the driver as his and many other rifles slid through. He watched as the occupants' faces lost all color—the sudden overwhelming display froze them in place. With eyes locked, Smith squeezed his trigger, as did many others pressed in alongside him. Blinking as all fired, the driver, along with his car, swerved from the pavement, which was now painted with streaks of red where white once had been.

Carlos sat watching as the snake image in his mind continued to strangle them. Had it not been for the gentle hand upon his shoulder, he would have already begun unwrapping from its grasp. Taking his eyes from the image in the mirror, Carlos looked ahead and asked as if they were just on a road trip, "How do you plan on shaking them?"

"I'm not."

Carlos could not believe her reply to his question. He quickly brought his full attention to Sierra and then back to the highway ahead. Just as she had felt his emotions at the ranch, Sierra could see that Carlos had not yet figured out just what she was thinking and could feel his uneasiness about it. She knew that he needed convincing.

"During our stop at the gas station, they clearly saw we were not carrying anything. I made sure of that. Now we have the element of surprise." Sierra smiled at the thought of what a surprise it would be for them.

"You have been planning this since then?" Carlos could not believe what he had just heard. Before she could reply, a thunderous roar made it impossible. The roar drew Carlos to the mirror, where he saw Sierra's plan begin to unfold. He watched as car after car turned into shredded metal. In his mind, Carlos saw the head of the snake die off as another took its place.

"Well, I didn't plan on this," Sierra remarked as she pointed at the cars ahead.

"What?"

The gunfire was making it virtually impossible to hear what she was saying. Carlos looked in the direction the hand that had calmed him was now pointing.

"That's the commander's Humvee!" he shouted.

Chapter 50

FRONT GATE

"We have a live one over here!" the medic called out.

Sgt. Lee ran over to where the medic stood—they both looked down at a man trying to crawl through the back hatch of what remained of the flipped SUV.

"Take care of him—we need to find out what he knows." As he turned to another soldier, Lee said, "Let Sergeant Karnic knows we have a prisoner and we will bring him to the gym once he is stable."

"Roger, Sergeant," the young soldier said, and was off at a full run to deliver his message.

Looking around at the destruction and thinking about what needed to be done next, Sgt. Lee took charge and sent out orders.

"When you have the prisoner stable, take two men and escort him to the gym."

"Specialist, let's get that vehicle off the road—we can use it for cover."

"Gunners! Are you ready to receive guests?"

Seeing that they were still reloading the 240 Bravo machine gun and knowing the answer did not stop Lee from asking—instead, it was more of a strong suggestion to get ready.

"Almost there, Sergeant!" the lead gunner cried out in response.

"When they arrive, nobody fires until I do! I fire first, and then we open up. Got it?"

"Yes, Sergeant!" came to him from all directions, and Lee knew they would be ready as he watched the preparations quickly being made. Then Lee watched as two of the men came past him with their prisoner. Sgt. Lee still could not believe that the Strong Cities Network, a branch of the United Nations, was operating within the borders of the United States.

"Who are you?" the prisoner asked Smith as he dragged him along.

Without thinking, Smith simply replied, "We, sir, are Americans," and waved the men along as he returned to securing the front gate.

All the way to the gym, men stared at the prisoner with disgust in their eyes. To them, he represented the reason why they were currently considered traitors to their country. Walking through the gym door, the two men released their grip on him and let his beaten body fall to the floor as if they were taking out the trash. Then they stood by his side and waited for Karnic to arrive. It was not a long wait—only a minute passed before they spotted Karnic walking through the doors at the far end of the gym. He was followed by the colonel and a few others.

His eyes drawn to the entrance at the other end, the prisoner looked to see what was heading his way. Still dazed by the flipping of his vehicle and from the low angle of the gym floor, he could not believe his eyes. The first man who entered looked as if his head were going to hit the lights high above, which caused fear to take hold of the prisoner. Then the prisoner focused on his bloodied uniform and thought of how little hope he had of walking away from this place.

"Pick him up." The sound of Karnic's voice terrified the prisoner that much more. The prisoner moaned as the soldier's grabbed hold underneath his arms to raise him to his feet. All the while, he attempted to prepare himself for the worst.

From the standing position, the prisoner could see that his eyes and mind were playing tricks on him. The man was not even close to the ceiling in height but still tall enough to tower over him.

"What is your name?" Karnic asked in a strong bass voice.

Looking the man up and down, Karnic saw clearly that the prisoner had to be in pain as he stood silently supported by his men. While making his observation, Karnic ordered, "Bring me a chair," and continued to watch the man— neither said a word.

Sitting down brought more groans from the prisoner as the two soldiers lowered him to the seat. The prisoner looked up at Karnic, who once again looked taller than he really was.

"*Grazie*," the prisoner said as he settled into the seat.

"*Prego*," Karnic replied, that being one of the very few words he remembered from his time in Italy. "So, my friend, what is your purpose here?"

"I say nothing," the prisoner said with only a touch of an Italian accent.

"Your English is pretty good. Where did you study?"

"I say nothing," the prisoner again replied.

Looking over to one of the men who had just carried him up, Karnic said, "Get us some coffee would you?" as if it were a question, not an order. Seeing the reaction on the man seated before him, Karnic could tell this was going to be easy. "While he is getting the coffee, which I have got to warn you is not going to be good but it does the job, how about we just relax?"

Karnic let out a little laugh as if he and the prisoner were old chums—he didn't bother to ask further questions, and within minutes, an aroma flooded the gym, followed by the soldier holding the cup.

"Thank you, Private," Karnic said as he took the two cups, held one out to the Italian, and took a sip of his own. After a little hesitation, the prisoner reached out for the cup presented to him and began to drink slowly.

"You are right to have warned me," the Italian stated as he took another drink. As the warmth of the drink made its way down, he could feel himself loosen up just a little.

"Well, I have had worse," Karnic said with a smile on his face.

"Me, too. Me, too." The Italian chuckled a little as he spoke.

Karnic observed that the man looked much older than him, and Karnic thought it strange that they would send someone of his age anywhere. "How did you end up here?" Karnic asked with real curiosity.

After a few seconds and another sip, Karnic could tell that the coffee had worked.

"You mean, for a man my age."

It was also obvious to Karnic that the man was no fool.

"I am Luciano. You know what it means?" the Italian asked Karnic as he took another sip. Once he was done, the prisoner did not wait for a reply before answering, "Light of the day."

Karnic stood and tried to understand how the prisoner's "light of the day" connected to current events. Did it mean a new beginning here? Did it mean the new light of the day will bring change? What? The questions kept coming to Karnic as he thought about it to the point that he had to ask.

"How does that connect to everything going on now?"

Taking a sip, the man looked at Karnic over his cup and then replied, "Nothing. I just like to tell people what my name means."

Feeling a little dumb, Karnic wondered if he was not skilled in interrogation, since the man seemed to be using his tactic against him. It was that, or the Italian was just a great conversationalist.

"OK, nice one, Luciano," Karnic said as he relaxed and prepared to play the game. "Listen, we do not want to do you harm, and once we are through talking at some point, we will let you walk out of here. We just don't understand why UN personnel are here on US soil. Can you help me with that?"

The Italian did—even though he did not know a great deal, it was enough. Over the next few minutes, Luciano explained how even being up in years he had been chosen because he spoke great English and how he had been first transferred to the SCN over a year ago.

The information did not set well with Karnic. "So this has been the plan for more than a year?"

"Yes," Luciano replied, a little taken aback by the aggressive manner in which Karnic had asked the question.

"Forgive me, Luciano—my anger is not toward you but toward the idea that my men and I were led here." Forcing himself to regain control, Karnic looked over to the colonel in disbelief.

"Oh, you were not led here. No, you and your men were to be made an example of."

"Example how?" Karnic was thankful about how things were going even though he was not happy about the content of the information. Finishing the last of his coffee, Luciano sat thinking about the question.

"Would you like more?" Luciano asked. Karnic was willing to cook the man a steak if it meant he kept talking.

"*Grazie*," said the Italian. One of the soldiers instantly headed off into the other room.

"Have you ever taken what is called a climate survey?" Luciano asked.

Wondering where this was going, Karnic answered, "Yes, but they were anonymous."

"No, they were not. It seems that they had a way to know who filled them out, and that created a list, which was given to us, of potential radicals."

"Radicals?" Karnic and the others in the room could not believe what they were being told. It was unbelievable to them that such a thing could have taken place, yet here they were.

"Yes, that is why we are here, requested by your government due to the large number in your armed forces." Hearing the door open, Luciano turned his attention to the soldier bringing him his coffee—he welcomed the cup as he felt the caffeine working its way through his bruised body.

Karnic's thoughts turned to the questions contained in the survey, and one stood out. "Would you obey orders to remove firearms from citizens of the United States?" Karnic blurted out. He looked around the room as the other soldiers did the same. "Would you follow orders to fire upon unlawful protesters in the United States?"

The questions had seemed pointless at the time—they'd been mixed in with a great deal of other pointless questions. Now it seemed unreal that answering *no* to such a question could have led to current events.

"At ease," Karnic said, and the room grew quiet. Karnic had to get more information while he could.

Sipping coffee from his the fresh cup, Luciano then continued, "Sergeant, you and your men were not supposed to escape—rather, you were to be put on trial for all to see."

Karnic raised his cup, took his final drink, and handed it off. Processing the new information, he asked, "Do you know how many of you are here?"

"No, but the number is high. Lists were given out for beginning to remove guns from the civilian population this morning. That is what we were preparing for until we received a call that your unit had been spotted."

Rage and disbelief filled the room, and it grew louder. Those present could not process what they had heard. Things were much bigger than they had seemed just ten minutes ago.

"What do they plan on doing now?" Karnic asked, focusing on what was to come.

"I do not know. I am here."

Believing his answer, Karnic had only one last thing to say before departing with the colonel. "Thank you, Luciano; we will see to your needs and send you on your way at the first opportunity."

With Marks close by, Karnic turned and made his way back to the door through which he had entered.

Chapter 51

DECISION MADE CLEAR

S tanding with both .45s and facing down overwhelming odds, Angelique felt
lucky that she was not standing alone facing down the Homeland Security
agents. She was thankful to see three men in the team that she had once trusted with her life. The one thing she wanted now was to get away with Ken,
Cameron, and Jeff and her family and to sort this out with Homeland Security.
Had it not been for Cameron, Ken, and Jeff on the team—well, the odds of
eight against one did not seem possible. Now, with four against five, she stood
with restored confidence.

Angelique clearly didn't see Jeff positioned to the rear just behind Ken, and
her attention turned to Johnathan. "Bring out my parents, and I will be on my
way!" she shouted out over the multitude of demands being thrown around,
most of which were demanding that others put down their weapons.

Movement just on the edge of her vision alerted Angelique's instincts to
take control, and one of her .45s moved to meet the possible threat. In a situation like this, many things that can be considered threats are not. This was not
the time for mistakes.

Angelique adjusted her vision to a possible threat that was slightly faster
than it took for the pistol to move. She watched Jeff raise his weapon and take
aim; Angelique's mind was sent into frenzy as she realized that the movement
was a clear. The Colt in her hand was now on him. As her finger began to

squeeze, Angelique shouted out "JEFF!" Her plea was muffled by the sound of rifle fire.

And then silence. The sound echoed away into the distance as everyone froze in place and looked in Angelique's direction. She still stood with both pistols in her hands; then Angelique twisted to the rear and then back to Jeff, as she watched him go limp.

Looking back once more at the vehicle she had dismissed earlier, Angelique's eyes locked on the smoking rifle that had fired the shot saving her life. Attached to the rifle resting over the side-view mirror was an arm covered in tattoos. She could see that the man inside was wearing an older woodland military uniform, with the sleeves rolled up to his large biceps.

As he gave her an upward nod, again Angelique felt that he was no threat to her and quickly focused back on what she had come there to do. Pointing both of her pistols at Johnathan, she gave her demands, which were heard by all.

"Bring out my parents!"

"Sorry, babe, can't do that. They are going with me." This was a side Angelique had never seen of the man, a side she had not believed was possible.

"You are now an accessory to the murder of a federal officer. All of you are!" Johnathan delivered the news while he struggled to get free of Ken's grasp.

"OK, this is over," said Angelique, closing the distance between her and Johnathan, keeping one pistol on him, and raising the other above her head. As she brought it down on upon his temple, the last thing he heard before unconsciousness was, "Johnathan, you're fired!"

Ken lowered Johnathan to the ground, just off the pavement, and collected his weapon, sliding it into his vest. "I think we all have had enough for one day, don't you, guys?" Ken asked. He said the name of each person remaining in the detail as he finished tucking the pistol away.

With their weapons still trained on Angelique and her new team, the people in the detail look around for guidance. Ken, their squad leader, had joined with the person they were after. One by one, the four of them slowly lowered their weapons.

Seeing that she would have no further resistance, Angelique holstered her .45s. She could see that Ken was still struggling with his decisions, but with only her parents' safety on her mind, it would have to wait. Angelique took two steps, reached out for a door handle, and opened a door of the black beast that was holding her parents inside. Looking in to where she expected the two of them to be, she found nothing but empty seats.

"Where are they?" she demanded as she turned back to Ken.

"Ann, they're not here," Ken replied, turning toward the forest and avoiding eye contact.

"Then take me to where they are." Angelique could not believe that she hadn't seen a third vehicle earlier. After walking over to Ken and stopping alongside him, she stood, letting her body language repeat the question.

"Ann, I'm truly sorry, but I do not know," Ken said with true feeling in his voice. He hung his head.

"They will stick to the main roads, and there is only one way east from here," said Angelique. "They couldn't have got far. Let's go!"

Ken spotted Cameron looking off in the distance.

"What is it?" Ken asked.

Then Ken saw them sitting on top of the hill: white SUVs with a blue dot on the hood.

"Shit! What are they doing here?" Ken asked Cameron, not expecting an answer. "Ann, we have got to go now!" Ken pointed at the convoy of white vehicles coming over the hill. Angelique instantly knew who they were from years of service, and the strategist in her fought against the desire to reach her parents.

"You men, lay your weapons down and run!" she ordered those who had shown their unwillingness to pick a side. Without being told twice, as they watched her hand rest on the pistol secured to her side, they did as she asked.

Todd, who had not said a word since stopping at a weird traffic stop that on any other day would have blown his mind, drew the rifle inside the cab of the truck. Seeing a familiar sight rolling down the road, he began turning his truck around back the way he had come. Because of the narrow road, it took a little while to turn the large truck around. While maneuvering the truck, he watched the blonde giving orders and the black SUVs becoming positioned across the road. After working the truck back in the other direction, Todd looked through the rearview mirror as Angelique, Ken, and Cameron hunkered down along-side the SUVs, preparing to fight. *That is a mistake*, he thought, shaking his head while pressing on the gas pedal.

"Thanks, Cameron, Ken," Angelique said and made eye contact with both of them as they positioned themselves for a fight. It was a wait that all three felt could have been longer. Fire began while the vehicles were still moving, and there was even more of it once they had stopped.

Angelique watched as bullets tore through from one side and passed through to the side of the SUV she was on. Having learned long ago that car doors do not stop bullets, Angelique gave hand signals to the others from her position where she used the motor of the bullet-riddled vehicle as cover to stop the incoming lead. Cameron and Ken both understood what she wanted and began firing from similar positions. Sliding down and rolling onto her belly, Angelique began returning fire by placing one round into each foot or tire in sight.

After firing a dozen shots, her surprise attack from under the SUV was over as she made her way back to the relative safety of front passenger side tire. Where she had been spraying bullets and making contact with the pavement, it had thrown up fragments, which had embedded themselves deep within her skin. Knowing this had been a mistake, she began looking for a way out, but there was nothing. Many of the cars to her rear had already been disabled from gunfire as their occupants huddled in fear.

"I'm OUT!" Cameron called to the others, catching Angelique's attention as she watched him duck back down. Assessing every direction for a way out, they concluded that the woods would be their only hope. The one thing stopping them was the fifty yards of open space between them and the woods. At this point, feeling there were no better options, they signaled one another that they were going to run for the woods. All three checked what ammo they had left and waited to make the run.

Angelique prepared herself to run faster than she ever had before. Looking over to her men, she gave them a quick nod and yelled out to them, "Go! Go! Go!"

She was unafraid of her enemies hearing. Just as they began their run, the sound of tires screaming against pavement overcame that of rifles firing and bullets striking, if only for an instant. Angelique was surprised until she remembered the truck with the driver who had saved her. She ran for it. Following her change in direction, Angelique felt no need in giving signals or calling out for them. None of them wanted to take the chance of crossing open ground.

Angelique didn't slow down—she used her momentum to carry her to the back of the truck. She landed one foot on the bumper, then flew through the air and into the bed of the truck. She was followed by Cameron and then Ken, who did the same and also let out sounds of pain as they landed.

Before the three had made contact, Todd's foot had already stomped on the accelerator pedal and propelled the truck forward once again, this time with extra cargo.

After traveling a safe distance away, Todd thought about those in the back and decided it was time for them to make their way to the front. He wanted to pull off on one of many gravel roads cutting their way through the rolling hills of the Ozarks. Locating a secluded area, Todd pulled in and watched his new cargo rise up and check out the area.

With her head just above the side rails, Angelique watched what looked like a life-size GI Joe step out of the truck.

"Looks like that is twice today you have saved my ass. Got a name?" she said to the man. Feeling as if nothing could be trusted lately, Angelique held one of her .45s just out of sight.

"Master Sergeant Todd Myers. Recently retired. And you?" He held a 9mm H&K pistol behind him and stood at parade rest while he addressed his new passengers.

"Angelique Carringer, Homeland Security."

Hearing what Angelique said, Todd slowly cocked the pistol carefully so that it would create little noise.

Seeing the reflection of his actions in the paint on the door, Angelique quickly responded, "Don't worry—I believe we have just been fired." Feeling that the man could have just let them die, she relaxed her body language and stood. She helped Cameron up and holstered her pistol.

"Looks as if you might be getting ready for something," she said, admiring the hastily loaded ammunition and weapons covering the bed on which they had landed.

"I ran into a little problem this morning," Todd replied, still not willing to let down his guard to the strangers.

"Guess you could say we all have. Didn't get up on the wrong side of the bed this morning—apparently I woke in the wrong bed instead." Making an attempt to ease things a little, Angelique put on a smile.

"What was all that back there?" Todd asked while raising his chin in the general direction of the firefight.

"Well, these guys and the others picked my parents up from their home, and I wanted them back." Stepping on the side rail of the truck as she made her way out of the bed, Angelique thought of how wrong it was to step with boots on the shiny black paint. Looking over and seeing where a number of bullets had made contact, she didn't give it another thought. "The other was—well, I really do not have an answer for that." Angelique looked over to Ken as he came alongside her.

"How about it, Ken. You know what that was?" she asked as if he might have been holding something back.

"No, they were not with us," Ken answered while looking at her and then back to Todd. The expression on Ken's face begged her to believe him.

"I do." Todd let them off the hook. "You two don't know?" He couldn't believe they wouldn't know. "How do you not? It has even been announced on the radio all morning."

"What has?" Angelique asked. Now very interested in what Todd had to say, Angelique gave him all of her attention, even as Cameron, walking strangely, made his way over to them.

"I think one of the many rifles I landed on molested me," Cameron said as he groaned and rubbed his rear. Though he irritated her, Angelique could always count on Cameron to make her laugh inside, even if the others couldn't tell.

"Carry on, Master Sergeant," Angelique said, seemingly dismissing Cameron's remarks.

"The UN personnel are going around confiscating firearms," Todd said.

Not knowing quite what to say, the three of them looked at one another in disbelief.

"Is that why you are running around with a trunkful of them? Because you heard it on the radio?" Angelique asked. Had she not just been in a firefight with them, she would have thought it a prank some DJ was doing to get ratings.

"No, I watched as they raided my neighbor's house while on my morning run," Todd replied. "After that, I made my way back home through the woods and threw what I could in the back of my truck." Turning his head to the side and looking up as if he had just remembered something, Todd blurted out, "Damn, I left my new tumbler on!"

"What?" Ken asked, not able to figure out how his brass-cleaning machine tied in.

"Nothing. I killed three and left the forth unconscious on my garage floor. Damn, I can't believe I did that." Todd let his hands fall to his side and relaxed his body while still holding his pistol.

"Hey, man, you did what you had to do," Cameron responded, shaking his head in approval.

"What? No, I just got it in, and now I will not get to use it. This sucks."

Neither Angelique nor the two men standing beside her followed along. Instead they thought it best to move the conversation forward.

"Where are you headed now, Master Sergeant?" Angelique felt that redirecting the conversation was the best move to make.

With his hands on his waist, Todd shrugged and replied, "No clue, hadn't planned on killing four people today and going on the run with most of my weapons."

Looking back into the truck bed, Cameron was overcome with one question. "There were more?"

The remark was met by a sharp elbow jab to the ribs from Angelique, followed up with a look that told him to pull it together before she responded to Todd.

"As much as I want to run after those who have my parents…" Angelique said, then paused to collect her thoughts before she continued. "We need to head for Jefferson City."

"What's there?" Todd asked—he was already interested, mostly due to not having any plans ready. At this point, he needed a plan.

"Karnic." As she said his name, Angelique felt as if the world were forcing them together.

Chapter 52

BUMPER TO BUMPER

"What's your plan for this one?" Carlos asked—he had decided at this point that he was just going to enjoy the ride and watched as they closed in on Cdr. Sawyer's Humvee.

"Well, it looks like we are going to be slowing down—might want to get ready!" Sierra said as she began lifting off the accelerator.

"Oh, now you want me to shoot. How about I just let you know the next time I need to piss, and you can tell me if I can go or not?"

"I have so many other clients; not sure if I will have time. I'll try to squeeze you in."

Rolling his eyes while rolling down the window, Carlos thought about how crazy Sierra had made him over the last few months. Then as he saw her reflection in the side mirror, he thought about how much he had enjoyed it. After twisting around and placing his knees in the seat to get a better position from which to return fire, Carlos hung out the window enough to have a clear view. He watched as one white car after the next pulled alongside them, only to be cut up by a multitude of rifles, and then fall back along the road.

"Those guys are stupid," he informed Sierra as he dropped back down into his seat and rolled his window up once again. "Smith and the rest are easily keeping them from overtaking us."

Sierra was growing impatient with traveling fifty-five. As fifty-five mph was close to the top speed of the Humvee, her truck or the Humvee were not going to get there any faster. The next four miles were going to be more frustrating than she could take.

"We had better let 'em know we are bringing company for lunch. Why don't you call it in? I'll have a steak, medium rare," Sierra said.

Carlos just ignored the last part, as he did most of what she said these days. He reached down and picked up the radio from the floor, where it had been thrown during the wild ride. He located the mic and saw that it was in working order. Raising it up to speak, Carlos realized that he didn't have a call sign, and at that moment, he could not think of one he really wanted to be stuck with.

Sierra saw Carlos sitting there with the mic in his hand, ready to speak but not doing so, and she knew instantly why he had not made the call. She helped him out.

"Texan dumbass, later we will work on that peeing schedule," Sierra said. She glanced over at Carlos and gave him a little smile.

Not wanting to get into a verbal match with her that he knew he would not win, Carlos simply pressed the button on the mic and began speaking.

"Ridge Runner, this is Texan. Over," Carlos said.

"Texan, we have been looking forward to hearing from you. Give us a si-trep. Over."

"Ridge Runner, unknown casualties. Ammunition unknown. Four miles out. Coming in hot. Commander's Humvee is in lead. Over."

"Texan, read you Lima-Charlie. We'll be ready. Over."

Chapter 53

ARRIVAL ON POST

Waiting near the radio for information since the last group had arrived, Robert was a little relieved to hear Carlos's voice. They had become close—something that comes easily when you are being hunted together.

Laying down the mic while keeping an eye on Robert, Karnic had begun to speak when the radio came alive once more. "Ridge Runner, this is Cardinal. Over."

"Go for Ridge Runner. Over," Karnic said—he didn't want to waste any time with proper radio etiquette.

"Ridge Runner, we are coming in with two. One privately owned vehicle, one Humvee. Be advised we have friendlies on our six giving 'em hell. Over."

"Roger, Cardinal. They just checked in. We are ready. Over."

"See you in four mics. Cardinal out."

As he began to exit the room, Karnic glanced over to Robert. "What do you say we go be social?"

Karnic did not wait for a response—he knew the answer. Robert moved to the same position as before and prepared himself for quick action by checking his rifle and steadying his aim.

Jumping into the nearby Humvee that sat waiting for his use, Karnic made his way to the front gate. He quickly went to see if everything was ready. Using a single thumbs-up or thumbs-down, he went from those positioned closest to him working his way to the outer perimeter along the tracks. As he stood along-side Smith, Karnic was confident that this would be a success.

"Everything in place?" Karnic asked Smith, who had prepared the welcoming party.

"Yes, Sergeant. The men know what needs to be done," Smith said with confidence he'd gained from the last group's failed pass.

Hearing the engines roar in the distance and head their way, Smith gave the order: "Here they come. Get ready, same as before!"

All men moved closer to the ground, tightened their grips on whatever weapon they held, and prepared for a fight.

Holding his rifle at ready while lying over the Humvee's hood, Karnic positioned himself to be ready. Seeing the first of the first group cresting the hill, he looked around at his men. There was no need in to give them further orders, for they all saw the van, followed by Commander Sawyer's vehicle. Satisfied with what he saw, Karnic's focus turned back to the rifle in his hands.

Gunfire could be heard in the distance as the first two vehicles crossed the track. As the Humvee approached Karnic's position, it slowed, and Sawyer shouted out to him from the unzipped window: "That girl has a hornet's nest on her. So be ready!"

Then, Sawyer signaled his driver to head on up to the main building of the armory. Forward they drove, with the lieutenant governor tucked safely inside.

Before Karnic could relay the message, Sierra came barreling over the hill with her wagon of destruction close behind. Sierra's vehicle picked up speed as it rolled down the hill, and Karnic could tell they were in a hurry. To his surprise, those who had just seconds ago been doing their best to stop them were no longer doing so.

Hitting the tracks at a high rate of speed, the heavy truck almost separated from the pavement beneath. Sierra didn't let up until they were back in the parking lot from which she had begun her journey.

Karnic looked back to the crest of the hill, then watched as they blocked the road with their vehicles.

"Smart," he said. "Be ready, men. They are sure to come at some point!"

Karnic jumped back into the Humvee and drove to check on the new arrivals. Driving up to the parking lot, he saw Robert running over to do the same. Even though the drive took seconds, Karnic felt as if the parking lot were miles away. Karnic hoped that nothing had happened to Sierra. The last thing he needed today was to go at it with her brother.

After the back gate swung open, Karnic positioned the Humvee just behind Sierra's trailer. Slowly those inside stepped out, their faces covered in black suit from weapons fire. The parking lot was showered with brass rolling from the trailer floor, as if it'd had a winning pull on a slot machine.

Walking over to them, Karnic could see that they had fought hard and for some time. Looking at the bullet holes covering the trailer's surface, Karnic dreaded hearing the casualty report. It had been a long morning, and it wasn't even noon. Sgt. Smith assisted Kate as they exited—they had blood running from both of their faces, some from the wounds they had suffered and blood from bullets striking others. Karnic ran over, as did Sawyer, who stopped as he spotted Kate.

"How bad you hit?" Sawyer asked, with a great deal of concern.

"It's nothing," replied Kate. Though it didn't look like nothing, Sawyer felt some relief in knowing that she was able to hop along with some assistance.

"Some shrapnel, but I believe I sprained my ankle," said Kate. "Doesn't that girl know trucks can't fly?" Kate was using humor to calm Sawyer's concerns about her wound.

"Smith, what happened?" Karnic asked while looking around. He spotted Robert talking with his sister and figured all must be well with her since Robert hadn't rushed over.

"She what?" Karnic asked after hearing that Sierra was the reason they had been pursued, Karnic wondered what had gotten into the girl.

"Yeah, I couldn't believe it either at the time, Sergeant, but I tell you it was great," Smith said, still high from the adrenaline rush—he looked ready for more. "Sergeant, we gave them hell. The highway is littered with them. With the exception of one young private with a concussion after a round to his helmet, we came out of it with little in the way of casualties."

"Very well. Go get yourself checked out; the day isn't over yet." Karnic said as he patted the young sergeant on the shoulder, Karnic thought it was time to have a talk with Sierra.

She wasn't hard to find. Karnic just followed the sound of Robert's voice laying down his set of rules to her. Karnic let out a short sarcastic laugh at the very thought. *Like that girl is going to listen.* As Karnic neared, Robert spotted him approaching over Sierra's shoulder and grew quiet.

Still a distance away, Karnic addressed Robert: "Can I have a word with your sister?"

Before the question was finished, Sierra turned slightly his way and seemed to struggle to pull the lollipop from her lips before she answered.

"Sure thing, cowboy," Sierra said with a flirtatious grin as her brown hair puffed up in the wind from under the dirty old cap.

Karnic stopped in his tracks, turned, and said, "I'll check in with you later."

He wondered where the hell she had gotten the sucker.

Chapter 54

UNDERGROUND

In a remote area buried deep underground, a portly man walked with his yes-men all trailing behind. All the yes-men displayed row of medals given to them for one insignificant duty or another with honor—the medals dangled from their pressed uniforms. Their shiny black shoes clattered as they followed the porky, childlike man, who was seemingly too big for the narrow passages. They waited for an opportunity to fulfill any need he may have.

They walked through the twist and turns. All could hear the labored breathing of their leader, yet none dared speak. Nearing their objective, they heard sounds of computers operating, keys being pressed, and orders being given. As they made the last of the turns, much like they had on previous occasions, the noises grew louder.

With their supreme leader entered the tight work space, all grew quiet. Orders stopped, typing ceased, and some people even stopped breathing. None of the occupants dared to draw the supreme leader's attention—past experiences had taught them that it was not a good idea.

One man stopped in the middle of giving an order, snapped to attention, and rendered greetings. His leader stood, unamused. Hanging from the ceiling just above his head was an image of Earth divided by longitude and latitude lines with only unlabeled landmasses represented. The image currently showed the outline of North America, across which three lines from opposing sides of the circle were traveling.

Speaking in his Korean tongue, the supreme leader addressed the man. "Is everything ready?"

The man quickly bowed before answering. "Supreme Leader, everything is as it should be."

The supreme leader was expressionless except for the look of boredom—he slightly lowered his head in acknowledgment.

"It had better be. We didn't spend the last year sending those things into space for it to fail," the supreme leader said. All in the tight area understood what he meant: a forced labor camp or, if they were lucky, death.

"We have only two hours to wait. It will take place soon, Supreme Leader."

With a slight wave of his hand, Kim Jong-un, the supreme leader of North Korea, ordered those in the room to continue. He walked over to where several large red-velvet chairs were positioned for his comfort—the chairs took up a quarter of the room in the tight work space. He sat. Those who followed remained standing off to the side and looked out over the room.

Once a beautiful servant delivered the supreme commander's favorite soft drink, he addressed the man seated to his left.

"Impressed yet? As you can see, it is as I said," the supreme leader said.

Not caring to gaze upon the man-boy, Chines diplomat stared about the room as his translator's voice came over his earpiece; the translator used his native tongue, Mandarin, which is spoken throughout most of China. With no fear of the supreme leader, the man, Chee, spoke his mind.

"We have thousands depending on this project. If it fails, so do you," Chee said.

Knowing that Chee meant what he had said, Kim sat in silence, drank his soda, and watched the images on the screen grow closer.

Chee turned to the man on his other side. "Are your people ready in the States?"

Without moving from the darkness, the man he had just addressed replied in English. "My people are the least of your worries if this doesn't work. We didn't allow that fat shit to develop nuclear technology for nothing. Just see that it works, Chee, and remember how this ends"

Chapter 55

THE UNKNOWN

"What's the plan?" Karnic asked three men who were seated in Marks office. None of them spoke—they all merely sat, looked at the others, and waited for suggestions. Karnic paced from one end of the room to the other as he went over scenarios in his mind. None of them played out to their advantage.

Karnic couldn't take the silence any longer.

"OK, what do we know?" Karnic asked. He looked over at the others. "We know martial law has been declared in Missouri but aren't sure how far it stretches. We know UN soldiers are at the front gate. By all accounts, the governor has run off. And we have over four hundred men and weapons." Karnic stopped in his pacing to address those in front of him. "We also have an inside man."

After opening the door to the office, Karnic signaled for one of the guards posted outside to come over.

"Locate Robert and bring him here. Go," Karnic said. Off the soldier ran.

"They are also planning on removing all personal firearms from individuals, Sergeant." The lieutenant governor added to the list. From the expressions on their faces, the lieutenant governor realized that they must not have known.

"Who is going to? The governor?" Sawyer asked, straightening up in his seat.

"They are planning on using the UN troops, along with those from our military they feel would do so. When I protested against the idea—well, you saw where I was." They could feel sorrow in his voice for not being able to stop the day's events.

"OK then, Governor. We need to get your voice heard. If we do not have the people behind us—" Karnic looked around the room. He continued calmly. "We all die here."

There was a knock on the door, and everyone focused on the person on the other side. "Enter," Karnic called out.

Karnic got right to the point. "Robert, we need intel from your buddy."

Without asking why, Robert pulled the phone from his pocket and dialed. After two rings, he hung up.

"It may be just a minute," he informed the group. "Anything particular you would like to know?"

"Yes, anything about our actions here and whatever other information he can relay," Karnic said. His theory was: keep it simple.

Ring. Ring. Ring.

A few minutes passed. Robert spoke with Sam while the other men watched and waited. Each man grew impatient as the conversation carried on.

"OK, stay safe, Sam."

It was time. The one thing every successful operation needed is information.

"What does Sam have for us, Robert?" Karnic asked impatiently.

"It looks as if the governor here is correct. They have set up firearms-check-in stations all around the state. UN troops are spearheading the operation and going door to door with a list of potential gun owners. A great deal of people are resisting, and there are a number of skirmishes taking place."

"Good God!" the governor said. "I told them that would happen."

"What about our actions? Any word on what they are sending our way?" Karnic asked—he was more interested in this than the other information provided so far.

"Nothing."

"Nothing?" Karnic asked, not believing Robert's answer to his question.

"That's right, Karnic. From what Sam told me, nothing has come over the wire. He feels as if it is being kept hushed up. He did say that the governor is supposed to speak today in Saint Louis."

"So they are planning on just containing us here."

While in deep thought, Karnic raised his right hand and rubbed the stubble on his chin. Sawyer recognized the look on Karnic's face and knew that Karnic was putting together a plan—one that Sawyer knew he was certainly to be happy with.

"Colonel, you know the community. Can you get a news crew in here?"

"Yes, I have someone I can call, but how do you plan on getting them to the armory?" Sawyer thought that Karnic had forgotten about the mass of UN soldiers blocking the way.

"Sir, they are going to have to take a train. Train tracks, that is."

Quickly understanding where Karnic was going with his plan, Marks began looking through his desk for the number he wanted. Locating the number, he began dialing while Karnic explained the rest of his plan.

"We have to get out the word about what is taking place, gentlemen. The only way they can gain total control is to do away with the Constitution, and that would require a civil war. After that they could simply say it failed and write up a new constitution."

Karnic felt as if he had put it all together. Now it was time to let the world know.

"Governor, you and Commander Sawyer here will have to convince them," Karnic said and gave Sawyer a pat on the shoulder as he spoke. Karnic knew that Sawyer hated being on camera. "While you two work on what you are going to say, I will let the front gate know to expect guests."

Karnic looked over to the colonel for a thumbs-up or thumbs-down about the reporters. He received an encouraging sight as the colonel's thumb went high in the air and was followed by, "Twenty minutes."

With that, Karnic exited for the front gate. He took Robert with him.

Chapter 56

GUESTS KEEP
COMING IN

M en of the U.C.M. waited and watched those atop the hill just past the front gate, waiting for them to make their move. Most waited to be struck down by Hellfire missiles from a drone flying high above—they would never see it coming. Still, they held their ground, tucked into shallow foxholes, ready to fight for what they believed in.

While keeping a close eye on the enemy perched atop the hill, Karnic climbed out of his Humvee and walked over to each position, as if he were daring the enemy to fire upon him. Seeing him walk around with such confidence gave his men confidence and eased their thoughts of what would most likely be the end result of their efforts.

After relaying information to each location, Karnic walked back to his Humvee and waited. It was a wait that seemed to never end. Throughout his tenure in the service, Karnic had frequently felt time drag. This time was different; this time he sat on the offensive in his own country. Karnic's thoughts turned to his grandfather and the stories of his last battle—not the sergeant who had helped get his grandmother out of Europe and had become his grandfather, but his biological grandfather. Karnic wondered if this was what his grandfather had felt as he and a handful of wounded men fought—just waiting to die.

The sound of gunfire snapped Karnic back to reality. His first thought was that they were making their move and not waiting for others to come. Making his way over to the front of the Humvee, which put the motor between him and incoming fire, Karnic soon noticed that nobody was firing back and no rounds were striking in their area. *Have they all gone crazy and started shooting at each other?* he mused while keeping an eye on the activity.

Karnic could see men dropping atop the hill, yet his men were not sending fire. He watched and waited. As he watched, the white UN vehicles flew to each side, reminding him of a rodeo when the opening shout released a big, black bull. Only this bull was a large four-by-four speeding through, followed by many others.

"Hold your fire! Hold your Fire!" Karnic yelled out as he watched the scene play out in front of him.

"Who is it?" Sgt. Smith called back.

Talking as if Smith were next to him, Karnic said, "I have no clue."

He counted six vehicles heading their way—somebody was holding a white T-shirt out the window of one of vehicles

"Friendlies coming in!" Smith hollered out to the men. Karnic stood watching and hoped it was true.

The lead truck approached the gate and as Karnic's men began returning fire at those remaining at the blockade, all hell broke loose. It did not take long for the firing to end. Knowing that they were outgunned, the remaining UN personnel ducked behind what was left of their vehicles.

The truck neared its intended position and slowed down. Looking over, Karnic could see that it had taken a great deal of fire.

"Angelique?"

Not believing his eyes and reaching up to rub them clean, Karnic took another look.

"We need a medic!" she screamed as loudly as she possibly could.

Still not believing his eyes, Karnic pointed.

"Main armory!" he responded and watched as the truck sped away.

Everything in Karnic's body told him to go after her, but the soldier in him knew that the mission had to come first. Doing his best to clear Angelique from his mind and refocus on what he had to accomplish, Karnic remained.

Minutes passed as he watched over his men, looked down the track, and, every so often, looked back at the armory. Just as Karnic thought of radio-ing back to the TOC, the sound of rumbling appeared—not the rumbling of thunder, but the sound made when tires bounce as they cross railroad tracks. Looking down the tracks, Karnic could see nothing through the trees. But the sound grew, and he knew it only could mean one thing.

"Cardinal, put on your game face—you are about to make the news."

Karnic was not one to break radio etiquette, but he knew just how much Sawyer hated being on camera.

Seconds later, a van appeared from the newly budding trees and blooming dogwoods—on its side, in bold lettering, were the words *ANA News*.

Well, they have come to the right place, Karnic thought.

"Smith, take first squad and check it out," Karnic said—he wasn't going to take any chances just because they had a van.

Smith was as thorough as he could be without a database to match IDs. He went through each piece of equipment and gave their vehicle a good going-over from top to bottom. To the news crew, it seemed a little over the top, and even more so by the time Smith had finished asking them a long series of questions.

By the time it was over, Karnic was confident that every precaution that could have been taken had been. He signaled to Smith to let the news crew on through and—though he felt it was unlikely that they could be in any shape to fight after the beating they had taken—he kept a close eye on the UN soldiers on the hilltop.

With the news crew back in their van and heading his way, Karnic quickly jumped in his Humvee. Pulling out onto the main drive just before them, he slowly drove them to the main armory, where the press conference was to be held. His mind didn't think as much about the news conference as much as it did about Angelique's surprise visit and those she had brought with her. Out of all the strange days Karnic had experienced, he ranked this one as number one.

Pulling into the lower parking lot just in front of the main building, Karnic could see Robert perched high above, looking out over the compound. Karnic wondered just how many times Robert had put the crosshairs on him since his sister had returned. Nevertheless, Karnic felt that things were a great deal safer with Robert on overwatch.

"This way, ma'am," Karnic called out to the reporter exiting the van as he stood alongside his Humvee. Carrying only a microphone, she had an easier time than her cameraman, who wrestled with the gear as he fought to keep up.

"I am Sandra Wheeler from Channel Three News. Good to meet you, Sergeant First Class." The woman reached out her hand to Karnic, who was a little taken aback that she knew military rank.

Reaching out and taking her hand, he had to ask, "Have you reported on the military much?"

"Why, yes. I was embedded with the 101st in Afghanistan four years ago."

"Well, this seems to have become just as dangerous of a place, ma'am. Let me show you the way." Letting go of her hand, Karnic gestured to where the door had once been. The cameraman was close behind them, and Karnic could see their shock when they took in what remained from the earlier battle—they looked from the bloodstained concrete on which they walked to the bullet-riddled facade of the main building of the armory.

Walking along in disbelief, Sandra Wheeler and her cameraman did not say a word—but once they were inside the entrance, that changed.

"Oh God!" Sandra said while surveying the carnage that lay before her. Dried blood and spent brass mixed with broken glass and shattered display cases covered most everything.

"How...how did all this happen today and nobody knew?" Sandra asked, letting out another gasp.

"Your questions will be answered soon, ma'am," Karnic said—he didn't want to waste time going over everything now and again in a few minutes. Continuing down the hall, they walked by rooms filled with wounded individuals being cared for.

Then Karnic heard her voice. Angelique. As he looked into the room, he saw her holding the hand of a man as medics worked to save his life. Karnic wanted badly to go to her, but he kept walking as he guided the reporter to a safe area to answer her questions.

Opening the door to the office, Karnic walked in first and introduced Sandra as she entered.

"Gentlemen, this is Sandra Wheeler. Sandra…" Unable to finish, he simply stepped aside.

"Lieutenant Governor, what are you doing here?" Sandra asked, snapping into reporter mode.

Seeing that Sawyer and Marks had everything moving forward, Karnic caught Sawyer's attention and, with a simple hand gesture, let him know he would be back. Then Karnic was off, shutting the office door behind him and making his way back to where he had last seen Angelique. As his anticipation grew, the distance between them seemed greater than it had just minutes ago.

Karnic made it to just outside the room where he had last seen Angelique and slowed down. Stepping around the corner and peering into the room, he saw that she was still there and that the medics were not moving as frantically as before. Leaning in, Karnic spoke her name softly.

"Angelique."

Getting no response, he spoke just a little more loudly.

"Angelique."

As she turned and caught sight of him, Angelique's heart began thumping hard and fast in her chest. She didn't know if it was due to the feelings she felt for Karnic or due to the current events, which she blamed him for. Lowering Cameron's hand and tucking it gently by his side, she turned to exit the room.

Stepping back from the door, Karnic took a deep breath as she approached. He wasn't sure just what he would say and thought that the best thing to do would be let her speak first.

Not saying a word as she exited, Angelique looked around, as if attempting a search for something. By going door to door, she found it. An empty room. Not caring what it once had been, Angelique walked in as if it were hers. Looking very confused, Karnic followed her in and stood just inside the door. Angelique kept her back to him as she finally spoke.

"Shut the door."

It was not quite the start he had planned, but at least it was a start. Karnic did as she requested. The door was secured. Turning to face her, Karnic hoped that the conversation would move forward. He waited in silence. Angelique was unable to stand still any longer. Pivoting on the balls of her feet, she spun to face him. That was not enough. Taking two long strides and drawing her fist back, Angelique let Karnic know of her anger as she planted her fist to the side of his face.

"What the hell was that for?" Karnic asked as he straightened up, not really moving much from the blow.

"Don't try to play me. You know damned well what."

Karnic suddenly realized why he had never married.

"You brought this to my front door and dragged me in!" Her anger could not only be heard but also felt by those in the hall through the closed door. Angelique was not one for crying, but she still fought back tears.

Karnic could not hold his silence any longer and a long-forgotten side of him began to show. Reaching out with both hands to her, he placed them on either side of her face an said softly, "Ange, I would not have done anything to put you in harm. My men and I needed a place we could control, and I knew the area well. That is all. I had no idea you would be there."

Raising her head slowly and meeting his gaze, Angelique began to relax and regain her calm. Then she spoke. "They took my mother and father."

Slight panic ran through Karnic's body. "Who did, Ange? Why?"

"Johnathan, Homeland Security. They were looking for you."

Angelique leaned forward and slid between his large arms as they closed in behind her. Resting her head upon his shoulder, she said nothing, only rested and focused on controlling her breathing. After a minute, Karnic felt it was time to learn more about what Angelique had been through—anything to take his mind off her warm breath on his neck.

Gently turning to the side and separating from her embrace, Karnic reached out to a nearby chair. He spoke as he pulled it over for her to sit on. "Tell me about it, Ange."

Five minutes passed as she brought him up to speed, starting with how she had been out of coffee and had taken her morning run down to their camp in the hopes of having a cup with him. While she explained the events, Karnic wished 138th had been on just another training mission—partially because he could have enjoyed a cup of coffee with her, but mostly for the men he had lost.

"And that is when we came across the mayhem all along the highway. I figured it had to be you, and when we saw the roadblock, we knew we had the right place. Cameron was hit on the way in. I tried to stop the bleeding, but it has been a while since I was in the sandbox."

Hearing Angelique say *sandbox* created many new questions Karnic wanted to know the answers to. Only those who had been deployed to the Middle East used that term. *Had she been there?* he thought.

Rather than ask now, Karnic thought it best to save those questions for later. Instead he focused on the now.

"Yeah, I was wanting to know about them. Who are they?" Karnic asked. He suddenly felt her hand in his and wondered if it had been there the whole time.

"They were at checkpoints set up by the United Nations looking for weapons. They didn't want to give them up, so we helped out."

"The guy who saved you, what's his story?"

"You're going to like him, Karl. Master Sergeant Todd Myers, retired. Well, forced to retire."

"Yeah, remind me to tell you the story later about those forced out of the military. For now, though, I have to get back—we are getting ready for a live news broadcast."

Chapter 57

⁓

THE BRIEFING

"Gentlemen, that is one hell of a story!" Sandra was excited and saddened by what she had just heard. She was excited as a reporter to have the opportunity to present such a story and saddened to have to do such a report. "I have to tell you, men, had you told me all this over the phone, I would have thought you were crazy. After what I have seen this morning, I know there will be no problems at the station breaking the martial law order. Just give me a few minutes to talk to my producer." Without waiting for a reply, she turned and exited the room with her phone in hand.

Looking at one another, they were satisfied with the conversation. There was only one thing left for them to do. Get ready.

Colonel Marks was the first to stand. He looked over at the lieutenant governor. "Sir, if you want to come with me, I'll show you where you can freshen up." Happy to take the colonel up on his offer, the lieutenant governor rose.

"Commander, would you like to join us?"

Sawyer sat and thought about the briefing. "No, I am good."

"See you back here in ten minutes then," Marks replied as he exited the office with the lieutenant governor.

From where she waited in the hall just outside the room, Kate watched the two men exit and wondered why Sawyer was not with them. She slowly made her way on her swollen ankle to the door and looked inside for him. There he was, still sitting in his chair. She could see that he was bothered. Making her way into the room, Kate could see the sparkle come back to his eyes as he looked up and spotted her.

Kate closed the door as she entered. Sawyer walked over.

"You shouldn't be walking around," Sawyer said. Concern poured out of him as he spoke to her.

"I'm fine, sweetie," Kate assured him. Almost before the last word cleared her lips, he tried to slow it down. After a minute, she pulled her head just enough to speak, but she did not let her arms loosen from around his neck. "What is bothering you?"

Sawyer didn't believe there was anything she could say that didn't sound like she was singing to him.

"Just nerves." He pulled her closer to him. "It is all good now, though."

Even though Sawyer and Kate hadn't known of the other's existence a week ago, those looking at them now would have thought they were newlyweds.

"I want you up there with me today, Kate. I need you there." Sawyer didn't let go the least little bit as he spoke.

"Anything you want, Commander," she replied in a flirtatious tone, doing her best to take his mind from the upcoming event.

A few more minutes passed as they stood in the center of the office in a tight embrace, and they probably would have remained that way, had it not been for a knock on the door. Breaking the hold they had on each other, Sawyer spoke.

"Yes?" Sawyer asked. He straightened his uniform.

A voice just on the other side came in response. "They are ready, sir."

"I will be right there."

Giving Kate one last soft kiss before opening the door, Sawyer looked at her and gazed into her eyes. "Kate, I love you."

Before she could respond, he opened the door, and there stood two soldiers waiting to escort him to the front of the building, where the briefing was to be held.

As they walked, he could feel her presence close by, giving him the strength he needed. Sawyer may have only been five foot eleven, but as he walked, he felt ten feet tall. Spotting the exit at the other end of the hall where a podium had been placed, Sawyer glanced back. After seeing Kate glow through her soot-covered face (due to the battle she'd fought earlier), he felt that everything would be OK.

Sandra walked over, meeting him at the exit.

"OK. As we discussed, the lieutenant governor will speak, and then you tell your story," Sandra said. Looking out over the grounds of the armory, Sawyer could feel eyes focused on him, and unlike any time before, it no longer mattered.

Robert was high above their heads, watching the movement of those at the barricade, knowing this would be an opportune time for an attack. Looking out with magnified vision, he watched for the slightest threatening movement and could see none—instead, there was nothing but calm bodies holding their weapons low, and this bothered him and caused him to look even harder and farther out to each side. Something did not feel right.

"Hello, I am Sandra Wheeler, Channel Four News, broadcasting live from where, hours ago, a bloody firefight occurred. It took place here between what we were told was a rogue unit of the Missouri National Guard and troops from the United Nations who were holding prisoner the National Guardsmen's comrades in arms. They have since freed the lieutenant governor of Missouri from a local jail cell and brought him here to speak. I believe that every American should listen closely to what these four gentlemen have to say, for our lives and the nation may depend upon it."

Directing the camera to the podium, the Sandra Wheeler said, "Governor."

Scanning each hiding spot that he would use in the distance, Robert saw nothing. He still felt as if there should be something, but the more he observed, the more he saw nothing.

"What are they up to?" Robert mumbled to himself. He was sure that if they wanted anyone dead, it would be the lieutenant governor.

Standing up straight with the stature of a politician, the governor began his speech. "My fellow Missourians and Americans, I bring you a most depressing story. A true story of how those in Washington have let us down."

"Let us down? What the hell?" Karnic whispered over to Sawyer with no one seeing. "I think it was a little more than that," he further stated and then focused on what the governor was saying.

"Every one of us has felt the pressure of the economy over the last few years and has had struggles—"

"NO!" Karnic shouted. No longer able to take the same political speech being given for years as he made his way to the podium shoving the lieutenant governor to the side. Surprised by the sudden force, the lieutenant governor stopped himself and began to head back in order to regain his position behind the podium. After seeing the largest fist in his life with one finger pointed in his direction, the recently freed lieutenant governor thought better of the attempt and stood up straight and silent.

"You know..." Karnic said and paused, deep in thought from behind the podium. "We are not here to give political speeches. That time has passed. We are here to tell you about what has happened. To tell you about the false imprisonment of your fellow man, about the thinning out of our military of men who say they will not fire upon you, about the families who have been driven from the land they have farmed for a hundred years, even killed for it by those in our government, and about the unconstitutional deployment of UN troops on AMERICAN SOIL!"

Karnic found himself losing control at the thought of what he had just said and tried to regain his calm. His fist came down with a rumble on the podium as he stared straight into the camera.

"This is the kind of shit you see happing on the ten o'clock news in other countries. How the hell did things get so off-kilter here in the land of opportunity? The one place where men and women voluntarily put their lives on the line, knowing they may never reap the rewards. What would those who destroy their own country and beliefs say to those who paid the ultimate sacrifice for this country? Sorry, but we have decided to take a different path."

Karnic held in his rage, but everyone could tell this was something he had to release from deep within.

"I DO NOT ACCEPT THAT!" he growled, slamming his cantaloupe-size fist down on the podium once more.

"I say, the HELL with tyrants and anyone else who wants to rule by tyranny. That is what martial law is, and it does not belong within the borders of the United States of America."

Every man who was not on watch gathered around. Every one of them could feel the power in Karnic's words.

"We ARE the land of the FREE. We ARE the BRAVE!"

He took a deep breath and then composed himself, but it did not last long. As Karnic began to speak, his emotions began to overcome him once more.

"We are at war. This is the time of rebirth for our country. No more will we have a GOVERNMENT THAT TRACKS our every move. No more will we have a government that WIPES ITS FEET ON THE CONSTITUTION. We are going to bring BACK this great nation and FREE IT FROM THE GRASP OF TYRANTS!"

His arms flying around as he spoke, Karnic's words flowed deep in every person present as they were broadcast all over the country.

Sawyer could see how drained his dear friend had become and stepped forward and placed a hand on Karnic's shoulder. Turning to see who was interrupting him, Karnic was ready to fight, but all the fight left him when he saw Sawyer standing there.

"I'll take it, my friend," Sawyer said in a calm voice. Karnic nodded to him as he stepped aside.

After looking back once more to Kate, Sawyer stepped up to speak and focused directly on the cameraman.

"We have fought long and hard to be here today, and we will fight long and hard tomorrow. We, the men and women of the United Constitutional Militia, will never stop living up to the oath we have taken."

Sawyer spoke with the presence of the great leader he had become.

"We ask that all those who have taken the same oath to defend the Constitution of these United States against all enemies, foreign and domestic, stand with us as we do so. To those who have not taken such an oath, I ask that you decide how important your country is to you and what you will do when they come for you or your family."

Sawyer showed no fear as he spoke, only the calm of a caring leader.

"There is nothing we, as Americans, cannot accomplish as long as we sta—"

Kate felt something wet splash on her skin as she heard the firing of two rifles, one close by and one off in the distance. As she raised her hands to see what it was, Sawyer fell behind the podium where he stood. Seeing the splattering of blood on her skin and clothing, she rushed over to him.

Kate did not know that she was screaming for help as she placed her hands over the holes in Sawyer's chest and back. He reached up and ran his hand along her cheek. Kate fell silent as his fingers slowly ran behind her ear and worked their way through her hair. She looked Sawyer in the eyes.

With tears racing from her eyes over her cheeks and dripping onto his face, Kate said, "I love you, too, Commander."

A smile began to appear on Sawyer's face. His fingers slowed their advance through her hair as the life left his body.

Made in the USA
Lexington, KY
17 April 2017